CONWAY
INCIDENT REPORT

Driver's Name: Travis Stockwell

Cab Number: 6

Date: June 7

Passenger Name: Peggy Saxon

Pickup Location: 5662 Rourke Way, Grand Springs

Final Destination: Vanderbilt Memorial Hospital

Description of Incident:

Sue Anne—

That pickup on Rourke Way turned into a two-alarm affair—and I _do_ mean two! Turns out that pretty little mom-to-be in the back of my cab decided she couldn't wait to get to the hospital. Guess I finally put all my years in the birthin' barn to good use. Yours truly, Travis Stockwell, delivered not one bouncing baby but _two!_

It was a little rough going for a while, but Mom, Virginia and little Travis John are doin' fine. And heck, I'm feeling like a proud daddy!

P.S. Can you believe she named her boy after _me?_

Dear Reader,

Sometimes your life can change in a heartbeat. For the residents of Grand Springs, Colorado, a blackout has set off a string of events that will alter people's lives forever....

Welcome to Silhouette's exciting new series, 36 HOURS, where each month heroic characters face personal challenges—and find love against all odds. This month, a pregnant woman in distress must rely on a handsome stranger to deliver her twins. But she gets more than she bargained for when the footloose cowboy insists on moving in and playing daddy to her adorable babies. Could this be love?

In coming months you'll meet a tough-hearted cop and a tender lady who join forces to solve a murder; a sexy tycoon who is searching desperately for a woman he has met only once; and an industrious reporter who has one chance to save his high school sweetheart—and his unexpected daughter. Join us each month as we bring you 36 hours that will change *your* life!

Sincerely,

The editors at Silhouette

36 HOURS

OOH BABY, BABY

BABY

DIANA WHITNEY

Silhouette Books

Published by Silhouette Books

America's Publisher of Contemporary Romance

Special thanks and acknowledgment are given to Diana Whitney for her contribution to the 36 HOURS series.

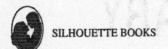

SILHOUETTE BOOKS

OOH BABY, BABY

Copyright © 1997 by Harlequin Books S.A.

ISBN 0-373-65008-6

Printed in U.S.A.

Diana Whitney

Twice a Romance Writers of America RITA finalist and a two-time *Romantic Times* magazine Reviewers' Choice nominee, Diana Whitney has sold twenty-four romance and suspense novels since her first Silhouette title was published in 1989. She has written for several Silhouette lines, including Romance, Special Edition, Intimate Moments and Shadows.

Diana has conducted writing workshops, is a frequent speaker and has written several articles on the craft of fiction writing for various trade magazines and newsletters. She is a member of Authors Guild; Novelists, Inc.; Published Authors Network and Romance Writers of America. She and her husband live in rural Northern California, and she loves to hear from readers. You can reach her at dhinz@oro.net, or in care of Silhouette Books, 300 East 42nd Street, Sixth Floor, New York, NY 10017.

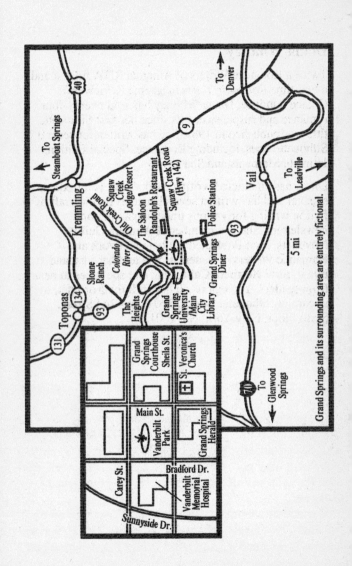

To Denver

To Steamboat Springs

40

9

Kremmling

Squaw Creek Lodge/Resort

Old Creek Road

The Saloon

Randolph's Restaurant

Squaw Creek Road (Hwy 142)

Police Station

Vail

To Leadville

93

Colorado River

Sloane Ranch

134

93

The Heights

Grand Springs University/Main City Library

Grand Springs Diner

131

Toponas

5 mi

To Glenwood Springs

70

Grand Springs Courthouse

Sheila St.

St. Veronica's Church

Main St.

Vanderbilt Park

Grand Springs Herald

Carey St.

Bradford Dr.

Vanderbilt Memorial Hospital

Sunnyside Dr.

Grand Springs and its surrounding area are entirely fictional.

One

Blackness gripped her like a fist. Outside, the wind howled, and rain pummeled the thin windowpanes. Thunder rumbled. Lightning cracked.

Inside, the silence of her heart was deafening. Terrifying. And so very, very lonely.

Peggy Saxon shifted on the worn sofa to massage the small of her back. It didn't help. The nagging throb simply wouldn't go away. She heaved her pregnant bulk sideways, seeking a semicomfortable position. The threadbare sofa arm poked her ribs.

Muttering, Peggy used a strategically tucked throw pillow to pad the exposed wood, then grabbed the tiny battery-powered radio from a nearby table. She needed something to drown out the roaring storm, the inner silence of desolation. She needed music. Voices. Even crackling white noise would be a distraction from desperate sadness, from secret fear.

On the radio, a tight male voice announced new road closures due to mud slides. Phone lines were holding, but the power company, having been flooded out by a massive surge of murky goo, still had no estimate as to when electricity would be restored. A state of emergency had been declared.

It was five o'clock in the morning. There was no light. No heat. The lovely mountain hamlet of Grand Springs, Colorado, was under siege. And Peggy Saxon was alone.

* * *

"Dispatch to unit six. Travis…are you there?"

Travis Stockwell ducked into the cab, knocked his hat off on the door frame and swore as his prized Stetson landed in the mud. He scooped it up, muttered and wiped the brim with a paisley handkerchief.

The raspy female voice boomed with familiar agitation. "Unit six, respond. Respond, dadgummit, or I'll be tossing out those fancy boots of yours and renting your room to the highest bidder."

"Aw, for crying out loud." Travis tossed the wet Stetson on the cab's front passenger seat, poked the soiled handkerchief back into his pocket, which was already crammed with a soggy pack of pumpkin seeds, and snatched up the microphone. "All right, already. This is unit six, soaking wet, so hungry I could chew cardboard, and so danged tired I don't give a fat flying fig what you do with that flea-bitten flophouse."

A long-suffering sigh crackled over the line. "Where'n Sam Hill are you?"

Travis squinted through the splattered windshield toward a weary group of guardsmen hoisting the gear he'd just unloaded. "Near as I can figure, about a half mile from the cutoff road to Mountain Meadows campground. I just dropped off the evacuation troop."

"What's your ETA?"

"I dunno. Thirty minutes, maybe sooner if the traffic lights are back on line."

"They're not. The whole town is blacked out. Oh, and don't take Orchard Road back into town."

"Mud slide?"

"Big one. Looks like it might have taken a couple cars."

Travis swore, slapped the steering wheel. "Maybe I should head that way to see if I can help."

The microphone crackled. "Jimmy's already en route

with a group of volunteers and a trunk full of shovels. I need you back in town. Every emergency vehicle in the area is tied up. City hall is scrambling for rescue transport.''

"On my way," Travis said, and flipped the ignition with his free hand. "Unit six out."

"Travis?"

"Yeah."

"You be careful, hear?"

"I will, sis." With that, he dropped the mike, shifted into gear and drove into the blinding rain.

Light blasted away blackness. The dingy duplex shuddered through thunder, screeched as if in pain.

Peggy gasped, suddenly awake, clutched her distended belly and struggled to her feet. An eerie energy crawled up her arms, lifting the fine hairs. Another flash, another roar. She covered her ears, bit her lip, may have cried out, but the sound was swallowed by a deafening crack and the reverberating crash of splintered lumber. Her scalp tingled, felt singed.

Peggy couldn't hear the scream but felt it explode from her parched throat. She wrapped her arms over her head, curled forward to protect the precious life in her womb. The house was collapsing around her. She knew it. She felt it. She heard the agonized shriek of fractured wood, of ripped nails. The floor rumbled beneath her feet.

Then the rumbling softened into silence.

She heard a thin sob, then realized it had come from her. Opening her eyes, she blinked into the darkness, seeing nothing but familiar shadows of doorways and lumpy furniture. Now, all she heard was the rain. The pounding, incessant rain.

Shaking violently, Peggy felt around the sofa cushions until her fingers brushed smooth metal, the flashlight that had been beside her throughout the long, black night. Her hand quivered around it, her thumb spasmed against the protruding switch. A beam of brilliant reassurance bounced from a wall.

She swept the light around the room, across the ceiling and over the floor, stopping briefly on the wall clock, which read eight o'clock. Everything was as it should be. No giant cracks, no collapsing timbers. The pocket radio had fallen under the coffee table, but the sparsely furnished room was otherwise tidy.

Peggy swept the light toward the front door, then veered left to aim the beam through the window and check the front porch—or rather, what was left of it.

The dilapidated decking had been crushed by an enormous pine that had once shaded the south side of the duplex and was now wedged against her front door. Judging by the angle at which the tree had fallen, she suspected that the other half of the duplex had borne the brunt of the damage. Fortunately, the unit was vacant, which meant her nearest neighbor was a quarter mile away.

Swallowing a sour surge of panic, Peggy told herself the damage probably wasn't as bad as it looked. Besides, the storm would be over soon. It had to be. The town couldn't take much more.

Peggy couldn't take much more.

She wiped her forehead, mildly surprised as a coating of icy fear came away on her fingertips. No shame in that. It was okay to be scared. As long as you didn't show it, didn't provide a weakness to target. Fear was a private matter, a respected adversary to be acknowledged, then controlled and ultimately defeated.

Peggy understood the process intimately. She'd fought fear all her life. She'd always won. Always.

Until now.

The grinding pain ripped her belly like a buzz saw, doubling her over. She had no breath to cry out, but her mind screamed for her. Fear surged victorious. She was in labor. She was terrified.

And she was alone.

Travis jammed the brakes, cursing. The cab fishtailed to a stop. In front of him, an impatient line of vehicles bunched behind an overturned big rig blocking both lanes of traffic. He sighed, tugged his hat down to his eyebrows and reached for the microphone.

"Unit six to dispatch." When there was no immediate response, he gave the mike button an impatient tap. "Aw, hell, Sue Anne, quit sucking soda and get on the danged radio. I don't have all day."

Actually, it appeared that he did have all day. That eighteen-wheeler wasn't going anywhere on its own, and Travis suspected it would be hours before the emergency team could spring loose the heavy-duty equipment needed to clear the roadway. At least the rain had eased to a dull drizzle, and it was just now becoming light—even though dawn broke hours ago.

The microphone emitted a juicy hiss. "Dang you, Travis, you are such a brat."

"Caught you, didn't I? You know, sis, there's a twelve-step program for people who can't control their cola. You ought to look into it." He held the transmission button down so he didn't have to listen to a sputtered reply, and squinted through the smeared windshield. "The interstate transition is blocked by a semi. I might be able to backtrack toward Virginia Road, but it'll add a forty-five to my ETA."

When he finally remembered to release the mike switch, Sue Anne was in midsentence. "About five miles from your location."

He frowned. "Say again?"

"We have an emergency relay from 911 dispatch. Pickup is at 5662 Rourke Way."

Travis was familiar with the street, a rutted two-lane cutting a rural swath around the outskirts of town. He jotted the address on a scratch pad affixed to the dash. "I'll be there in ten."

He hung a U-turn, stomped the accelerator and sped away.

Breathe, breathe, breathe.

Short, shallow breaths. Pant like a dog. That's what the book said, wasn't it? Or maybe it said to take a deep breath and hold it. Peggy couldn't remember. It had been more than three hours since her first pain, and suddenly, dear Lord, she couldn't remember.

If only she'd taken the Lamaze classes her doctor had suggested. But she hadn't, because the classes were geared for couples and she'd been too embarrassed to go alone. So she'd bought a handbook on childbirth, read it cover to cover and thought she was prepared.

Only now she couldn't remember what the book said, what she was supposed to do.

Squeezing her eyes shut, Peggy willed herself to be calm and to focus on what she'd learned. Short breaths. Yes, she was sure now. Short breaths during labor, deep breaths during crowning, when it was time to push.

To push.

Oh, God.

The contraction eased, allowing panic to bubble like bad beer. It was too soon, Peggy thought frantically. Too soon. She wasn't due for three weeks. She wasn't ready to give birth, not ready at all.

Her heart raced, pumping icy perspiration out of every pore. She licked her lips. They were rough, cracked. Dry as dirt.

The doctor was waiting at the hospital. When she'd phoned a few hours ago, he'd told her that everything would be all right. And she wanted to believe him. She *did* believe him.

The image of kind blue eyes and a rumpled, grandfatherly smile warmed her heart. Dr. Dowling had been good to her. He understood how difficult things had been since Clyde left, and had gone out of his way to spend extra time during her appointments, time to calm, to soothe her. Peggy longed for that comfort now, for the gentle touch of proficient hands, the resonant, parental voice that made her feel safe and secure.

He was waiting for her. At the hospital. Now.

Where the hell was that cab?

A glance at the front window confirmed that morning had indeed come. Cold, wet. Gray. The fallen tree loomed enormous, its massive trunk blocking all but a bleak sliver of gloomy sky.

The thought occurred to her that there was no way for her to get out through the front door, no way for anyone else to get in. But Peggy couldn't worry about that now, because a viselike tightness was working its way from the base of her spine to around her belly.

Breathe, breathe, breathe.

The pain swelled, twisted, sliced like a dull blade. Tears sprang to her eyes. She curled forward, wanting to scream, but her lungs were in spasm.

Breathe, breathe, breathe.

Peggy gritted her teeth, dug her fingers into the sofa cushions and imagined a hundred innovative ways for the ex-husband who'd abandoned her to die ugly.

Travis was horrified. He pulled onto the dirt shoulder behind a clunky old sedan and fervently hoped he was at the wrong address. Even in the gray, rain-dark pall he could see that anyone left inside that crushed structure needed an ambulance, not a cab.

He exited the checkered taxi and headed toward the duplex, veering around a massive root ball jutting from soaked earth. Closer examination revealed that except for the porch, now a splintered nest of rubble under the toppled tree, the dwelling itself seemed to be relatively unscathed.

Shading his eyes, Travis squinted between blowing pine boughs and saw a snapped porch beam had crushed one of the unit's two doors. The other door was undamaged, but completely blocked by the tree trunk, which he judged to be about four feet in diameter.

He cupped his mouth and shouted, "Conway Cab. Anyone in there?" A movement behind one of the windows caught his eye. He shifted toward the unit on the left, thought he saw a shadow inside the room. Before he could focus, the shadow seemed to collapse, melt in upon itself and was gone.

Shifting, Travis grabbed a sturdy limb and hoisted himself up onto the fallen trunk, hoping for a better look, but gray light threw his own reflection back at him, obscuring his view inside. A windblown whip of pine needles stung his face. He swatted at it, lost his grip and dropped back to the mucky ground.

The sky darkened again. Clouds swirled, boiled black. The wind whistled a warning and began to howl.

Travis swore and pulled up his jacket collar until wet denim chafed his earlobes. He longed for warmth, the arid desert heat, the soft crush of dry sawdust beneath his boots. Cheering crowds. Bellowing livestock. Rawhide rasping his palms. The pungent smell of animalistic power, of sweating victory and bloody defeat.

Ah, he missed it. Just a few more weeks and he'd be back on the circuit, back where he belonged. Travis could hardly wait.

Ducking into the wind, he gripped the brim of his hat and circled back around the giant root ball toward the rear of the old duplex. A five-foot wooden fence creaked against the wind.

"Great," he muttered, automatically wrapping a protective arm around his taped ribs. At the moment, climbing a fence didn't much appeal to him, but there didn't seem to be a whole bunch of options. A quick glance around confirmed nothing but a few vacant lots backing up to a conifer forest. No help there.

Issuing a pained sigh, he hoisted himself up and over, wincing as he dropped into the yard. He straightened slowly, waiting for the pain to ease. Doc had warned him that ribs fractured that badly were slow to heal. Slow? Hell, that wasn't the half of it. A snail could've crawled to Texas by the time Travis had mended enough to take a decent breath. He was better now. Not great, but better.

Travis straightened and stretched out the kinks. After a quick glance around the barren square of fenced grass, he strode to the back door of the first duplex, peered through the mullioned window and tapped on the glass.

There was no response, but Travis focused through the galley-style kitchen into the living room of the duplex. There were no lights inside, only slight illumination from a sliver of daylight breaking through the partially blocked front window. He saw the outline of a sofa, the triangular shadow of a lampshade and a table of some kind. His gaze narrowed, focusing on the floor beside the table. Something was heaped there, a crumpled silhouette that could have been a wadded blanket or a bundle of laundry.

But the bundle was moving. The crumpled silhouette was a person. A person in trouble.

Travis frantically rattled the knob. It was locked, so he took a step back and kicked the door in. In less than a heartbeat, he knelt beside a woman who was curled on her side, making strange hissing sounds through her teeth.

He laid a tentative hand on her shoulder. "Ma'am?"

She opened her eyes, huge pools of emerald terror in a colorless face.

Travis's breath backed up his throat. "It's all right," he muttered with considerably more confidence than he felt. "You're going to be fine, ma'am, just fine."

Her eyes widened, then squinched shut. To his shock, she formed her lips into an O and began to pant. He blinked, wondering why she would be overly warm when the room was colder than a barn in winter. For some odd reason, he noticed the bulge of her abdomen long before the reason for it struck him. When it did, he danged near went into shock.

"Oh, no," he murmured, utterly transfixed by the realization. "No, no, ma'am, you can't do this...not now. Please, lady—"

Her cheeks flexed with each quick puff.

"Oh, Lordy—"

Puff, puff, puff.

"Ma'am, please stop. This just really isn't a good time—"

A shudder jittered through her body, then she suddenly went limp as a squashed snake and her breath slid out with a long, slow hiss.

Travis sat back on his boot heels, wiped his forehead. "Yes'm, that's better. Much obliged."

She looked up, her eyes bright with moisture. "What are you doing here?"

"Conway Cab Company, ma'am." He licked his lips. "You did call for a cab, didn't you? Oh, well, sure, sure you did, but maybe, ah—" he swallowed hard "—maybe under the circumstances, an ambulance would be a better choice."

Her gaze narrowed. "Golly, what a swell idea."

He flinched, feeling stupid. Every ambulance in town was tied up on emergency duty, which was why he'd been called out in the first place. "I guess you've already tried that."

"I guess I have, cowboy."

Flustered and completely out of his element, Travis blurted, "Can't you put this off for a while? I mean, this is a really, really bad time to have a baby...." His voice trailed away as her eyes thinned into mean little slits. Obviously she was well aware of that fact and didn't appreciate the reminder. He cleared his throat. "Okay, sure, no problem. We'll, ah, just mosey on over to the hospital and ah—ma'am?"

As another contraction tightened, she bit her lip, made a peculiar vibrating sound deep in her throat, then started to pant again. She bent like a safety pin. Beads of sweat slicked her face. Her skin was white as death.

Travis was beside himself. Flustered and completely out of his element, he didn't have a clue what to do. Instinctively reaching out, he patted her shoulder, then let out a yelp as she snatched up his hand and damned near crushed every bone in it. Since there was no way short of amputation to pry himself out of her spasmed grasp, he gritted his teeth and waited for her pain—and his—to pass.

Several long seconds later, she released him and fell back exhausted. Her hand dropped limply onto the floor, and she issued a soft, guttural moan that touched Travis to the core.

He flexed his fingers, grateful that they still moved, then wiped a gentle thumb over her delicate brow that was the copper-gold color of a summer sunset. "Can I get you a glass of water? Maybe a wet cloth to, you know, cool you down some?"

A flash of pink moistened her lips, then was gone. "Thank you, but I'd really like to leave now. My doctor is waiting."

"Oh, sure." He glanced around the room, suddenly panicked. "We can't get out. The front door is blocked."

This was clearly not news to her. She sighed and wiggled a weak finger toward the kitchen. "That way."

Travis considered that. "Even with me giving you a boost, it'll be a mite tricky getting over that fence, what with your condition and all."

She stared at him as if the word *stupid* had appeared in neon welts across his forehead. "As exciting as that sounds, I'd prefer to use the gate."

"The gate," he repeated, feeling more idiotic by the moment. He hadn't seen a gate, but then again, he hadn't spent much time looking for one. "Right. The gate."

When she struggled upward, he helped her to her feet, then held on, fearing she might collapse. If it weren't for his sore ribs, he would have carried her—

"My valise," she whispered.

"Excuse me?" He followed her gaze to a tapestry bag on a table beside the kitchen door. "Oh."

He braced an arm around her. She took a shaky step forward, then suddenly went rigid as another contraction hit her.

Travis swallowed hard, tightening his grip to hold her upright. "You're doing fine," he murmured as she puffed and shuddered. With his free hand, he stroked her upper arm, offering the same quiet encouragement he'd have used to gentle a skittish mare. "Just a few more seconds...that's right...breathe real short-like...that's good, ma'am, that's real good."

A rush of air escaped her slack lips. She sagged against him, gasping. She was just a slip of a thing, really, barely big enough to rest her head against his shoulder. Faded freckles were scattered across the bridge of her nose, and the scent of sweet flowers wafted from hair that tangled around her shoulders like a curly mass of poppy red fire.

A protective surge swelled up in his gut, an odd sensation

that made him want to whip out a saber and fight the world to keep her safe. At the moment, that meant getting her to the hospital.

Travis tugged down his Stetson, grabbed the valise and ushered the exhausted woman to the cab.

"Aa-a-ah!"

The cry from the back seat sent chills down Travis's spine. He looked in the rearview mirror, and could have wept. The poor woman was contorted in pain, white as death except for a bright trickle of blood where she'd bitten her lip. "Hold on, ma'am. We'll be there soon."

Her features relaxed slightly. She licked her lips and gave a weak nod.

Focusing on the road, Travis swerved around a large rock dislodged by the rain, then slowed to forge a muddy puddle. Black sludge splattered the cab's hood and fenders. Travis's brother-in-law, who owned the cab company, was a spit-and-polish stickler, but at the moment Travis didn't much care. He concentrated every ounce of his attention on his mission, which at the moment was traversing a winding gravel pathway that was pitted, potholed and edged with a quivering mass of muddy muck.

Navigating Virginia Road had always been a challenge; now it was a nightmare, But with paved interstate access still blocked by the overturned big rig, this was the only available route into town.

Squinting into the dreary late morning light, Travis saw the hairpin curve up ahead and touched the brake with his boot.

A blood-curdling shriek came from the back seat.

Travis jerked his eyes from the road to the mirror and back again, but it was too late. The mud slide loomed like a mountain. And they were heading right for it.

Two

Travis yanked the wheel. The woman shrieked. The cab spun doughnuts on wet gravel, then sank to its hubcaps in the mucky shoulder.

He gunned the engine. The tires spat mud and sank deeper. Logically, Travis understood that the vehicle was irretrievably mired, but panic was not a logical emotion. He jammed the cab into first gear and stomped the gas pedal to the floor. The engine revved madly. Black goo shot from beneath the spinning tires.

"Aa-a-ah!"

A quick glance into the rearview mirror confirmed that the situation in the back seat was not going at all well. Sweat trickled into his eyes. He snatched up the microphone. "We've got big trouble! Send an ambulance to Virginia Road, about three miles down from the turnoff. For God's sake, hurry, Sue Anne. We're fixing to have a baby here!"

The radio crackled. "Say again?"

"A baby, a baby!"

"Ayeee-ee!" The woman gasped, bolted upright. "It's coming! Oh, God, it's coming!"

Travis spun in his seat. "Not yet, ma'am, please. Help is on the way. Just hold on a few more minutes, okay?"

She went limp and fell back against the door, panting. "I need to push."

"Oh, Lordy, don't do that!"

"I have to."

"No, no, you don't." Frantic, Travis dropped the microphone and hoisted his torso over the headrest far enough to grasp her cold hand. "Think of something real calming, you know, like a pasture of grazing horses or maybe a pretty little creek. That always helps me to hold off during, uh, well, you know."

She gave him a look that could freeze meat.

Travis swallowed hard. "I guess maybe you're not in the mood to think about that sort of thing right now."

Her eyes were green slits. "Oh, I'm thinking about it, cowboy. Believe me, I'm thinking about it— Ah! Oh! Oh!"

As the contraction hit, she clutched his wrist with both hands, hauling half his torso into the back seat. Behind him, a voice cracked over the radio, but Travis couldn't deal with that because the thrashing woman with a death grip on his arm was shrieking distinctly unladylike epithets along with horribly graphic, gender-specific alterations she planned to perform on a man named Clyde.

Sue Anne's voice crackled from the radio. "Travis! Travis, pick up. I'm patching you through to Vanderbilt Memorial's ER. *Travis!*"

The driver's headrest pressed Travis's throbbing ribs as he teetered over the seat back, struggling to extricate himself from the woman's clenched fingers. When he freed himself, he scooped up the microphone.

Before he could scream into the speaker, a crisp, female voice crackled out. "This is Dr. Jennings—"

Travis plunged his thumb on the mike switch. "Help!" he blurted. "She wants to push!"

"How close are the contractions?"

Travis shifted a wary glance toward the thrashing woman. "One right after another. Geez, they just won't stop."

"Can you see the baby's head?"

"Huh?" Travis frowned at the microphone. 'You're kidding, right?"

The doctor gentled her tone. "My name is Amanda. What's yours?"

"Travis, ma'am."

"Well, Travis, you're going to deliver this baby—"

"The hell I am!"

"And I'm going to help you."

"Uh-uh, no way." Travis shook his head so hard his hat shifted. "This is *not* going to happen—"

"It's *coming!*" the woman screamed, then curled forward, teeth gritted as her face folded in on itself.

Travis dove into the back seat, dragging the microphone with him. "She says it's coming!" he shouted, yanking the mike cord taut. "What do I do?"

The doctor's voice was crisp, competent. "Remove her clothing and see if the head is crowning."

Defeated, Travis issued a pained sigh, licked his lips and mumbled, "I'm real sorry, ma'am, but we, ah, need to adjust your skirt and such."

The woman bared her teeth, allowed him to do what had to be done, then snarled like cornered prey.

Taken aback, Travis wiped his forehead, blinking at the woman who appeared ready to rip out his Adam's apple and shove it up his nose. But he saw something else in her eyes. He saw terror.

Her snarl slipped into a broken sob. "Please," she whispered. "Help me."

Travis's heart melted. "I will, ma'am. Don't you fret. I'll take real good care of you and your baby."

Her gaze was skeptical, but tinged with hope. "Have you done this before?"

"Hmm? Oh, sure. Dozens of times." Since the reassurance seemed to calm her, Travis chose not to mention that all of his previous patients had hooves.

A split second later the woman was convulsing again, locked in the throes of the worst contraction yet. Travis grabbed the mike. "The baby's coming, all right. I can see its head."

"Good," the doctor said. "You'll need something to grip the child with. Do you have a towel, or any kind of clean cloth?"

"Well, ah." Travis plucked at his muddy shirt. "I don't think so."

"Valise," the woman mumbled when the pain eased.

"Hmm?" Travis followed her weak gesture to the tapestry bag on the floorboard. "Oh. Wait a minute, Doc." He snapped the bag open and pulled out a handful of items, including a couple of adult-size nighties, a robe, some baby gowns and two tiny blankets. "Okay, I got some stuff." A guttural moan caught his attention. He froze for a moment, then stuttered, "Sh-she's going at it again, Doc. Oh, Lordy, the baby's coming *out!*"

"Reach down and support the child's head," Dr. Jennings said brusquely. "During the next contraction, ease the shoulders out of the birth canal."

Instantly forgetting the doctor's instruction about using a cloth, Travis dropped the flowered nightie, lurched forward and made a clumsy grab for the tiny wet skull. "Its eyes are open. It's looking at me—"

The woman sucked in a rasping gulp of air, squeezed her eyes shut and pushed for all she was worth. A wriggling infant slipped into Travis's waiting hands...then squirted right out of them. The baby landed fortuitously on the woman's stomach, where it emitted a startled gasp, screwed up its purple face and began to howl lustily.

Travis fell back, horrified by how close he'd come to dropping the slippery little guy. He didn't know squat about babies—hell, he'd never even touched one before—but it didn't take a genius to realize that bouncing one off the floorboard was a really bad idea.

The exhausted woman peeled open an eyelid and smiled. "A boy," she murmured. "A perfect little boy. Isn't he beautiful?" She beamed expectantly.

Travis eyed the ugly, wrinkled creature and decided God would forgive a small lie. "Yes'm, he's real pretty."

The radio crackled. "Travis? What's going on there?"

He took a shuddering breath and picked up the microphone that was dangling over the headrest by its cord. "The baby's here, Doc, and it's yelling something fierce."

Dr. Jennings chuckled. "Good job, Travis, but your work isn't done yet."

After answering several questions about the child's appearance and the mother's condition, Travis managed to follow the doctor's instructions about clearing the infant's nose and mouth, then used a strip of flowered cloth to tie off the umbilical cord. He'd just draped one of the blankets over the still-howling child when the woman went rigid.

"Ma'am?" Travis blinked sweat out of his eyes. "Oh, Lordy, ma'am, why are you doing that again?"

She gritted her teeth, curling forward.

"Something's wrong, Doc!" Travis dropped the mike, snatched up the wrapped infant from her stomach and looked frantically around. His gaze fell on the open valise, which conveniently resembled a small bassinet. After hurriedly tucking the wrapped infant inside, he turned his attention to the woman and nearly went into cardiac arrest.

"Holy smokes," he hollered into the microphone. "She's having another one!"

"Well, Travis," Dr. Jennings replied calmly. "At least now you know what to do."

Peggy let her head fall back against the cab door, eyes closed, lips slack. A world of blackness spun around her, sucking her in. Her mind wept.

From a distance, she heard the familiar voice urging her with a desperation that touched but couldn't move her. "Push! Please, ma'am, you have to push."

"Can't," she murmured, overwhelmed by the effort of the monosyllabic utterance.

Wet hair stuck to her face, clung to her quivering eyelids. She didn't have the strength to lift her hands, yet felt gentle fingers stroke her skin, smoothing the damp strands away. The touch was so tender, so loving. She forced her eyes open and saw his face. Rugged yet young, not much older than she was. Round eyes, dark with worry, fringed with a stub of golden brown lashes. A mouth that was full, sensitive. Lips that were moving.

She strained to hear. "Your baby needs help," he was saying. "I know it's hard, but you have to try, ma'am, you have to."

The contraction struck like an earthquake in her soul. Her back arched without permission, throwing her backward, shaking her, pummeling her, battering her body without mercy. The world darkened as her eyes rolled up into her skull.

"*Push*, ma'am! Oh, Lordy. Doc? She can't, she just can't. You've got to get her some help...please, Doc, she can't take no more."

The voice was coming from somewhere, everywhere. Peggy focused on it, used it as a lifeline to bring herself back from the brink.

Your baby needs help, ma'am.

Peggy forced her mind away from the white light of unconsciousness.

Your baby needs help.

The young cowboy's words echoed in her mind, giving her strength.

Your baby.

She drilled her fingernails into the upholstered car seat.

Needs help.

She thrust her head forward until her chin struck her chest, then coiled forward, using every ounce of strength she could muster. Stars broke through her mind. Lights flashed. Blood roared past her ears like an exploding ocean.

She fell back, panting. Drained. Empty.

Empty.

With immense effort, Peggy opened one eye and saw the limp little body lying on her abdomen. The cowboy was alternately wiping its tiny mouth and talking into the microphone. A dull hiss in her ears kept her from hearing him, but she could tell by his grim expression that something was very wrong.

Blinking sweat from her eyes, Peggy tried to touch the precious infant, but her hand felt like lead. The cowboy dropped the microphone, snatched up a wad of cloth—one of her nightgowns, she thought—and began to vigorously massage the tiny body.

Slowly the droning hiss dissipated and Peggy could hear again, although sound was distorted, distant. She tried to speak, couldn't, coughed, tried again. "What's...wrong?"

The bleak-eyed cowboy didn't look up. "Nothing, ma'am. You've got yourself a pretty little girl, and everything's fine, just fine."

But it wasn't fine at all. Even in her exhausted stupor Peggy could see that the baby was smaller than her brother, and more lethargic. Her color was odd, too, kind of a dusty lavender that made Peggy's heart flutter in fear. "My baby...?"

"Don't you fret." The flowered fabric came apart in his hands. He used a strip if it to tie off the cord. "I'm not going to let anything happen to your baby." As he spoke, he continued to massage the limp little limbs, then he bent down and puffed gently into her tiny mouth.

A lump rose into Peggy's throat. Hysteria bubbled from her lips. "God...oh, God... Please, please—"

The infant's arms twitched, once, then again. A tiny foot kicked the air. There was a squeaky sputter, then the baby's chest heaved.

"That's right, darling," the cowboy murmured. "Take yourself a big old breath. There you go, sweetheart, there you go."

In response, the baby pulled up her knees, flailed her tiny fists, screwed up her face and belted a howl even louder than her brother's had been.

Peggy exhaled all at once. Tears sprang to her eyes. "Oooh." She bit her lip, overcome with joy and relief.

The cowboy's shoulders rolled forward. He lifted his hat, wiped his face with his forearm and heaved a shuddering breath. "You go on and holler all you want," he murmured to the wailing infant. "You got a right to be mad."

He tucked his hat back over a disheveled shock of sun-streaked brown hair, then awkwardly wrapped the thrashing infant in a blanket. His hands were huge, clumsy, endearingly gentle. When he brushed a sweet kiss across the baby's soft little scalp, Peggy's heart swelled until she thought it would explode. She'd never seen a man, any man, exhibit such tenderness. It touched her to the marrow.

Peggy cradled her daughter in the crook of her arm, loosened the blanket to marvel at the perfect little body and, of course, to count each miniature finger and teensy toe. Gratitude surged into her throat, nearly choking her. She swallowed, struggling to speak. "I don't know how to thank you."

He shrugged, clearly uncomfortable. "I didn't do much."

"You saved her life."

The second shrug was more like a twitch. "She's a gutsy little gal," he murmured, angling an admiring glance. "Just like her mama."

That's when Peggy saw it, the telltale moisture clinging bright to his stubbled cheeks. Their eyes met and held. Something special passed between them, something warm and wonderful. Something that changed her life.

Shortly after the second birth, the ambulance arrived and Travis was shuffled aside in the chaos. While the medics tended to the new mother and her twins, he stuffed his hands in his pockets and ambled through the gray drizzle, stopping occasionally to peer through the wet cab window at the frenzy of activity.

A gurney was pulled from the rear of the ambulance and wheeled to the open cab door. Travis strained to watch, but was pushed aside by a burly EMT as the weak woman was lifted out. A baby fussed. Travis thought it was the boy. He was attuned to each infant's distinctive sound. They were a part of him now.

He stretched upward, trying to see, but caught only a quick glimpse of matching bundles whisked to the waiting ambulance. The gurney wheeled by. Another glimpse, this time of flaming hair spread on white linen, a pale face, eyes closed, beautiful in its purity, smiling in repose.

Someone slapped his shoulder. Someone shook his hand. Travis paid little attention. He was busy watching the ambulance doors close.

A moment later, the vehicle sped away, lights flashing.

Alone now, Travis pulled down the brim of his hat, folded his arms and propped a hip against the cab fender to wait for the tow truck. But his mind replayed the morning's events over and over and over again. After twenty-

eight years of living, Travis Stockwell had finally figured
out what life was about.

He'd never be the same.

Vanderbilt Memorial's emergency room was packed
with patients, clamoring with chaos. A rash of blackout-
induced traffic accidents and storm-related injuries had
strained the ER's resources to the breaking point.

Peggy, who'd been wheeled to a curtained examination
area, was distressed when her twins were immediately
whisked away. She struggled to sit up, was overcome by a
wave of dizziness and managed only to prop herself up on
one elbow.

A flurry of activity bustled just beyond her cubicle, uniformed personnel rushing with purpose while civilians wandered aimlessly like shell-shocked soldiers.

One civilian caught Peggy's eye, a bewildered gentleman
with glazed eyes. His handsome face was expressionless,
and he shuffled back and forth, eyeing the activity around
him as if it were the most perplexing thing on earth.

A nurse appeared and took hold of his arm. "There you
are, Mr. Smith. We've been looking for you."

The man focused, then frowned. "Smith?"

"For the moment," the nurse mumbled, distracted as a
gurney encircled by medics whizzed past. "At least until
we locate your family and find out who you really are."

"Family?" The man's confused expression broke Peggy's heart. He touched the bandage on his head and
flinched. "Smith," he murmured. "Martin Smith."

"That's right." The nurse sighed and ushered him away
before Peggy could get her attention.

When another uniformed woman appeared just beyond
the cubicle's open drape, Peggy waved weakly. "Nurse!
Please, can you help me?"

The woman glanced around, issued an empathetic smile
and hurried over. Peggy clutched her frantically. "Where
have they taken my babies?"

"Up to Pediatrics," the nurse replied, peeling Peggy's fingers from her wrist.

"But they're all right, aren't they?"

The nurse managed a frazzled nod. "I'm sure they're perfectly healthy, Mrs. Saxon, but we need to examine them. It's routine for newborns."

"Why can't I go with them?"

"Dr. Dowling wants to see you first. He's with a patient right now, but he'll be down shortly." She patted Peggy's hand, then rushed off in response to a colleague's call.

Peggy lay weakly against the pillow. Her body was drained, but her mind was a frantic contradiction of fear and relief. It was over. Her babies were safe and healthy, thanks to a certain cab-driving cowboy with puppy brown eyes. She shuddered to think what might have happened if he hadn't been there.

She bit her lip, shaking off the frightening image. It didn't matter what might have been. All that mattered was that he *had* been there, a stoic stranger who'd saved her babies' lives, probably her life, as well. And she didn't even know his name.

"Peggy?"

She turned her head and recognized Marsha Steinberg, a member of the city council's administrative staff. They didn't know each other well, but their paths had occasionally crossed at city hall where Peggy held a clerical position before taking maternity leave.

The portly woman hurried over. Her eyes were red, as if she'd been crying. "My stars, child, what are you doing here?" Her bloodshot gaze shifted, then her lips thinned into a weak smile. "Why, you've had those babies. And so soon, too." She clucked her tongue and bit her lip. "Time goes by so fast. In the blink of an eye, things change. Lives begin. Lives end." Her voice quivered, choked to a sob. "So fast."

Peggy felt a chill. The woman was clearly distraught, and this *was* a hospital. "Is something wrong, Marsha? Your family...has there been an accident?"

She shook her head, sniffed and forced a smile. "Gracious, look at me, all teary-eyed when this is the best day of your entire life." She forcefully patted Peggy's hand, rattling a jangle of bracelets encircling her thick wrist. "Now, where are those beautiful babes of yours? I just can't wait to see them."

"Upstairs," Peggy murmured, following the woman's gaze to where a familiar, bleak-eyed man was speaking with an equally grim physician. "Is that Hal Stuart?"

A fresh spurt of tears beaded the older woman's lashes. She nodded and snatched a tissue from the box beside Peggy's bed.

Peggy frowned. "I thought he and Randi were leaving for their honeymoon right after the wedding."

Marsha's face crumpled like a wet shirt. "There wasn't any wedding," she wailed, then burst into tears.

Stunned, Peggy didn't know what to say. The marriage of Hal Stuart and Randi Howell had been touted as the social event of the season. It had been front-page news for months, and since Hal was the mayor's son, half of city hall, including Peggy, had been involved in finalizing preparations at Squaw Creek Lodge, which had been braced for the biggest nuptial bash in Grand Springs history.

Marsha blew her nose, snatched up another tissue and frantically dabbed her eyes. "It was horrible, simply horrible. The guests were seated, the organ was preparing to play the Wedding March, and then—poof!"

"Poof?"

"The lights went out."

"Oh. The blackout." Peggy relaxed slightly. "Well, they'll have to reschedule, I suppose...."

"No, no." Shaking her head until her gray curls bobbed,

Marsha clasped a palm over her mouth, struggling for composure. After a long moment, she straightened, wiping her palms on her suit skirt. "The bride is gone."

"Gone where?"

"No one knows. She just...disappeared." Marsha clasped her hands and angled a compassionate glance toward Hal Stuart, who was still engrossed in somber conversation. "The poor man," she murmured. "Poor, poor man."

Exhaling, Peggy shoved a tangle of hair from her eyes and tried to grasp what she'd learned. Or more important, what it all meant. She'd seen Randi Howell a few times, usually at city hall when she and her fiancé, Hal, had dropped in on the mayor. As Peggy recalled, Randi was stunning in an outdoorsy kind of way, with dark blue eyes and a wild mane of curly black hair that seemed ready to explode from the braids she favored.

Peggy had thought her rather shy, because she rarely spoke unless spoken to, and avoided eye contact. It seemed odd that a meek, apparently pliable young woman would be drawn to a man of such opposing temperament. Certainly no one had ever accused Hal Stuart of being timid. Brash, yes. Perhaps even controlling. But never timid.

As much as Peggy liked Hal's mother, Olivia, she'd never much cared for the mayor's ambitious offspring. There was something, well, furtive about him. Shifty.

And, of course, to Peggy's way of thinking, Hal Stuart had one other fatal flaw. He was male.

Peggy didn't exactly dislike men; she simply didn't trust them, and with good reason. Still, there were exceptions. A certain heroic, cab-driving cowboy came to mind—

"Poor Hal," Marsha murmured again. "He's devastated, positively devastated."

Pushing away a niggle of guilt at having thought ill of a man who was clearly troubled, Peggy managed an empathetic smile. "It's a shame the wedding didn't go as planned, but I'm sure Randi will turn up soon, they'll talk things out and everything will be just fine."

Marsha waved that away as irrelevant. "Randi Howell is no loss to a man like Hal Stuart. He was too good for her to begin with. But he and Olivia were so close—" She sobbed into the tissue, perplexing Peggy even more.

"I don't understand. What has Olivia got to do with the wedding?"

The woman's shoulders shook with the force of her sobs. "No one knew," she blubbered, nearly incoherent now. "She seemed so vibrant, so strong. No one knew her heart was weak."

A chill skittered down Peggy's spine. "Has something happened to the mayor?"

Marsha shuddered, sniffed, clutched Peggy's hand. "Oh, my dear, her assistant found her on the kitchen floor shortly after the lights went out."

"A heart attack?" When the woman nodded miserably, Peggy clutched the bedclothes. Olivia Stuart was a brusque woman, but a kind one. She'd gone out of her way to help Peggy through one of the most traumatic times of her life. Peggy adored her. "Oh, God," she whispered. "Not Olivia."

Snatching another tissue, Marsha blew her nose again, then fixed Peggy with red-rimmed eyes. "I'm so sorry, dear. I know you were close."

"People recover from heart attacks all the time. I know it's serious, but she'll be all right, won't she? She has to be all right."

Marsha gazed back toward the spot where Hal Stuart had been standing. He was gone. She closed her eyes a moment, then faced Peggy. "No, dear, she won't be all right. Olivia is dead."

* * *

It was late afternoon before Peggy was moved up to the maternity ward. As promised, the twins were brought to her, whereupon she promptly unwrapped them again to study every appendage on their pink, healthy little bodies. Satisfied and brimming with maternal love, she dressed them carefully, then cuddled her beloved infants until the floor nurse insisted she needed rest and whisked them back to the nursery.

An hour later Peggy was awake, restless. She couldn't sleep because her stitches hurt and her mind was awash with conflicting emotions—love for her beautiful new babies, mingled with terror at the responsibility of raising them alone, and profound grief at the death of a woman who'd been her friend.

Life was so fragile, so precious.

An image flashed through her mind, a fleeting memory of glowing brown eyes, a tender kiss brushed across her newborn daughter's brow. The stranger had saved her baby's life, and she couldn't even recall if she'd thanked him.

At that moment, her memory of the man became so crisp, so clear, that she could literally see him standing there, hat in his hands, eyes shifting with shy, western charm that was oddly endearing. She smiled at the apparition.

It spoke to her. "I, ah, didn't mean to disturb you, ma'am."

She blinked, frowned. "It's you."

Looking perplexed, he aimed a quick glance over his shoulder, then eyed Peggy warily. "Yes'm, I guess it is."

She pushed herself up and wiped a tangle of hair from her eyes. "I didn't think I'd ever see you again."

Startled and a bit crestfallen, he backed toward the open door. "I just wanted to, uh, see how you were doing. I'll be going now—"

"No!" She bolted upright, whipping back the covers as if preparing to chase after him. He froze, his eyes huge.

"I'm glad you're here," Peggy said, wondering where that peculiar bubbly voice had come from. "I really wanted to see you again."

That seemed to unnerve him. "You did?"

"Of course. I wanted to thank you."

"No need, ma'am."

"You saved my children's lives, and probably mine, as well. I'd say that deserves at least a modicum of gratitude." She cocked her head, amused by his obvious discomfort. "Isn't this where you're supposed to say, 'Aw, shucks, ma'am, it weren't nothing'?"

He widened his eyes, then narrowed them, but a smile played around the corner of his mouth. "You poking fun at me?"

"That depends."

"On what?"

"On your promise never to reveal to a living soul anything I did or said in the back of that cab."

His grin broke free. "Such things are a private matter."

"You're a good man, Mr.—" She cocked a brow in question.

"Stockwell, ma'am. Travis John Stockwell." He stepped forward, extending his hand.

Peggy took it, feeling the abrasion of calluses against her palm. This was a man who did more than drive cabs, she realized. These were work-worn hands, with strong fingers toughened by years of hard labor. Clyde's hands had been soft.

Clyde had been soft.

"Ma'am?"

"Hmm?" Blinking up, Peggy realized that she still had a grip on the cowboy's hand and was studying his softly haired knuckles as if they contained universal secrets. She released him reluctantly. "Well, Mr. Stockwell—"

"Call me Travis." His dark eyes twinkled with good

humor. "All things considered, I think we'd best be on a first-name basis."

She felt herself blush, but couldn't keep from smiling. "In that case, I'm glad to meet you, Travis. I'm Peggy Saxon."

"Peggy." The name slid off his tongue sweetly, with a soft twang that made it sound almost exotic. "That's real pretty." He regarded her intensely for a moment, then glanced around the room. "So, the babies are doing okay?"

"They're wonderful, pink and healthy and full of vigor." To her horror, a sudden gush of tears stung her eyes. "The doctor said that my daughter probably wouldn't have made it if you hadn't cleared her airway so quickly. I'm so grateful—" She bit her lip, irritated by the rush of emotion. "Hormones are such a pain. I'm normally not much of a crier."

The poor man looked stricken. "No, ma'am, you're sure not. You're the bravest woman I know."

That startled her. "You must not know many women."

He coughed, shifted his hat to his left hand and wiped a well-defined and decidedly muscular forearm over his brow. "Truth is, I don't have much chance to, uh, socialize. Not that I couldn't," he added quickly. "It's just that the rodeo circuit keeps me traveling so much there's never enough time to get to know folks."

Peggy brightened. "You like to travel?"

"Yes'm, I guess I do."

"That must be so exciting. When I was a little girl, I used to pour over maps and crayon circles around all the places I wanted to visit." She issued a nostalgic sigh and leaned back against the pillows. "Then I grew up."

Travis eyed her intently, started to speak, then thought better of it. He studied his boots, then aimed another glance around the room, seeming visibly disappointed that the babies weren't available. "Guess I should go. You need your rest."

She waved that away. "I'm too keyed up to rest. Do you want to see the twins?"

His eyes lit like neon. "Yes, ma'am, I sure do."

"So do I. I hate sitting here, waiting for some nurse to bring me my own children." Pivoting carefully, Peggy lowered her feet to the floor.

Instantly, Travis stepped forward to grasp her elbow. "Are you sure it's okay for you to be out of bed?"

"It had better be. I'm going home Monday."

"So soon? You're still looking peaked and all."

"The doctors said I'll be fine."

"Guess they know best," he muttered, although clearly he disagreed. He slipped a protective arm around her waist. "Lean on me, ma'am."

"Peggy, remember?"

"Yes, ma'am, Peggy."

She chuckled. "Cowboy, you are just too much."

Travis flopped on his hat to free both hands and helped Peggy down the hall toward the windowed wall of the nursery. They saw the activity from several feet away. Peggy felt Travis stiffen, hesitate. Her heart leapt into her throat.

She pushed away and stumbled forward on her own. A moment later he caught up and braced her as she pressed her hands against the glass. Inside, a team of medical personnel surrounded a Plexiglas incubator, their worried eyes focused above sterile masks. Frantic activity announced a tiny life in peril. Peggy couldn't see the infant they were working on, but knew it could be one of her own precious babies. She was distraught. She was terrified.

But this time she wasn't alone.

Three

Travis felt like he'd been kicked in the gut.

He tightened his grip on the frantic woman, urging her away from the nursery window. "Let's go on back now. You ought to be resting."

Peggy yanked out of his grasp just as a woman in a white, nurse-style pantsuit emerged from a nearby doorway. There was a stethoscope poking out of her breast pocket, so Peggy latched onto her. "What's going on in there? Please, is something wrong with one of my babies?"

The nurse spiked a quick glance through the nursery window and smiled sadly. "That's the preemie nursery." She added a deflective nod down the hallway. "Your babies are in the next room."

Peggy's breath rushed out all at once. She sagged bonelessly into Travis's arms. A warm, liquid feeling spread through his chest. He tried to ignore it, but a sweet fragrance wafted up from her hair, and the feel of her soft weight against him made him feel, well, kind of knightly.

It was a stupid sensation. Travis wasn't anybody's knight in shining armor. Even the fleeting image made him feel like a fool. Still, there it was, a protective instinct so strong that it shook him to his boots.

When Peggy's gaze shuddered toward the incubator, the nurse's did, too. "That's Christopher," she said with a sad sigh. "He was born late last night, only it was a little too soon for him, so he has some problems."

Peggy's lip quivered. "Will he be all right?"

"We hope so."

Peggy looked up at Travis, her eyes wide with concern, moist with sympathy. "The poor little thing. His mother must be so frantic."

The nurse's lips thinned into an angry line. "One would think so. Unfortunately, we have no idea where she is. A security guard saw her slip out through the north-wing exit, but he didn't realize that she was a patient, and since we were having trouble with the hospital generator at the time, things were a bit chaotic."

Peggy was horrified. "You mean she simply walked away and abandoned her baby?"

"So it seems."

"How can that be?" Peggy whispered. "How could any mother do such an evil thing?"

The nurse made a conspicuous attempt to soften her disapproval with a forced smile. "Christopher's mother wasn't much more than a child herself. She may have been overwhelmed by the responsibility of motherhood. We hope she'll be back when she's had a chance to think things through."

Travis followed Peggy's gaze to the incubator, which was partially exposed now that most of the medical team had moved away. Apparently the crisis was over. Electronic screens reflected rhythmic peaks and valleys, and inside the clear plastic box, hooked to a vicious assortment of tubes and wires, was the tiniest human Travis had ever seen in his entire life.

One doctor in surgical scrubs remained with the infant, gazing through the Plexiglas with an incredibly sad expression, but the rest of the group were already removing their masks, exiting the area with tight faces and rounded shoulders.

The nurse nodded at the red-eyed physician still hovering over the incubator. "That's Dr. Howell."

Peggy glanced up. "Randi Howell's brother?"

"Yes. It's been a horrible time for poor Noah. First his sister disappeared on her wedding day, then Olivia's death, and now this poor little preemie struggling for life without anyone to love him."

Travis knew Peggy was going to cry even before the first surge of moisture brightened those meadow green eyes. He made eye contact with the nurse, who understood his silent question and took Peggy's arm, urging her down the hallway.

The woman's smile broadened. "Your babies are doing beautifully, Mrs. Saxon."

Peggy sniffed, brightened. "Are they?"

"Indeed, and they're just gorgeous. Let's go have a look, shall we?"

"Oh, yes." Breathless, Peggy wiped her wet cheek, focusing on the window toward which she was being tactfully guided. "Oh...oh, there they are! Aren't they beautiful, Travis?"

"Uh—" he gulped "—huh." Clearly, childbirth had affected the poor woman's vision. To Travis's good old twenty-twenty sight, the red-haired infants in question resembled a matching pair of rumple-faced orangutans. "Umm, how come they're all wrinkly?"

Peggy laughed, a delightful, melodic sound that sent happy chills down his spine. "Patience, Mr. Stockwell. God just hasn't had a chance to iron them yet."

Oddly enough, that made sense. Travis nodded dumbly, his gaze locked on the tiny faces blinking up from their Plexiglas bassinets. The boy, so designated by a blue-striped stretch cap, had loosened the tight infant wrap and was placidly gumming his fist. The pink-capped little girl completed a giant yawn, then stared straight at Travis as if thinking, "Hey, I know you!"

A lump rose in his throat, nearly choking him. They may

not be the prettiest babies he'd ever seen, but he was absolutely convinced that they were the smartest.

"The staff adores them," the nurse was saying. "They're such good babies. Have you decided on names yet?"

Smiling, Peggy touched the window, flexing her fingertips against the glass. "What was the name of that road we were stuck on?"

Travis blinked. "Road? Oh, you mean Virginia?"

"That's it." She bent forward, wiggling her fingers at the little girl. "Hello, Virginia Marie. Mommy loves you." Angling a glance over her shoulder, she smiled. "Marie was my mother's name. And as long as we're performing introductions, Travis John Stockwell, I'd like you to meet Travis John Saxon."

If he hadn't been gripping Peggy's elbow, Travis would have fallen smack on his face. He opened his mouth, closed it, tugged his hat brim and stared at the floor. "I get it. You're having fun with me again, right?"

She straightened, eyes sparkling. "If you mean I'm enjoying your stunned expression, yes, I guess I am. But Travis is a fine name, strong, sensitive, gentle—" her gaze jittered and dropped "—just like the man who carries it. I want that for my son."

Travis licked his lips and shifted. "I don't know what to say, ma'am—"

"Peggy."

"Yes'm, Peggy, it's a real honor—and I appreciate it, really I do, only…"

She cocked her head. "Only what?"

"Only your husband might not be real excited about having his son named after a broken-down rodeo bum."

For a moment, she simply stared at him, with that tousled mane of hair spiraling around her face like a fountain of flame. Her complexion had pinked up considerably, although she was still extremely fair, and the smattering of freckles were standing at attention like a platoon of rust-colored soldiers. Even without a speck of makeup, Peggy Saxon was one incredibly beautiful woman.

Travis wondered why he hadn't noticed that before.

She pursed her lips and tapped a bare foot. "First off, *Mr.* Stockwell, I take umbrage at the term 'bum.' You're a fine man, and I won't allow you to make light of yourself."

Completely taken aback, he murmured, "Yes'm, sorry," then winced at the foolish response.

Ignoring his discomfort, she appraised his body from scalp to toe and back again, with such blatant admiration that he felt his neck heat. "Second, nothing about you is visibly broken-down, and even if it was, I also consider that term to be derogatory and therefore off-limits when referring to my son's namesake. Last but not least, I have no husband." She speared him with a look. "Does that about cover your list of objections?"

Travis swallowed hard. "Yes'm, I believe it does."

Issuing a pained sigh, Travis settled into the lounger and cooled his forehead with a can of soda. "I'm plumb tuckered. Having babies sure wears a man out."

In the corner of the Conways' converted den, Sue Anne swiveled away from the dispatch center to toss her brother a sour look. "Try shoving a ten-pound watermelon up your nostril and I might consider feeling sorry for you."

He popped the soda can, took a long swallow and wiped his mouth with the back of his hand. "Yep, women sure got it easy, just lie back and puff like a hound while us menfolk do the real work." He ducked as a throw pillow whizzed past his head.

Travis retrieved the pillow and tucked it behind his back. "A mite touchy, eh, sis?"

She scowled at him. "I told Mama I wanted a kitten. She came home with you."

"And you've been bullying me ever since."

"It's a rotten job, but someone has to do it." She smiled sweetly. "You have to admit I'm good."

"Best bully in the whole danged world, next to that fat-knuckled little horse apple who used to steal my lunch money."

Sue Anne angled a smug grin. "Who do you think hired him?"

"No fooling?" Travis hiked a brow. "Well, I'm glad to hear that. Takes some of the guilt off me for ripping pages out of your diary and pasting them up in the boys' bathroom."

Sue Anne roared to her feet. "You did *what?*"

Travis tipped back his hat, propped the soda can on his knee and launched into an exaggerated falsetto recitation. "'I'll just die if Daniel Harris doesn't ask me to the spring hop. He's so-o-o dreamy. Every time he looks at me, my heart flutters and I get all gooey inside—' *Hey!*" He flung up his forearms to ward off another pillow, two magazines and a tissue box. "Cripes, sis, chill out, will you? I was just joshing."

Travis peeked out from under his crossed forearms to judge the extent of his scowling sister's ire. Her brows were puckered, but not enough to form a pleated bridge across her nose. That meant she was perturbed, but not dangerous. At least, not to Travis. A stranger would have taken one look at that glowering face and run for his life.

Sue Anne Conway kind of had that effect on folks. By any standard, she was an imposing woman. Only an inch shorter than Travis, she outweighed him by twenty pounds and had been three-time women's barrel-racing champion before settling down with the only man who'd ever beat her at arm wrestling.

After skewering her brother with a narrowed stare, she plopped back into the dispatch chair, ruffled a choppy shock of short brown hair and smoothed her oversized I Brake for Cowboys T-shirt. "Lucky for you the radio console is bolted to the desk, or I'd jam the danged thing in your ear."

"Love you, too, sis."

"Yeah, yeah." Sue Anne sniffed, shrugged, but couldn't hide a smile. "I love you, too, kid."

Travis had never doubted that for a moment. His sister was the only stable person in his life, not to mention the only family he'd had since their no-account father drank himself to death on Travis's sixteenth birthday. Even though Sue Anne had been busy with her own family, she and Jimmy had welcomed the orphaned adolescent into their home.

But not for long. At eighteen, Travis had struck out on his own and had soon earned a reputation as one of the best bronc riders on the circuit. The rodeo became his home, leaving Travis free, mobile and emotionally unencumbered. He liked it that way. And on those rare times when irritated livestock used him for a doormat, Travis always limped back to his sister's house to sulk and lick his wounds until the call of the whispering wanderer made his boots itch.

Times like now, when he'd been grounded for weeks with a bruised liver and a chest full of cracked ribs. Heaving a pained sigh, Travis retrieved the wet package of pumpkin seeds and shook a few into his palm while the dispatch console hissed to life.

A familiar voice drawled, "Unit one to dispatch. You there, babe?"

Sue Anne swiveled around and flipped the switch. "Hi, sweet cheeks. Where else would I be?"

"Never know. Good-looking woman like you must get lots of offers."

"'Course I do. Why, there's a whole line of hopefuls queued in the parlor, just waiting for me to come to my senses and let one of 'em sweep me off my feet."

"And right pretty feet they are, too." Jimmy Conway's voice crackled with humor, but was slurred with fatigue. "Listen, hon, I'm outside city hall, getting ready to roll. Seems a pipe break opened a big ol' sinkhole outside an apartment unit up on North Nash Street. I can't take but half a crew. Buzz Ted, will you? See if he can pick up the rest."

"Ted's on his way in." Sue Anne focused on a mural-size city map tacked up on the wall to her left. "He should be a couple of miles from you. I'll divert him."

"Thanks, cupcake. Unit one out."

A moment later, Sue Anne was on the radio with the oldest of her two sons. At twenty, Ted Conway was a chip off the old block, a hard-working, hell-raising, good ol' boy who'd tear his shirt off for a buddy and risk his life for a stranger in need. Like his father, Ted was boisterous, adventurous and salt-of-the-earth good.

His younger brother, Danny, was less active and more sensitive than either his father or brother, but was every bit as committed to the down-home ethics that had made the entire Conway family one of the best liked and most respected in Grand Springs. Having just graduated from high school, Danny was already firming up college plans despite objections from his chagrined father, who'd always assumed that both of his boys would enter the family business.

If Jimmy had been disappointed that his youngest preferred computers to cabs, Sue Anne had been quietly pleased, not so much by her son's choice of career but by his fortitude in pursuing that choice. Sue Anne was the backbone of the family, the champion of choice, probably because she'd had so few options in her own life.

At thirteen, she'd been thrust into the roles of mother to a six-year-old brother and housekeeper for a drunken slug of a man who'd never known the meaning of the word *parent*. If it hadn't been for watching Jimmy Conway, Travis wouldn't have had a clue what a father was supposed to do. Jimmy was a good dad, a real good dad. He instinctively knew the right thing to do, to say. He'd raised himself a pair of danged fine sons, too.

But Jimmy had a good dad himself. Travis had long accepted the sad fact that a man who never had a real father could never expect to be one.

Which was exactly why Travis had long ago vowed to never, ever have kids.

"Travis?"

"Hmm?" He looked up, blinked and saw Sue Anne frowning. "Sorry. Guess I was lost in space."

"So what's new about that?" She smiled, a maternal, loving kind of grin that always made Travis feel, well, special. "You look tired, kid. Why don't you go take a nap or something?"

The reminder made him yawn. He rolled his head until his neck cracked, stretched and set the soda can on the table. "Maybe later. Right now, things are still pretty much a mess out there. As soon as the garage finishes washing and fueling unit six, I'll be on my way and see where I'm wanted."

At the word *wanted*, Peggy Saxon's face popped into his mind with startling clarity. Eyes like a field of spring clover, hair that sparkled like a wood-stoked campfire, and a tweaked-up nose spattered with the cutest freckles he ever had seen. Now, there's a woman who could make a man crazy with want.

Apparently, Travis's eyes glazed, because before he knew it, Sue Anne was on his case again.

"Doggone it, Travis, you're so danged tuckered you can't even keep your wits about you. There's no way I'm letting you back on the streets."

He yanked off his hat, ruffled his hair and issued a frustrated sigh. "That's not it, sis. I was just thinking about— Aw, hell." He slapped the Stetson against his knee before resettling it on his head. "She's all alone, you know? She hasn't got anybody at all."

Sue Anne blinked. "Who's all alone?"

"Peggy…er, Mrs. Saxon."

"Ah, the twins lady."

"Can you believe those poor babies are going to grow up without a daddy?"

Sue Anne shrugged. "We did. Long as they've got a mama, they'll be okay." She widened her eyes, realizing what she'd said. "I'm sorry, hon. I didn't mean—"

"I know, sis." He leaned back, understanding that his sister feared his feelings were hurt, but not certain how to explain that when it came to their mother, he couldn't recall enough to have any feelings at all. "I know you and Mama were real close, and I know how much you miss her. Thing is, I don't, because I can't remember anything about her."

"I wish you could." Sue Anne fiddled with the microphone cord. "You missed out on so much, Travis. That pains me."

"I didn't miss out on nothing. I had you." He glanced up and sighed. "Aw, geez, you're not going to tear up on me, are you?"

"Getting a cold, that's all." Sue Anne sniffed and cleared her throat. "I shouldn't have left you so soon."

"You didn't leave me. You got married. There's a heap of difference."

"You were just a kid."

"I was nine, old enough to take care of myself."

"No, you weren't." Sue Anne rubbed her eyes with the back of her hands, just as she'd done years ago when she'd been a tearful sixteen-year-old creeping into her baby brother's room to tell him she was running off to get married. "I should have taken you along instead of leaving you with *him*." She spit the last word out like a bad taste, then issued an irritated grunt and spun back to the console. "Go take a nap, Travis."

"Is that a boss-type order, or a mommy-type order?"

She glowered over her shoulder. "You aren't too big to whup, boy."

"Hell, no one's too big for you to whup." Travis stood, rolled the kinks out of his shoulder and strode across the room. "Jimmy still have those chain saws out in the shed?"

Sue Anne was on her feet now. "What are you up to?"

"Same as always, about five foot ten." Grinning, he tipped his hat. "If you need me, I'll be on Rourke Way. You've got the address."

With that, he sauntered out the door, whistling.

From her third-floor window, Peggy gazed out at the dark town. A few lights were visible in the distance—glowing windows in the police station across the square and in a squat building down the block that she thought was the telephone company. Apparently, those locations were relying on generators, as was the hospital. Everything else was black, cold. Dead-looking.

She shivered.

"What are you doing up, Mrs. Saxon?" The night nurse scurried across polished linoleum, whispering loudly enough to rouse the other occupant of the ward, a woman who'd given birth only a few hours ago. "It's after midnight," the nurse scolded. "You should be sleeping."

"It's too hot to sleep."

"There's not enough power for air-conditioning," the nurse murmured, stopping beside Peggy's abandoned bed long enough to indulge in a pillow-fluffing frenzy. She looked up and brightened. "A sponge bath might make you feel better. Shall I bring a water basin and a washcloth?"

"No, please don't bother. I'll be fine." She gazed back out the window, fighting fingers of fear that she couldn't quite identify and was powerless to control.

Clucking her tongue, the woman snagged Peggy's arm, hustling her back to bed. "My dear, you really must get some rest. You've a big day on Monday. If the blackout is over, you and your beautiful little ones will be going home. Isn't that wonderful?" Without waiting for an answer, the nurse tucked in the bedclothes, patted her patient's stiff shoulder and left the room.

Peggy winced, swallowing a sudden surge of tears. She wasn't really going home. Home was a cheery clapboard house a thousand miles away, a place where her beloved mother had once baked cookies, bandaged skinned knees and hugged away loneliness. There had been nothing on earth that Peggy's mom couldn't fix with a loving kiss, a soothing word. She'd raised her daughter alone, without the slightest hint of financial or emotional support from the husband who'd abandoned the family when Peggy was barely four. Her mother had worked, slaved, sacrificed everything for her child. When she'd died, Peggy's entire world had collapsed.

So Peggy didn't have a home anymore. All she had was temporary use of a dilapidated structure in a town of friendly strangers, a town in the throes of crisis. Like her mother, Peggy had been abandoned to raise her family alone. Unlike her mother, Peggy didn't have the foggiest notion how that could be done.

Although Peggy had squirreled away as much money as possible during the past six months, her only income while on maternity leave was a small unemployment stipend that was barely enough to cover the rent. She'd have to dip into her small savings for food, baby supplies and medical costs until she could return to work.

And then what? Even if she could afford the exorbitant price of good day care, how could she hand her precious children over to strangers?

How could she not? She had to work, had to support her babies.

"Oh, God, Mama," she murmured into the darkness. "I wish you were here."

Then she turned into her pillow and wept.

The moon was out. Travis thought that a good sign. No more rain, at least for a while. Grand Springs could dry out, clean up. Clear the roads.

The last item was the most important, at least to Travis's mind. He gazed past Sue Anne's frilly curtains to the sturdy pickup with the weatherproof Fiberglas shell that had served as his permanent home for more years than he cared to remember. It was a good truck, dependable as a well-broken roping horse. He and that old diesel had ridden a lot of miles together, seen a lot of fine country. Grand Springs was a nice-enough place, but it was small, kind of stifling for a career cowboy like Travis John Stockwell.

Travis John.

He smiled, turning away from the window, savoring the image of a screwed-up little face framed by wispy feathers of auburn hair. His namesake. Lordy, the thought sent a proud shiver down his spine. It was almost like being a daddy.

Or, at least, it was as close as Travis would ever get, since fatherhood had been crossed off his list a long, long time ago. Kids were too special, too vulnerable to be stuck with a broken-down rodeo bum—

Peggy Saxon's decisive voice boomed into his mind. *I take umbrage at the term 'bum.' You're a fine man, and I won't allow you to make light of yourself.*

Properly chastised—again—he felt himself flinch, then grin stupidly into the darkness. No one had ever scolded him for thinking too little of himself. Truth was, he kind of liked it, liked the spitfire spunk in Peggy Saxon's eyes as she'd stood up to him without a second thought. Most women were kind of wishy-washy, always trying to please a man, butter him up with wiles and such. Not Peggy. She wasn't afraid to stand up in a man's face and tell him what was on her mind. Travis liked that.

And he liked her, too. Feisty women intrigued him. He admired their spunk and independence. Most of all, he liked that they didn't need him.

Not that he minded helping folks out now and again, but he didn't want to be needed, to be smothered by the clingy weakness of those who didn't have enough gumption to face the world on their own.

Peggy Saxon wasn't like that, he decided. She was a tough woman, and smart, too. He liked the way she spoke, using educated speech the way rich folks used money—by tossing it around without a worry in the world. He admired that, admired her.

There was just one small problem. Travis couldn't seem to get the gutsy little redhead out of his mind. For a man who'd already taken the road as his lady, that was bothersome. And it was scary.

Four

On Monday morning, Peggy had just finished stuffing a plethora of complimentary baby supplies into a brown paper tote when a soft knock caught her attention.

Travis Stockwell hovered in the open doorway with one hand behind his back and the other clutching a bouquet of flowers. He hesitated, entering only when invited by Peggy's bright smile. "'Morning, ma'am." He shuffled his feet, glanced down at the colorful flowers as if seeing them for the first time, then extended them awkwardly. "I thought these might brighten your day some."

She took them gently, reverently, taking time to inhale the sweet fragrance of budding yellow roses nested in a cloud of white baby's breath. "They're lovely," she murmured, touched by the simple gesture and genuinely surprised because she hadn't expected to see Travis Stockwell again, hadn't seen him since Saturday evening. "You didn't have to do this."

He shrugged and flexed his free hand a moment before tucking his thumb in a belt loop beside a silver buckle embossed with the outline of a bucking horse. "All new mommies deserve flowers, you more than most."

Cradling the cellophaned bouquet, Peggy regarded the lanky cowboy with gratitude. Thankfully, he was too much a gentlemen to point out the obvious fact that she had no one else to bring her flowers, or to offer congratulations on the birth of her babies. "I appreciate this more than you know, Travis. Thank you."

His smile was quick, nervous, positively devastating—a flash of white teeth, a sexy sparkle that lit his dark eyes like amber flame. Peggy sucked in a breath, licked her lips, lowered her gaze and noticed a furry gray tube protruding from the crook of his arm. She blinked. "What in the world...?"

Travis followed her gaze. "Oh, almost forgot." Grinning proudly, he held out two of the most adorable stuffed elephants she'd ever seen. One of the creatures wore a squishy blue velour cowboy hat. The other wore a pink one. "For the babies," he explained when she simply stood there laughing. "Kids like stuffed animals."

She covered her quivering mouth. "So I've heard."

Frowning, he raised the blue-hatted elephant to stare into its beady black eyes. "Shucks, Homer, I think the lady's making sport of you."

Peggy could barely contain herself. "Homer?"

"Yes'm, and this here—" he held up the pink-hatted animal "—is Bertha. They're twins, you see, so I thought it was, you know, appropriate."

"Oh, yes, quite appropriate," she murmured, wiping her eyes. "It's just that I've never seen an elephant wearing a Stetson."

He looked stung. "They're Texas elephants, ma'am."

"Ah, well, that explains it."

"Yes'm."

"Are you from Texas, Travis?"

"Born and raised," he replied, setting the furry toys on the bed. "Been gone a long time, though." Before Peggy could follow up with another question about her new friend's past, he nodded at the open valise. "Looks like you're all packed."

"Hmm? Oh, yes. I just have to call a cab...." She angled him a look and found him grinning at her.

He clicked his boot heels together. "At your service, ma'am."

She smiled and heaved a soft sigh. "Peggy, remember?"

"Yes'm, Peggy."

"Hello-o-o!" A cheery nurse strode into the room with a wriggling bundle tucked in each crooked arm. "Are we all ready to go home?"

Peggy brightened, reaching out to take her blinking little daughter from the nurse. "Yes, all ready. Hello, sweetheart," she cooed, tickling her daughter's feather-soft cheek. "Mommy loves you." Virginia peered up as if trying to focus. She yawned, which tickled Peggy immensely. "I think she knows me."

"Of course she does, dear. You're her mommy." The nurse turned to Travis, eyed him quickly, then held out little Travis. "Here you go, Dad."

Travis's eyes nearly popped out of his head. He took a quick step backward, locking his hands behind his back. "Uh, thank you, ma'am, but I, uh—" his frantic gaze scraped the room "—I might squash him or something."

Peggy took pity on the poor fellow. "Mr. Stockwell is a friend," she explained to the nurse, who promptly raised a brow. Peggy adjusted Ginny's wrapping and reached out with her free arm. "I'll take T.J."

Travis lit up. "T.J.?"

"Umm." Peggy cradled her sleepy son beside his bright-eyed sister. "Using initials as a nickname is quite the rage these days. I think it suits him, don't you?"

"Sure does," he agreed, eyeing the infant with an almost parental pride. "Sounds real manly."

"Manly, hmm? Then, perhaps I should reconsider."

The edge on her voice took them both by surprise, and she immediately softened the comment. "It just seems a bit premature to project my son into a state of divine machismo before he can even burp by himself."

"Yes, ma'am—ah, Peggy. Kids need a chance to be kids, and that's a fact." He tipped his hat back, regarding her intently.

Peggy strongly suspected that he'd have said more about her apparent aversion to manliness had the maternity nurse not been flitting around the room, ears tweaked, eyes sparkling with interest.

When an awkward silence indicated that there would be no further discussion on the subject, the nurse sighed and rubbed her hands together. "All right, then. I presume the doctor has already discussed postpartum care and so forth. Do you have any other questions?"

Peggy felt the blood drain from her face. Questions? Dear God, she had a million of them, not the least of which was how she could possibly give both of her precious babies the nurturing care they deserved when she'd barely learned how to take care of herself. There was so much to think about. Breast-feeding, she'd discovered, wasn't nearly as natural as the books had implied. She'd assumed that babies instinctively understood what to do. Well, they didn't, and this morning's feeding had been a frustrating ordeal for all of them.

The instructional nurse had soothed, encouraged and re-assured her that a learning process was perfectly natural, and the babies would soon become quite proficient at filling their own little tummies. But what if they never learned how to suckle? And even if they did, Peggy was such a novice at motherhood, she feared doing something horribly wrong. What if she got confused as to which baby had been fed and which hadn't? Worse, what if her body couldn't produce enough breast milk to satisfy both infants?

And God forbid, what if they became ill? Would she know what to do? She'd read a million books on infant care over the past few months, but had little hands-on experience caring for babies. None with babies as tiny as her own. She shifted the tiny bundles in her arms, fighting a surge of panic.

"Mrs. Saxon?"

"Hmm? Oh, no questions, thank you."

"Well, then." The nurse glanced around, frowning. "Have you chosen to take advantage of our Mommy's Helper program?"

The program in question cost more than a month's rent and wasn't covered by insurance. Peggy refused to look up. "It, ah, won't be necessary."

"So you've made other arrangements for in-home assistance?"

"Yes."

From the corner of her eye, she saw Travis's eyebrow hike up and sent him a pleading glance. He frowned, but thankfully said nothing. The last thing Peggy's pocketbook needed was enforcement of the hospital's policy for post-partum patients without in-home assistance. She barely had enough to meet the insurance co-payment for two nights, let alone four.

So Peggy had lied. Again.

In the space of five short minutes, she'd lied about having questions, she'd lied about having help. Guilt pricked her, but only a little. There'd been a time in her life when she'd been naively truthful, gullibly sincere. Lies had wedged like chicken bones in her throat, choking her into silence. But that had been years ago. A lifetime ago. Before her illusions had been shattered.

Virtue, she'd discovered, was not a universal concept. Guile was the key to survival. And Peggy Saxon was a survivor. She had to be. Her babies were counting on her.

The drive home from the hospital was quiet, thoughtful. In the back seat, the twins were fastened in matching car seats that doubled as baby carriers, gifts from Vanderbilt's maternity staff. Peggy sat between them, a hand resting on each flannel-wrapped little tummy while she gazed out the window, lost in thought.

Power had been restored about six on Sunday morning. Traffic lights were on line and functioning. Gridlock had eased as mud-clogged roads were cleared and abandoned vehicles reclaimed. Grand Springs residents emerged to dig out and tally their losses. The blackout was over, but the effects lingered. The town itself would never be quite the same.

Peggy certainly wouldn't. Her entire world had been transformed since Saturday. She was a mother now. A *mother*. The sacred word frightened her, but she cherished it all the same and prayed she'd be worthy. Her babies were so precious. They deserved every wonderful thing life had to offer, health and happiness and the joy of knowing they were loved.

And they *were* loved. Deeply. Desperately.

The cab slowed, swerved to the right. Peggy idly glanced out the window at a bustling group of chain-saw-wielding workers clearing storm debris. She paid them little mind. Every block swarmed with weary residents repairing shattered shingles, hauling broken tree limbs and dragging ruined carpeting to cluttered curbs. Neighbor worked with neighbor, a familial shouldering of shared crisis. Peggy admired that, envied it.

But she wasn't really a part of it. Never had been. A community's social fabric was knit too tightly to assimilate a person so flawed that she'd been abandoned by her own father. Or her own husband.

Or both.

"Ma'am?"

Peggy blinked up and saw Travis pivot away from the steering wheel to stare into the back seat.

"You feeling all right?"

A bit dazed, she realized that the cab was no longer vibrating, because the engine had been turned off. "Yes, I'm fine. Why have we stopped?"

"You're home, ma'am."

Frowning, she focused out the side window and saw several beefy workers marching toward the cab. "Home?" she murmured, eyeing the duplex, which was in the process of having its porch reframed by a construction crew. "Who are these people?"

"Just a few friends of mine." Travis pushed open the driver's door, flashing a grin over his shoulder. "Thought you might need a bit of help hoisting that big old tree off your porch."

Tree. Of course, that's what was different. Peggy scooted forward on the seat, peering over the headrest to stare out the front windshield. "Ohmigosh. It's gone."

Well, the fallen pine wasn't exactly gone, but it had been sliced into manageable hunks and hauled into the yard, where it was apparently in the process of being chopped into firewood.

She gasped as the back door flew open, and cringed as a meaty, grinning face poked inside. "Whoo-ee! Look at those purty little babes. Ain't they sweet." A pair of china blue eyes crinkled at the corners, focusing on Peggy from beneath a hairy buzz of sandy-colored brows that matched the man's military-style crew cut. "You must be the proud mama. Pleased to make your acquaintance, ma'am. I'm James T. Conway. My friends call me Jimmy."

Before she could withdraw, the ruddy-faced fellow had clamped one of her limp hands between two of the biggest, beefiest palms she'd ever seen in her life. "I, ah—" Her gaze darted toward the front seat. It was empty. She was trapped. "It's nice to meet you, Mr. Conway."

"Jimmy," he replied cheerfully. Releasing her, the brawny guy reached beneath Virginia's carrier and unsnapped the seat belt. Before Peggy could protest, he'd expertly unlatched and raised the padded plastic carrier handle and hoisted the carrier, baby and all, out of the cab. "You'd be little Ginny," he said, holding the carrier up so his huge red face was inches from her daughter's tiny button nose. "Just look at them big ol' eyes. You're a beauty, you are. Your poor mama's gonna have to whack them boys off with a shovel."

Horrified to see her precious daughter in the oversize clutches of a complete stranger, Peggy struggled out of the cab. "Mr. Conway, please—" Someone took hold of her elbow.

It was Travis. "Watch your step, ma'am. Wouldn't want you to slip and, ah, skin nothing."

"Thank you," she murmured, glancing up at him. When she looked back toward Jimmy Conway, he'd been joined by a younger version of himself who was toting T.J.'s carrier. A stunned glance behind her confirmed that the back seat of the cab was now empty.

"That's my nephew Ted," Travis said genially. "You've already met his daddy."

"They have my babies," Peggy said foolishly.

Ted looked up, grinning just like his father. "They're real pretty, ma'am. Real pretty."

"Uh, thank—"

"That little Travis? Lemme see that boy." Jimmy snagged T.J.'s carrier, which Ted relinquished without protest. "Well, danged if he don't look like you, Travis." Travis narrowed his eyes but said nothing.

Peggy hurried forward, hands extended. "Thank you for your assistance, Mr. Conway. I'll take them. Mr. Conway…?"

James T. Conway—Jimmy to his friends—had hoisted both carriers to eye level and was marching across the yard making peculiar kootchie-coo noises at the tiny occupants.

Horrified, Peggy turned to Travis for help and found him with his head in the trunk. "That man has my babies!" she blurted.

Travis straightened and passed the tapestry valise and a fat package of complimentary disposable diapers to Ted. "Jimmy likes kids."

Reaching back into the trunk, Travis retrieved the two stuffed elephants. Ted took them, too, then nodded happily at Peggy and followed his burly father into the duplex while Travis snapped his fingers at a slender, dark-haired teenager just beyond the cab's hood. "Danny, come take this bag, will you?"

"Sure, Uncle Travis." The boy leapt forward, snatched the tote of complimentary baby supplies and gave Peggy a shy smile. "Congratulations, ma'am. You must be very proud."

The handsome adolescent was a younger version of Travis, with dark, puppy-dog eyes and a smile like a Texas sunrise. Peggy couldn't help but smile back. "Thank you, Danny. Yes, I'm very proud." Noting a few wood chips nested in the young man's ruffled hair, she nodded toward the partially cut stack of firewood. "Did you do that?"

"Some." Danny actually blushed. "Dad and Ted did most of the work. They're the muscles of the family."

Travis slammed the trunk. "And Danny's the brains."

Flushing wildly now, the boy peeked from beneath a fringe of thick, dark eyelashes that Peggy would personally have killed for. "Don't let Mom hear you say that. She always claims that if brains were gunpowder, men still couldn't blow their own noses."

"Your mama's right," Travis said, chuckling. "Women rule the world, and that's a fact." He took Peggy's elbow, escorted her a few feet toward the house, then stopped abruptly. "Oops." He loped back to the cab, reached in the open window and retrieved the yellow rose bouquet.

A moment later, Peggy stepped onto the freshly laid planks of her porch, clutching her lovely flowers. Still dazed, she hesitated and glanced toward two smiling construction workers who were shuffling nearby, brushing sawdust off their sleeves and looking exceptionally pleased with themselves. "This is—" words nearly failed her "—wonderful," she finished, feeling emotion clog her throat. "I never expected this. I—I can't believe how much trouble you've all gone to for me."

Travis lightly nudged her with his elbow. "Aw, shucks, ma'am, it weren't nothing."

When she stared up at him, he winked, reminding her of how she'd used the same words to tease him at the hospital. "Touché, Mr. Stockwell."

He shifted, used a fingertip to push back his hat and furrowed his brows into a frown that couldn't conceal the amused sparkle in eyes that reminded her of sun-warmed cognac. "There you go, using them fancy foreign words on a poor old country boy."

Danny edged by them, pausing at the threshold. "Don't let him yank your chain," he told Peggy. "Uncle Travis turned down a mathematics scholarship and speaks three languages." The boy swiveled aside to let his uncle's booted foot kick empty air.

"Smart aleck kid," Travis mumbled, swatting his hat against his lean, denim-clad thighs. "Young'uns nowadays have no respect for their elders."

"Why did you turn down a scholarship?"

Clearly uncomfortable, he shrugged, flexing his fingers around the Stetson's brim. "I guess riding horses appealed to me more than fussing with figures. Besides, the thought of spending four years chained to a textbook gave me hives."

"So how did you learn so many languages?"

"Where I come from, most folks speak passable Spanish.

I picked up their way of talking, along with a smattering of French from some French-Canadian cowboys I ride with up in Quebec.'' He tugged the crew neck of his T-shirt. ''I took the liberty of unlocking the place, in case someone got thirsty or had to use the, ah, you know, facilities and such. Hope you don't mind.''

''No, I don't mind at all.'' Peggy stepped across the threshold, glanced over her shoulder and fought a smile. ''Just one other question, Mr. Stockwell.''

''Yes'm?''

''Do you speak all those languages with a Texas accent?''

''Why, yes, ma'am, I reckon I do.''

''Just checking.'' Her grin popped free, then froze as she stepped into her living room and saw Jimmy Conway finger-wrestling her two-day-old son.

''Heck of a grip,'' Jimmy told T.J., who peered up from his carrier while his baby fist clamped the man's sausage-size index finger. ''Why, I'd bet a month's beer money you're gonna be a champion calf roper when you grow up.''

Travis strode inside, hooked his hat on a floor lamp and scowled down at his brother-in-law, who was perched on the edge of the sofa, leaning over the coffee table where the infants were side by side in their carriers. ''Get your grubby paws off that baby,'' he snapped at the big man. ''You're not sterile.''

Jimmy glanced up, surprised. ''Sterile? Hells bells, Travis, babies eat dirt and suck their own toes.''

''Ms. Saxon?'' Danny hovered in the kitchen doorway. ''May I have a drink of water, ma'am? I'm feeling kind of parched.''

''Hmm? Oh, help yourself, Danny.''

''Yes'm, thank you.''

''I put the diapers on the dresser,'' Ted announced as he

emerged from the tiny bedroom Peggy had fixed up as a nursery. "One package won't last too long, though. One of Mom's friends had twins a few years back—"

Jimmy looked up. "You talking about Alma?"

"And I remember her saying those babies went through two packs a day." Ted frowned, scraping a fingernail over his sparsely whiskered chin. "Or was it one package every two days?"

"I always liked Alma," Jimmy said to no one in particular. "Ugly woman, but she baked right tasty pies."

Danny poked his head out of the kitchen, clutching half a glass of water in one hand and wiping his mouth with the back of the other. "Can I get you something, Ms. Saxon?"

"Ah, no thank—"

"I can pick up extra, if you want."

Peggy's jittery gaze swung back to Ted. "Excuse me?"

"Diapers, ma'am. Alma liked the kind with little Velcro doodads to, you know, keep 'em from falling off."

"Strawberry-rhubarb was the best," Jimmy mumbled. "One bite made a man feel like he'd died and gone to heaven."

"Sure you wouldn't like a glass of milk?" Danny asked. "Milk's real good for you."

Jimmy's eyes glazed dreamily. "The crust was so danged flaky, makes my mouth water just to think about it."

Ted flopped on a lounge chair and swiveled Virginia's carrier around so he could tickle her chin. "About six packages oughta last a while, depending on how often they have to, well, you know."

"Maybe I oughta stop by Alma's, see if she's been doing any baking lately."

"How about orange juice? Vitamin C is good for you, too."

"Yep, six packages oughta do it, long as they don't get the runs."

Overwhelmed, Peggy swayed slightly and was immediately propped up by firm hands and a strong shoulder.

"You'd best sit," Travis murmured, his face close enough that moist breath warmed her cheek. "You're looking peaked."

She made no protest as he plucked the bouquet from her limp grasp, laid it on an end table, then slipped a solicitous arm around her waist and guided her toward the sofa.

"Move it," he growled.

In response, Jimmy immediately retrieved his finger from T.J.'s tenacious grip and stood, backing away as Travis gently lowered Peggy to the sofa. "Is there something we can do for you?" Jimmy asked, clearly concerned.

The question was aimed directly at Peggy, but it was Travis who answered. "Yeah, you can leave," he snapped, plainly annoyed. "Can't you see the lady is plumb tuckered by all your yapping?"

Ted rose quickly, rubbing his palms on his jeans. "Oh. Sure." He sidled toward the door, crablike, his head bobbing. "Sorry, ma'am. Didn't mean to cause no distress."

Danny scuttled from the kitchen. "You're all out of milk and juice, ma'am—" His eyes widened at Travis's narrowed stare. "Oh, sure. Sorry." He flashed a nervous smile, then darted out the front door.

Jimmy planted himself beside the sofa, frowning, oblivious. "Would you like an extra pillow, ma'am?" he blurted, gesturing to the cushion on which she was seated. "After the boys was born, Sue Anne always found comfort in settling herself on something soft and kinda squishy, you know?"

Travis moaned.

Jimmy blinked. "What'd I say?"

"That's all right," Peggy murmured, although she was

certain her face must be glowing. "I'm fine, Jimmy, but thank you for, uh, your concern."

"What the lady needs," Travis growled between his teeth, "is peace and quiet."

"Sure she does," Jimmy mumbled, his attention riveted on Virginia's sudden yawn. He grinned broadly. "Now, just look at that. Ain't that the cutest thing? You know, she must have her daddy's eyes, because..." His grin faded when he caught sight of Travis's thunderous expression. "Oh. Sure. Gotcha." Reflexively, he touched two fingers to his buzzed scalp as if respectfully tipping a nonexistent hat. "Was a pleasure to meet you, ma'am."

"It was a pleasure to meet you, too, Jimmy." Peggy started to rise, was stopped by a sharp throb and settled for a sincere smile. "I don't know how to thank you for all you've done."

"We was proud to help. If you need anything, you just call, hear?" His blue eyes gleamed.

A moment later, the screen door squeaked open, then swished shut. Peggy let her head sag back into the cushions and sighed. Her head was swimming. "Gracious," she murmured. "Talk about testosterone overload."

Travis cleared his throat. "Sorry, about that. Conway men do tend toward the rambunctious, but they don't mean any harm."

Her eyes fluttered open. "They're charming, absolutely charming."

"They are?"

"Umm." Smiling, Peggy leaned forward to straighten Virginia's carrier and tidy T.J.'s blanket. "I have to admit having so many Conways in the same room is a bit overwhelming, but I've never had more attention or felt more pampered in my entire life."

Travis was silent a moment. "I'm sorry to hear that."

Something in his voice, sadness perhaps, or disapproval, made her look up. "Excuse me?"

"A woman like you deserves a lot more than someone offering a glass of milk, or volunteering to pick up a few diapers."

Peggy averted her gaze the moment she felt the telltale sting of tears. When, she wondered, was the last time anyone told her that she actually deserved care, deserved concern, deserved anything at all? She couldn't remember, although it had certainly been before her mother's death. During her three years with Clyde, she'd been repeatedly told what *he* deserved and how she failed to provide it, but he had never concerned himself with his wife's needs. Or anyone else's, for that matter. Clyde had always been, well, Clyde. Peggy supposed she couldn't fault him for being exactly what he was.

But she did.

The sofa cushion dipped. "Are you feeling ill? Should I call the doctor?"

She turned her head away, dabbed her eyes. "No, no, I'm fine. I'm just—" She paused for a breath, then faced the gentle-eyed man seated beside her. "I'm just very touched, Travis. Touched and grateful for the kindness you and your friends have shown me. I never expected it."

His regarded her with wise eyes and a grim smile. "No, ma'am, I can see that, but it surprises me some."

"Why?"

"Because where I come from, folks just naturally do for one another, and friends, well, friends are like family." He cocked his head, absently running his knuckles over his hat-ruffled hair. "How long have you lived in Grand Springs?"

"A few months." Eight, to be precise. She continued to fuss with T.J.'s blanket, oblivious to the infant's growing irritation. "We moved here last fall so my husband—my ex-husband—could capture a mountain winter on canvas.

He's an artist, you see. Unfortunately, the world has yet to discover his talent.''

Travis nodded but said nothing.

Peggy licked her lips. ''Not that he didn't bring in his share of the bacon. He found other work to supplement his income. In fact, he was working at the lodge last winter. Ski instructor.'' Peggy wiped her face, forcing a thin smile. ''He, uh, taught people to ski.''

Travis nodded again, but not the out-of-habit-but-bored-stiff kind of nod. Instead, he was watching intently, offering every ounce of his attention. For Peggy, it was a startling revelation. She'd initially presumed Travis to be a typical example of the strong, silent type, but he wasn't. Rather, he was a man who listened, who actually cared what others had to say. It was a unique talent, one with which Peggy had little experience.

After a long moment, Travis shifted beside her. ''So, did he?''

Peggy gave him a blank stare. ''He who?''

''Your husband.''

''Oh. What about him?''

''Did he paint his snow pictures?''

''A few.''

''And then?''

She looked away. ''He left town last January.''

''You didn't go with him.''

It wasn't a question. Clearly she hadn't gone with him, and she had no intention of discussing the reason why. ''To tell you the truth, Mr. Stockwell, I'm feeling a bit fatigued.''

He lowered his eyebrows. ''Yes'm, I'm sure you are.'' At that moment, T.J. flailed a tiny fist and emitted a fussy gurgle. ''The babies, too, I reckon.''

''He's probably getting hungry,'' Peggy said, leaning over to unfasten the carrier's safety harness. She lifted the warm little body to her shoulder, cooing against his cheek. After a moment, she glanced up, seeing Travis still sitting there. "Well. Thank you again for all your help. I can't tell you how much it means to me, but I'm sure you have better things to do than hang around here."

"Nope, not a thing."

A slow heat crawled up her throat. "I'm going to feed the babies."

He nodded, then widened his eyes in comprehension. "Oh, right." He stood so quickly that his shin bumped the table, startling Virginia, who threw out her tiny arms and began to wail. "There, there, darling." Travis reached down as if to touch the crying infant, then flexed his fingers and withdrew, looking stricken. "I'll, ah, just wait outside."

Peggy stopped him as he made a move for the door. "Travis?"

He looked over his shoulder. "Yes'm?"

"I'm fine, really. You don't have to, well, hang around."

"I'll be leaving soon."

"How soon?"

He gave her a devilish grin. "Why, just as soon as your in-home assistance shows up," he said.

And Peggy's heart sank.

An hour later, both babies were fed, changed and tucked into the two mismatched cribs Peggy had found at a local flea market. T.J. was already asleep, but Virginia was bright-eyed and alert. Peggy adjusted her daughter's gown, then pulled a lightweight crib blanket over her. "Precious girl," she murmured, stroking a silky little cheek. "Do you know how much Mommy loves you?"

A dribble of milk oozed from the corner of her mouth. Peggy dabbed it with the soft burp towel hanging over the crib slats. She'd just redraped the towel when the room started to spin. The dizziness lasted only a moment, but it was long enough to weaken her knees.

God, she was so tired, so very, very tired. Motherhood was obviously an exhausting profession. Peggy desperately needed sleep.

Using the walls to steady herself, she tiptoed out of the nursery and down the short hall to her own room, collapsed onto the bed and fell into a deep, dreamless slumber.

Peggy jolted upright, awakened by a baby's cry. She rubbed her eyes, swayed and planted her palms on the mattress to keep herself upright. There was a brief surge of panic as she realized that she didn't know whether she'd been asleep for minutes or hours. She swung her feet to the floor, testing the strength of her legs. Thankfully, they held her up.

The baby's wail filtered down the hallway, then stuttered to silence. Pushed by a rush of adrenaline, Peggy sprinted into the nursery, skidded to a stop and nearly had a heart attack on the spot.

A strange woman was stealing her baby.

Five

The woman turned, tightening her grip on the tiny baby girl nested at her shoulder. Peggy's heart, jolted by shock, raced in fear. She stepped back, bumped into a large, warm body and spun around with a yelp.

Travis reached out as if to steady her, eyed her raised fists and thought better of it. "I see you and Sue Anne have met," he said, nodding toward the brick of a woman who flashed a warm, vaguely familiar smile.

Bewildered and disoriented, Peggy dropped her arms, turned and stared at the dark-eyed, dark-haired person who was tenderly cuddling tiny Virginia in her mannish, muscular arms. "Sue Anne...your sister?"

"Guilty as charged," Sue Anne said cheerfully. "I've got to tell you, hon, these are two of the cutest babes I ever laid eyes on. Now I see where they got those adorable feathers of red hair. Whoa, sweetie!" She turned her face toward the blinking infant. "My, that was a big one. Betcha feel better now, hmm?"

Peggy moistened her lips, fighting the urge to leap forward and rip her child out of the stranger's arms. "I'm pleased to meet you, but why— I mean, what—"

"What am I doing here?"

"That question did flash through my mind."

Chuckling, Sue Anne laid Ginny back into the crib, cooed once, tweaked the tiny little cheek and straightened, eyeing her brother with blatant amusement. "Tell her, Travis."

Peggy swung her gaze around, scraping him with a look. "Yes, Travis, if you wouldn't mind."

"Well, ma'am," he drawled, barely able to contain a smug smile, "looks to me like your in-home assistance finally got here."

"My *what?*"

"Guess I'll be moseying along." With that, Travis tucked his hands in his pockets and sauntered out, grinning like a cat with feathers in its teeth.

Peggy sagged against the wall for a moment, then hurried over to check each of her babies. T.J. was on his back, sound asleep. Virginia was awake, but yawning. Peggy inspected her daughter carefully, checking each and every baby appendage.

"Not that I wouldn't like to steal a couple of those sweet little toes," Sue Anne said with a knowing sparkle in her eyes. "But I figured the child might be needing them someday."

Peggy turned, propped her hip against the crib and regarded the woman, realizing that her smile had been familiar because it was very much like her brother's. The siblings shared the same whiskey-colored eyes and full, flashing grin, but the resemblance stopped there. Travis was lean and slender, with a tight, rounded rear that made blue jeans look like denim skin. Sue Anne, who was wearing a square-dance plaid shirt and a pair of courageous Levi's, was built like a tractor, squat and square, with shoulders broad enough for a man to envy. Peggy recalled that Jimmy Conway's shoulders were larger, but not by much.

Recognizing the blatant appraisal, Sue Anne laughed. "Believe it or not, I'm the spitting image of our mother. Travis takes after Pa. Except Travis isn't a wimpy, drunken fool."

"I see."

There was enough ice in the comment to make Sue Anne wince. "Guess he didn't mention that I'd be dropping by."

Peggy folded her arms. "It must have slipped his mind."

"Honey, nothing slips my brother's mind. He's got a reason for everything he does or doesn't do." She cocked her head, smiling kindly. "My guess is that he didn't want to be on the receiving end of the look you're giving me right now. Most men would rather be gut-gored than face off with an angry woman, and Travis isn't any different. Except in his case, you can add babies to the list. He's scared to death of the little critters, which is why it's so comical he got stuck delivering yours. First babies he's ever touched in his life, as far as I know. If he had his way, they'll be the last, too." Her eyes twinkled. "But somehow, I doubt he'll have his way on that. Thing is, he's a stubborn cuss, and he's been fretting about you."

"Why? He barely knows me."

"How much does a person have to know to recognize someone in need?"

"I am not *in need*—"

"Sh, now, don't get your dander up. Everyone can use a helping hand now and again. There's no shame in that."

"Peggy sucked her lips between her teeth, feeling inadequate, fighting tears.

"Hormones," Sue Anne commented with a knowing gleam in her eye. "After my babes were born, I cried at detergent commercials."

Peggy sniffed. "I feel silly." Not to mention fat, bloated and besieged by postpartum uterine contractions that made her wonder if she was going back into labor. "Listen, Mrs. Conway—"

"Sue Anne."

"Sue Anne, I really do appreciate your concern, but it isn't necessary for you to take time away from your family on my account."

"It is to Travis." Sue Anne brightened. "Say, you must be neigh onto starving by now. I got a casserole in the oven."

A spicy aroma wafted down the hall, making Peggy's mouth water. "Casserole?" She wandered to the doorway, sniffing appreciatively. "As in real food?"

"Nothing fancy, just chicken and noodles, but I figured you'd be too tuckered to fix anything nourishing for yourself." Sue Anne scanned Peggy as if sizing up a prized hog. "Looks like you haven't been filling your plate for quite a spell. You're nothing but bones. But don't you worry, hon, we'll fatten you up in no time."

Peggy angled a morose glance down at the tummy pouch that threatened to pop the elastic on the only pair of pre-pregnancy slacks she could squeeze into. "Fattening is the last thing I need."

"Leftover flab, eh?" Sue Anne clicked her tongue on the roof of her mouth. "Well, don't worry about that, sugar. It'll tighten up. After Danny was born, my belly sagged so low I could squeeze it between my knees."

"Really?" Peggy felt her spirits lift. "I thought it was just, you know, me."

Sue Anne's laugh was deep, resonant and warming. "Heck, no hon, we're all sisters when it comes to the pains of womanhood. There's nothing happening with you that hasn't happened to most all of us at one time or another."

For some odd reason, Peggy found that immensely reassuring. "What about, well..." Embarrassed, she made little scratching gestures at the sides of her abdomen.

"Stretch marks?" At Peggy's miserable nod, Sue Anne's eyes warmed with sympathy. "They'll fade some."

"They won't go away?"

"Think of them as a merit badge, the purple heart of motherhood." She tossed a sisterly arm around her. "Are your stitches giving you grief?"

Peggy rolled her eyes and nodded.

"A real pain in the butt, hmm?" Sue Anne grinned at her own joke and gave the new mommy's shoulders a squeeze. "And speaking of pain, let's talk breast-feeding. Just wait until your little sharks get teeth."

For the next few hours, Peggy's fear and loneliness dissipated in a rush of giggles and girl talk. With twenty years of mothering experience under her ample belt, Sue Anne anticipated and answered all of Peggy's questions, and shared tips on caring for babies—tips that hadn't even been hinted at in the parenting books Peggy had read. Sue Anne even helped give the twins their first bath, which was more a damp mop job than the full submersion wash, which she suggested could wait until their little umbilical cords had healed.

After the sponge bath, when the twins were clean and comfortable, Peggy was flushed with exhilaration along with more self-confidence than she'd felt in a very long time.

Then, with T.J. cradled in Peggy's arms and little Ginny nestled in Sue Anne's, they spent hours talking—about nothing and everything, about midnight feedings and the horrors of breast pumps, about diaper rash and maternal insecurity, and about the very real pressure of just being a woman.

Sue Anne was able to expose Peggy's fears without exploiting them, to rationalize seemingly irrational emotions, and to offer valuable reassurances. By evening's end, she'd become the confidante Peggy so desperately wanted, the sister she'd never had, and the mother she'd lost—all rolled up into one wisecracking bundle of effervescent energy.

Even more important, Sue Anne became exactly what Peggy needed more than anything in the entire world. She became a friend. Which was, Peggy suspected, exactly what Travis Stockwell had in mind.

"You mean you just left her *alone?*"

Sue Anne hiked a brow and flopped on the sofa, balancing a bowl of buttered popcorn in her lap. "What did you expect me to do, roll out a sleeping bag on her living room floor?"

Travis slapped his hat on his thigh and muttered an oath. "Yes, dadgummit, if that's what it took. Peggy just had those babies Saturday. It's not right, her being left to fend for herself and all."

"She's just fine. Ted, hand me that flipper." Sue Anne tossed a few kernels into her mouth while her oldest son, who was hunched cross-legged on the floor, felt around the carpet for the television remote. He found it and handed it over without taking his glassy eyes from a babes-in-bikinis beer commercial flickering across the screen.

Standing behind the sofa, Travis tossed his hat on a table, planted a hand on each side of his sister's shoulders and shouted at the top of her head. "What if something happens? What if one of those babies gets sick?"

Sue Anne tipped her face back, grazing her frustrated brother with a bland stare. "Peggy Saxon's a bright woman, Travis, and she's good with those babies. A natural mommy. She'll deal with whatever comes." She refocused on the screen, aiming the remote. Her thumb jerked.

Ted spun around. "Hey!"

"I wanna watch the news," she mumbled, continuing to flip channels as Jimmy ambled in from the kitchen with a half-eaten sandwich in his hand. Sue Anne spared him a glance. "Is Danny still handling dispatch?"

"Nah." Jimmy smacked his lips and dropped into a worn recliner. "There ain't been no calls for a couple of hours, so he flipped the switch to speaker and went on to bed.''

Since there was only one cab on duty during the slow overnight shift, the switch in question would sound an audible alarm throughout the house if a call came through dispatch. Most nights were quiet enough, which allowed the Conways to sleep undisturbed while the bored night cabbie snoozed through his shift parked by a quiet curb somewhere in town.

Jimmy finished his sandwich and eyed the bowl on his wife's lap. ''That popcorn?''

''Roasted maggots,'' Sue Anne replied, tossing the remote aside and settling back to watch the news. ''Want some?''

Jimmy leaned over and scooped up a handful. ''Hmm, hot buttered maggots. Yum.''

Clearly revolted, Ted, who'd been known to loose his lunch at the sight of a kitchen ant invasion, left the room, muttering. A moment later, his bedroom door slammed.

''More for us,'' Sue Anne said, grinning broadly to indicate that had been her plan in the first place. Jimmy concurred with a grunt, then dug another huge handful out of the bowl.

Travis was about to bust. ''Forget the danged popcorn. What about Peggy?''

Jimmy looked up, his cheeks bulging. ''Wha' about her?''

''Don't talk and chew at the same time,'' Sue Anne growled. ''Didn't your mama teach you no manners?''

Properly chastised, Jimmy swallowed. ''Yes, honey pot.'' He heaved sideways in the chair, turning his attention back to Travis. ''So, what's wrong with Ms. Saxon?''

''Sue Anne left her alone, that's what. Alone.'' He shot an accusatory stare at the back of his sister's head, which responded by jerking around as if it had been physically poked.

She glared at him. "Dang it, Travis, she's a grown woman, and she don't need no baby-sitter. If she wants help, she can pick up the phone."

"And how long would she have to wait before help arrives?"

"Oh, sorry, Travis—"

"She's miles out of town. Why, a person could choke to death before an ambulance could even get out of the downtown garage."

Jimmy nodded. "That's true."

Sue Anne cowed him with a look. "No one is going to choke to death, or bleed to death, or die in their dadgummed sleep. Peggy and the babies are just fine." She swiveled on the sofa and fixed her brother with a killing stare. "Got that, Mr. Always-Looking-For-Trouble? Nobody is sick, and *nobody is going to get sick.*"

"Wouldn't dare," Jimmy mumbled, feigning interest in the televised news program while his wife glowered.

Travis puffed his cheeks and blew out a breath. Part of him understood that his fear for Peggy went far beyond normal concern for a fellow human being, but he couldn't help himself. He was consumed by thoughts of her, by memories of her vulnerable eyes, and the way her lips tightened when she was trying to be brave.

Travis Stockwell knew what it felt like to be alone and afraid. That's how he'd spent his entire childhood—alone, afraid, waiting for his father to stumble home from the bar, terrified that he wouldn't make it; terrified that he would. Sober, Silas Stockwell had been frightened by his own shadow. Drunk, he'd feared nothing, not even God. Why should he? Whiskey had made him omnipotent. And it had made him mean.

Travis had always feared his father would die in a bar

fight, crumpled in a pool of his own blood. Instead, Silas had expired in his own foul bed, a skeleton of a man ravished by the cancer that had eaten a vicious path from his liver to his brain. Sixteen-year-old Travis had watched helplessly and been filled with unbearable despair.

Despite having endured years of cruelty and beatings and drunken rage, in the end Travis had cried for his father, for the man he could have been, for the man he'd become, and for the legacy of disillusionment he'd bequeathed his only son.

"Oh, almost forgot." Sue Anne's voice popped the sad bubble of his thoughts. "You got mail today, something from the pro rodeo association. Looks like a flyer."

At the moment, Travis couldn't have cared less. "Shouldn't have left her alone," he mumbled to no one in particular.

Sue Anne heaved an exasperated sigh. "Oh, for corn's sake. Quit that dadgummed pacing and come sit down."

"I don't want to sit down."

"Then go jog around the block or something. You're driving me nuts—"

"Hush," Jimmy said suddenly, pointing at the screen. "They're talking about the mayor."

Frowning, Sue Anne fumbled for the remote and hiked up the volume.

"Collapsing at her home before her son's wedding..." The bespectacled anchorman shifted and stared into the camera. "Mayor Stuart was transported to Vanderbilt Memorial, where she later died. Sources confirm that the mayor's final word, 'coal,' may have been a reference to the zoning vote on a strip mining operation that had politically pitted Mayor Stuart against her son, Councillor Hal Stuart, who favors the development. In other news—" the photograph of a man Travis vaguely remembered seeing at the hospital flashed across the screen "—police are requesting citizen assistance in identifying an apparent amnesia victim. The man, who calls himself Martin Smith, was first spotted by the occupants of a vehicle trapped by a mud slide...."

The newsman continued his report, but Travis was distracted when Sue Anne suddenly lowered the volume. "Terrible thing about the mayor," she murmured, hitching her arm over the sofa back and swiveling around to meet her brother's gaze. "I met her once, over at Higgen's Five and Dime. Seemed like a real nice lady."

"Good tipper," Jimmy added, reaching for his wife's can of soda. "Gave me ten for a two-dollar fare."

Sue Anne tucked her legs up and scratched her choppy hair. "This sure has been a weird week. The storm, the blackout, the biggest social event of the season going to hell in a bucket when the bride takes a powder, then the groom's mother meets her Maker worrying about fossil fuel...."

She paused, clicked her tongue and had just shifted her monologue into general political commentary about the ills of society when Travis jerked to a stop, staring at the television. "Turn it up." Sue Anne tossed him an annoyed glance, but complied.

"Third rape in the area since May... Although a police spokesman denies that the incidents are related, a reliable source confirms that the possibility of a serial rapist is being investigated."

When a map flashed on the screen, superimposed with large red *X*s, Travis gripped the back of the sofa. "My God, that's just a few blocks from where Peggy lives."

Sue Anne drew her brows together in a worried frown. "Now, Travis, don't go getting your shorts in a twist—"

But Travis wasn't listening. He'd already grabbed his hat and hit the door running.

The cranky sound floated into Peggy's slumber, disrupting the most marvelous dream about a moonlit night and a romantic cowboy who bore a striking resemblance to Travis Stockwell.

She issued a disappointed sigh as the dream dissipated, and the fussy little noise became more demanding. She sat up, rubbing her eyes, and automatically whipped off the covers. A moment later she was padding toward the nursery, stifling a yawn.

She turned on the hall light to illuminate the twins' room without flooding it with blinding brilliance, and went directly toward T.J.'s crib. His little face was screwed into a purple mask of pure displeasure.

"There, there," she murmured, scooping the firm baby body into her arms. "Mommy's here."

T.J. shuddered, then emitted a startled wail that roused his sister, who was clearly irritated by the interruption. With her cranky son nested against her shoulder, Peggy moved to her daughter's crib.

"I know," she whispered softly, laying T.J. beside his sister so she could tend them both. "Your brother is a noisy roommate, isn't her?" Ginny blinked up, her tiny chin puckered and quivering.

It was, Peggy realized, a miniature duplicate of Clyde's chin. She wondered why she hadn't noticed that before. Scrutinizing her daughter's adorable little face, she also saw that Virginia's nose tweaked upward like her father's.

Her father.

A venomous anger hit Peggy like a body blow. Clyde Saxon didn't deserve the title of father. He was a coward and a cad, and Peggy was irrationally infuriated that his blood ran in the veins of her beautiful babies. It was her fault, of course. If she hadn't been so gullibly naive, she'd have recognized the selfish serpent beneath the superficial charm. She never would have married him.

But as much as it galled her to admit it, she was secretly

grateful to Clyde. If not for him, she wouldn't have been blessed with her precious children. They were everything to her. They were her life.

Suddenly, her heart filled to overflowing as she gazed at her beloved infants laying side by side, rigid and wailing, united in baby outrage. Yes, she decided, Clyde did have one redeeming characteristic. From his gene pool this extraordinary life had sprung.

Peggy's anger dissipated as suddenly as it had evolved. She smiled down at her children and lifted T.J. into her arms. "I think," she murmured to both of them, "that dry diapers and a midnight snack will make you feel much better."

Unconvinced, Virginia continued to fuss and flail her tiny fists while Peggy tended her brother. The changing process went efficiently, if not expertly. Still, Peggy was pleased. After all, she'd never changed a diaper in her life until this morning. Or was it yesterday morning? She glanced at her watch. Well after midnight, so technically it was Tuesday. She'd lost track of time.

She was a mother. Peggy could still hardly believe it.

"In less than twelve hours, you'll be exactly three days old," She told T.J., who didn't seem impressed by the revelation. She tidied his gown, then repeated the changing process for his sister, who was immediately calmed by her mother's touch. Peggy took a deep breath, smiling down at her precious babies. "There. Not bad for a rookie, hmm?"

The question so excited T.J. that he flung his fists, hit himself in the nose and let out a wail that was instantly matched by the howl of his startled sister.

Peggy's confidence crumbled. "Sh, it's all right, sweeties, Mommy's here. Mommy's—" she winced as they hiked up the volume "—here," she finished lamely.

Clearly, the situation called for considerably more than

her esteemed presence in the room. They were hungry. Both of them. At the same time.

Responding to her infants' cries, Peggy's breasts became engorged, painful. Two breasts. Two hungry babes. Fortuitous enough, but the thought of simultaneously juggling two feeding infants made her break out in a cold sweat.

She sighed, scooping up T.J. while Virginia thrashed with righteous indignation and struggled to focus newborn eyes. "Sorry, sweetie," she murmured to her wailing daughter. "You'll have to wait a few minutes. Your brother asked first."

By a quarter of two, both infants had drifted into a satisfied slumber, and their exhausted mother returned to the sanctuary of her own tiny room. Peggy's shoulders ached. Her head throbbed, and she was so tired she wobbled when she walked.

Her bed, invitingly tousled by her abrupt departure, beckoned like a lover. She sighed, crossed the room and glanced out the window. Something struck her as odd. She stopped, lifted a blind slat for a better look and saw a strange vehicle parked at the front curb behind her car.

A nervous skitter slipped down her spine. The full moon splashed the vehicle's hood, providing enough illumination to confirm that Peggy had never seen it before, and she was certain it had no legitimate reason to be there.

From the corner of her eye, she saw a shadow duck around the side of the duplex. A large shadow. A man's shadow. Someone was out there, a sinister presence creeping beneath her bedroom window. Peggy had never been more terrified in her life.

Six

The cat's eyes gleamed feral in the moonlight. Back arched, the animal froze for a split second, then shot past the fence into the shadowed safety of the woods.

Crouched beside the porch, Travis flipped off his trusty penlight, blew on the lens, then spun it like a bone-handled revolver and tucked it into his jeans pocket. He sat back on his boot heels, rubbing his stiff neck. The startled cat was the third varmint he'd chased off since midnight, none of them two-legged.

Which suited Travis fine. A puny penlight was enough to frighten off raccoons and pussycats, but it wouldn't provide much protection against an armed felon. If it came to that, Travis would rely on the element of surprise. The way he figured it, criminals were gutless cowards who preyed on the weak and would wet themselves if confronted by someone their own size.

At least, that was his fervent hope. Heroism wasn't really Travis's thing. He much preferred leaving valor to those whose palms didn't sweat at swaying tree shadows. But a cowboy's got to do what a cowboy's got to do.

He stood slowly, bones creaking as he stifled a yawn. When he turned toward the street, light erupted all around him, a blinding brilliance that made his eyes water.

"Freeze. Police!" The command boomed from the core of the radiance. "Get down! Down on the ground. Get down now!"

Startled and confused, Travis raised a forearm to shade

his eyes. Something leapt out of the light, grabbed his wrist and twisted him around.

It was a chaos of grasping hands, bellowing voices, an unintelligible din of pandemonium. Before he could take a second breath, he'd been flipped over the freshly chopped tree stump, bounced off the newly stacked woodpile and was sprawled on the ground, sucking dirt. His sore ribs shrieked at the indignity. Someone yanked an arm behind his back, shoved his wrist up to his shoulder blades. A knee bludgeoned his spine. A rock bit into his cheek. Rough hands dug through his pockets, emptied them. Cold metal wrapped his wrists, clicked tight.

Then, as quickly as the swarm had descended, it rose up, leaving Travis flat on his belly, winded, bulldogged and tethered like a thrown steer.

"Find a gun?"

"Nah, just his wallet and this."

Twisting his head, Travis saw a uniformed police officer displaying the penlight to someone beyond his view. He felt the vibration of feet around his prone form, saw several pairs of shoes and estimated that he was surrounded by at least three, possibly four officers.

A moment later, two of the cops flanked him and hauled him to his feet. He swayed there, spitting grass, and cast a woeful glance at his beloved Stetson, which lay on the ground dangerously close to a pair of tromping feet. "My hat," he managed to mutter. "Don't step on my danged hat."

The officer on his right gave his manacled arm a jarring jerk. "You won't be needing it, pal."

Not need his hat? Travis blinked up, alarmed by the heresy. Why, a cowboy without his hat was like, well, like a cop without a badge. He cleared his throat, tried to speak rationally despite a distracting film of wet grit on his tongue. "I'm pretty sure I wasn't doing whatever it is you think I was doing."

The policeman who was grasping his shackled wrist shot him a cynical stare.

Travis tried again, more succinctly this time. "You're making a mistake."

"Sure, buddy, sure." Clearly unimpressed, the policeman squinted toward the front porch, then turned toward a fellow officer who was using a massive flashlight to search the yard, presumably for evidence. "Hey, Charlie. Is that the RP?"

Charlie glanced toward the duplex. "Yeah, I imagine. Dispatch said the prowler report came directly from the resident."

Travis frowned, followed the policeman's gaze and saw Peggy Saxon's horrified face peering out the front window. His heart sank halfway to his boots.

A moment later, the porch light flashed on and she dashed out, clutching her robe at the throat. "Travis?" Her eyes were huge. "Ohmigosh, Travis, is that you?"

He tried to smile, but his lips stuck to his teeth. "You oughtn't be out here, ma'am. You'll catch a chill."

Peggy's jaw drooped like a gate with a broken hinge.

Officer Charlie stepped forward. "Mrs. Saxon?" She closed her mouth, managing to nod. "You know this fellow?"

For a moment, she simply stared at Travis, stunned. Then her eyes narrowed into mean green slits. "It would serve you right if I told them that I'd never seen you before in my life," she snapped.

Travis hung his head. "Yes'm."

"What in the world are you doing here?"

"Well, thing is..." He paused, opting for a diversionary tactic and flashed his trademark grin. "So, how'd you and

Sue Anne get on? She said those babies were cuter than a pair of big-eyed calves—''

"Cut the bull, Stockwell." She folded her arms, glaring at him. "You were spying on me, and I want to know why."

"Spying? Why, no, ma'am, I wouldn't do any such thing. I was just, well, passing by and, ah…" Alerted by her furrowed frown, Travis realized that Peggy Saxon wasn't the least bit fooled, and had no intention of buying a load of hooey, no matter how tempting the price. She wanted the truth, and if the angry wrinkle of her darling amber brows was any clue, she wanted it now.

But danged if she wasn't pretty when she was mad. Those green eyes flashing, and that pert little nose all scrunched up—

Peggy tapped an impatient foot.

Travis rolled his shoulders forward and sighed. "It just didn't seem right, you being alone your first night home with those babies. And when I heard that there'd been, ah, some trouble around here, I figured I could catch a few winks in my truck so I'd be close by in case—"

"Trouble?" Peggy blinked once and spun toward the squat, ruddy-faced policeman who had a death grip on Travis's left bicep. "What kind of trouble?"

Startled, the officer tipped his hat, his gaze darting to Travis, then back to Peggy. "There've been a few incidents, ma'am," he admitted. "Some women have been, uh, assaulted."

Even in the pale moonlight, Travis saw the color drain from her face. "Oh."

An older officer with a bushy mustache loped back from the street clutching Travis's wallet and the portable two-way radio he kept in his pickup truck. "The truck checks out," the officer told Officer Charlie. "No wants, no warrants registered to Travis J. Stockwell. He's clean, too," he added, nodding at Travis.

The ruddy-faced policeman seemed disappointed. "Maybe he's been using that scanner to keep tabs on the police."

"It's not a scanner," the mustached officer replied. "It's just a CB radio." He glanced up at Peggy. "We can still take him in for trespassing, if you want, ma'am."

To Travis's horror, she pursed her lips as if considering the option. "Trespassing? Oh, no, Peggy, ma'am, I wasn't trespassing." He straightened, shaking his head so violently he could feel his hair vibrate. Words rushed out, nervousness accentuating his Texas twang until it was thick enough to hang a hat on. "Something was moving out yonder in those woods, heading straight for your backyard. I couldn't rightly tell what it was, so I just moseyed over for a quick look-see—"

Peggy interrupted. "What was it?"

"Ma'am?"

"The 'something' that came out of the woods. What *was* it?"

"Oh." He coughed and studied his boots. "It was, umm, well, a cat."

Officer Charlie chuckled. The ruddy-faced officer snorted in disbelief.

"What color was it?"

Travis looked up, perplexed. "The cat, ma'am?" She gave an irritated nod. "It was orange, I think, and kind of striped."

Peggy turned away, but not before Travis saw the telltale quirk of that sweet little dimple. At that point, he realized that she had no intention of having him arrested.

He exhaled all at once, then managed a reproachful stare. "Why, ma'am, if I didn't know better, I'd swear you were just funning with me. 'Course that can't be true, on account of a fine lady such as yourself being too well bred to enjoy watching a man sweat like a pig in a butcher's kitchen.''

"You're mistaken, Mr. Stockwell. I'm enjoying it very much.'' Peggy unfolded her arms and fiddled with the lapels of a robe that Travis now noticed was worn through at the elbows. "You took ten years off my life,'' she muttered. "I ought to let them have you.''

He let his head droop forward, then rolled his eyes up and widened them, using the same whipped-puppy expression that used to melt Sue Anne's heart whenever she got perturbed at him. "Yes'm, Peggy, ma'am. I'm real sorry.''

A smile twitched the corner of her mouth. "Nice try, cowboy.''

"Excuse me?''

"I learned a long time ago that you can avoid stepping in it if you recognize the smell.'' She heaved a sigh, shoved back a tangle of fiery hair. "Lucky for you, I've been feeding a little orange-striped stray. There's a food bowl on the back porch.'' She turned to Officer Charlie. "I'm terribly sorry for the inconvenience, Officer, but apparently there's been a misunderstanding. I won't be pressing charges. You can let him go.''

"You sure, ma'am?'' When she nodded, albeit reluctantly, Officer Charlie moved around to remove the handcuffs.

Travis rubbed his wrists, retrieved his wallet, CB radio and hat, and cast Peggy a woeful look as the ruddy-faced policeman hauled him aside to give him what appeared from Peggy's vantage point to be a stern lecture.

Peggy sagged against the porch rail, drained and oddly disoriented. She wanted to be angry. Dammit, she *was* angry. When she'd seen that slinking male shadow outside her window, she'd nearly fainted in terror. Her hands were still shaking.

If Travis Stockwell could be believed, he'd been trying

to protect her, a concept that boggled her skeptical, independent mind. No man had ever put himself out for Peggy before, not her husband, not her father, not even the hormone-pickled, adolescent dog who'd escorted her to the prom, then abandoned her for a tipsy blond cheerleader rumored to be taking all comers behind the high school gym.

That had been a hard lesson, one of many that had taught Peggy not to expect much from the male of the species. Men, even relatively young ones, were transitory at best. At worst, they were deceitful, selfish and downright cruel.

Clearly, Travis Stockwell did not represent the worst of his kind, which to Peggy's mind meant that he was basically amicable, probably decent, a person who would treat others with respect for however long he chose to hang around.

Naturally, Peggy didn't hold Travis personally responsible for the emotional wanderlust afflicting his gender. She was, however, acutely aware of his maleness. From the brim of his Stetson to the scuffed toes of his stamped leather boots, Travis Stockwell was pure, unadulterated man. That kept her wary. It also affected her in deeper, more disturbing ways.

The rev of a car engine broke into her thoughts. As she glanced up, one squad car was pulling away from the curb. The other had already hung a U-turn and was speeding into the night.

Travis stood awkwardly at the foot of the porch steps, hat in his hands, shifting from foot to foot like a scolded child. "I'm real sorry to have upset you, Peggy. It was the last thing on this earth I meant to do."

"I know that, Travis." The fact that he'd finally dropped the formality of calling her "ma'am" didn't escape Peggy's notice. It made them seem closer, somehow. More like friends. She smiled, fidgeted with a loose thread on the cuff of her robe and was suddenly embarrassed by her shabby attire. "Your intentions were honorable enough, but I wish you'd have let me know what you were up to."

"I figured you'd just say you didn't need watching out for and send me packing."

"You figured right. Still, it was a kind gesture and I appreciate it."

The porch light illuminated his strained expression as he glanced over at his truck and back again. "So, have the babies been keeping you up tonight?"

"Among other things."

He actually blushed. "You should go on inside, then, try to get some rest. G'night, Peggy."

For some reason, she felt a small surge of panic as he turned to leave. "Wait! I mean..." Her voice trailed off as he glanced expectantly over his shoulder. "Can I, ah, get you anything?"

"Ma'am?"

"A glass of water, something to eat. I could make coffee."

"It's three in the morning."

"Ah, yes, so it is." She tangled her fingers together, locked them at her waist, but made no move to reenter the house.

Travis shuffled his feet and peeked up in that endearing manner that, although clearly manipulative, was nonetheless appealing. "You can sleep easy, Peggy. If you need me, I'll be right outside."

"I won't *need* you, Mr. Stockwell."

"Now, don't go getting your back up."

"My back is perfectly fine, thank you."

"Yes, ma'am, it sure is." He smiled, a brilliant flash that lit up the night and melted her heart.

Then a strange thing happened. Their eyes met and held. Travis's smile faded into an expression of awed confusion.

Peggy stood there, frozen, transfixed by a peculiar radiance emanating from his mystified gaze. He was looking at her as if he'd never seen her before, never seen any woman before. There was a reverence in his eyes that took her breath away, and a sensual promise that sent her heart into frantic palpitations.

With some effort, Travis jerked his gaze away, took a shuddering breath, held it, then puffed his cheeks and blew it out all at once. His Adam's apple bounced. He squared his shoulders and pulled on his hat. "G'night."

"Good night."

She steadied herself on the porch rail, watching him cross the yard with long, slightly bowlegged strides. When he reached his truck, he gazed over the pickup's roof, stared at her for a long moment, then yanked open the door and slid behind the wheel.

Peggy still hadn't moved. She should, of course. She should go inside, lock the door and get whatever sleep she could muster before the twins woke up for their next meal.

But for some reason, she couldn't move. Could barely breathe, in fact, and was utterly riveted by the moonlit silhouette moving inside the truck cab. He slumped down in the seat, tugged his hat brim over his eyes and settled in, apparently for the rest of the night.

Despite his prior comments, the realization that he wasn't leaving took her by surprise, jolted her numbed body into reaction. She spun smartly and went into the house, locking the door behind her. Her hand twitched over the light switch before she withdrew it and went to bed, leaving the porch light on.

The next morning, Travis's truck was gone. Peggy had expected that, but she certainly hadn't expected her heart to throb with disappointment at the sight of a vacant curb. But she couldn't afford to consider the worrisome implications of what she was feeling. Her babies were awake, and they were hungry. They were her entire life now. They needed her. She'd never be alone again.

"Dammit, Sue Anne, it's flat. Can't you find tires that a pebble can't pop?"

The radio crackled. "If you wouldn't ride a cab like a prized bronco, you wouldn't blow 'em out every time you take a corner."

Stretching the microphone cord, Travis hooked his arms over the cab's open door and stared morosely at the flabby hunk of flattened rubber. A squirt of steam hissed from the hood vent. He sighed and pressed the mike button. "Now it's overheating. Danged piece of junk."

"Unit six was the best we had until you got your clumsy paws on it. In the past month, you've blown three tires, bent the blasted axle and thrown the muffler halfway to Wyoming."

There was no malice in Sue Anne's voice, but the reminder irked him just the same. Under the best of circumstances Travis hated driving a cab. When things went wrong, that hatred bubbled into irrational fury. "It's not my fault this cheapskate town can't fix potholes."

"You don't have to hit 'em doing sixty."

"Time is money, right, sis?"

"Not when it's your time and my money." Papers crinkled, as if Sue Anne was shuffling call-out sheets. "Oh, by the way, you don't have to spend any more nights crouched in front of Peggy's house. They caught the rapist."

Travis stiffened. "When?"

"Just before dawn, trying to crawl into some woman's window over on the west side of town. Her dog wasn't none too happy about it, either. By the time the cops got there, his pants were shredded and the rotten louse was begging to be arrested."

"Good. They ought to skin the perverted SOB and nail

his hide to the wall." Travis shifted, licked his lips. "Uh, how did you know about last night? Me being at Peggy's, that is."

"Hmm? Oh, she mentioned it when she dropped by to return my casserole dish."

"She *dropped by?*"

"Uh-huh, on her way back from the laundromat. Oh, and she also brought three of the fattest strawberry-rhubarb pies I ever saw. When Jimmy lays eyes on 'em, he's going to think he's died and gone to heaven. And they're home-baked, if you can believe it. Peggy says baking calms her nerves, although it beats me where she found time—"

"How?" Travis blurted.

"The usual way, I imagine. First you buy strawberries and rhubarb at the market, then you roll out a crust—"

"I mean, how did she get there, what with those little babies and all?"

A patient sigh filtered through the mike. "In her car, Travis. Believe it or not, the woman actually knows how to drive. Shocking, isn't it? Next thing you know, they'll be letting her kind vote."

The vision of Peggy and the twins tooling around in the old rattletrap parked by her curb made Travis cringe. "She oughtn't be out so soon."

After a long moment, Sue Anne said simply, "She's alone, Travis. She doesn't have much choice."

"Smile, sweetums. Don't you want your daddy to see how pretty you are?" Peggy aimed the camera, pausing as T.J. cracked a massive yawn. A moment later, he turned unfocused eyes toward her, and she snapped the picture just as Virginia whipped a tiny fist in front of her face.

Sighing, Peggy set the camera down and straightened her daughter's red gingham dress, which matched her brother's tiny shirt. The babies, cuddled side by side on a blanket-draped pillow propped on the sofa, looked like perfect little dolls, adorably irresistible. Once Clyde saw how beautiful his children were, Peggy had no doubt that he'd come to his senses and become part of their lives.

Not that Peggy needed her ex-husband—she'd spent a lifetime convincing herself that she didn't need anyone— but her babies were another matter. They needed their father. More important, they needed to grow up secure in the knowledge that their father cared about them. There was nothing more hurtful, more traumatic to a child than parental abandonment. Peggy could certainly attest to that, and was determined that her beloved babies not suffer the same feelings of guilt and shame that had haunted her own childhood.

But that wasn't going to happen. Peggy simply wouldn't allow it.

She moved to the right of the sofa, changing angles as she focused the inexpensive camera that she'd carried on a three-year odyssey across the U.S. "Look at Mommy, Ginny. Oh, sweetheart, don't go to sleep. Just one more picture, okay? For Daddy."

A throat cleared behind her.

Startled, Peggy nearly dropped the camera as she spun around and saw Travis standing just outside the front door, which had been left open to encourage a hint of breeze into the sweltering room.

Travis shifted awkwardly, then tipped his hat with one hand while holding the other out of sight behind his back. "Sorry, ma'am. Didn't mean to startle you."

Pressing a palm over her racing heart, Peggy straightened and laid the camera on a lamp table. "I think I'm getting used to it. You seem to have a penchant for appearing at the most unexpected times. And the most opportune," she added with a smile. "The twins are all duded up for their first photo shoot. I was hoping someone would drop by so I could show them off."

"First pictures, huh? Bet they look real cute." He hoisted up on his boot toes, trying to peer over the sofa back. Since that was impossible from his vantage point just outside the front door, Peggy invited him in. The screen creaked open. Travis took a couple of hesitant steps into the room, just far enough to peek down and see the gingham-garbed infants. His eyes lit up, but all he said was "Wow."

Peggy proudly smoothed Virginia's dress and used her thumb to brush back an errant strand of T.J.'s soft red hair. "Pretty spiffy, hmm? The outfits were a gift from my friends at city hall. They gave me a shower right before I left on maternity leave."

"They look—" Travis paused while his Adam's apple gave a nervous jerk "—real fine."

The poignant glow in Travis's eyes did strange things to Peggy's heart. It was an expression of reverence, of wonder, of almost paternal pride. A lump of pure sadness wedged in her throat, because in her dreams, that expression of blatant admiration had always been in the eyes of the twins' father. She'd imagined Clyde gazing down at his beautiful children, bonding with them, declaring his determination to be a real father to them, to be an integral part of their lives.

Peggy had no choice but to believe that dream would come true some day. The alternative was too devastating to consider.

Travis suddenly laughed as T.J. stared up and emitted a bubbly gurgle. "Hey, I think he knows who I am."

He was clearly so thrilled by the prospect that Peggy didn't have the heart to inform him that his tiny namesake's eyes couldn't yet focus beyond the distinctive blur of bright colors and moving objects. "Of course he does. After all, you're the first person he saw on his way into the world."

That seemed to please Travis immensely. "Yeah, I guess so."

As he leaned forward for a better look, Peggy spotted a white bag clutched behind his back. "What's that?"

"Hmm?" He straightened as he followed her gaze. "Oh, a peace offering." His shoulders rotated in a sheepish shrug, then he held out the bag, exposing the logo of her favorite takeout chicken establishment. "I figured that you probably didn't get much sleep last night, what with the, uh, excitement and all—"

"You mean having the police in my front yard at three in the morning?"

He squirmed, scratched his ear and avoided her playful grin. "Yes'm. I, well, I thought maybe you'd be too tuckered to cook."

"I'm always too tuckered to cook real food, but I love to bake." She snatched the bag he offered, her mouth watering as she peeked inside. "Umm, biscuits, potato salad, all the fixings. Oh, gracious, this is just too wonderful. My stomach is applauding."

"I know. I can hear it." His smile broadened. "There's enough for two, in case you're in the mood for company."

Peggy didn't respond. She was already in the kitchen pulling plates out of the cupboard.

An hour later, Peggy pushed away crumpled bags and empty boxes, leaned back in her chair and massaged her stomach. "I'm stuffed to the gills."

Travis glanced up from the drumstick he was devouring, swallowed and washed the final bite down with a half glass of milk. "You sure you've had enough? There's a wing left."

She eyed the tiny morsel, poised between them like a crispy raffle prize. "If I take one more bite, I'll pop."

"Well, we wouldn't want that." Travis snagged the final piece, disposed of it quickly, then wiped his greasy fingers with a paper towel. He regarded her, transfixed by her sated smile and surprised by the sharp arousal it evoked. Lowering his gaze, he laid the crumpled towel beside his plate. "I was fixing to bring some of your pie back for dessert, only Jimmy and Ted got there first. Danny was pretty riled, on account of getting home too late for a taste."

He peeked up in time to see her amber brow quirk adorably. "Now, you're not going to tell me that two people ate three pies in one sitting."

"Okay, I won't tell you." Travis leaned back, smiled. "But I've got the empty pie plates in my truck. Sis washed them up and asked me to bring them by. I was supposed to tell you they were real good, too. 'Course, I wouldn't rightly know, because those greedy hounds didn't leave so much as a crumb."

"Oh, they were good, all right. I bake a mean pie, if I do say so myself. My mama taught me." She cocked her head, giving Travis a sparkly little smile that made his gut tighten some. "But I wouldn't want you to take my word for it. If you were to come by around dinnertime tomorrow, I just might have another one cooling on the stove."

"Maybe I'll take you up on that."

"Good." She sighed, pushed away from the table and cocked an ear toward the nursery, where the twins were snuggled in their crib for a nap. "Still quiet," she murmured, turning a quick glance toward the clock. "If I'm lucky, I'll get the kitchen cleaned up before they remember it's dinnertime."

Travis snagged a plate out of her hand. "You rest up. I can wash dishes."

She widened her eyes, seeming genuinely surprised that

he'd offer to rinse a couple of plates. "You don't have to do that."

"It'd be my pleasure."

"Well…" She blinked a couple of times, then her shoulders relaxed. "All right, then. Thank you."

It only took a few minutes to toss away the take-out wrappers and tidy the kitchen.

After Travis finished placing the washed plates in the drainer, he followed Peggy into the living room and stood there, shifting from foot to foot, knowing he should leave but oddly reluctant to do so.

After a moment, Peggy flashed a nervous smile and twisted her fingers together. "Thanks again for dinner. It was wonderful."

Travis shrugged as he settled his gaze on a stack of books and shoe boxes piled on the floor in the corner of the living room. "You must really like to read," he blurted stupidly, then covered the idiotic comment by striding over to lift the top book in the pile and flip through it, feigning interest. *"Rocky Mountain Majesty,"* he read, then glanced down at the next book in the stack. *"Highways of the Heartland?"*

She crossed her arms and aimed a bland smile at what he now realized was a pile of travel guidebooks. "I grew up in an old section of Cleveland, where my entire world was a fifth-floor view of squalid brick buildings and ugly pavement. When my mother showed me pictures of lush Alabama forests and meadows where she'd played as a girl, I couldn't believe there were places so beautiful. I made up my mind that someday I'd see everything for myself."

"And did you? See everything, that is."

She crossed her arms to shield her heart. "Clyde and I spent a lot of time traveling, if that's what you mean. I loved seeing new places, and he loved painting what we saw, so things worked out well for both of us."

"Clyde's your husband?"

"Not anymore."

Since Peggy clearly wasn't going to elaborate, Travis replaced the book on the stack and noticed the lid was ajar on one of the shoe boxes. It was filled with photographs. "Are those pictures of your trips?" he asked, hoping she'd respond to the hint and invite him to examine them.

Peggy turned away without reply, wiping her palms on her thighs. "I'm going to check on the twins. They should be awake by now."

Travis waited until she'd reached the hallway door. "You're going to send him the pictures you just took of the babies, aren't you."

She stiffened, steadying herself on the jamb.

Travis sighed. "I don't mean to pry, Peggy—"

"Then, please don't."

"But I can't quite figure why a man would settle for pictures of his own kids when he ought to be with them." Travis saw her jaw twitch, knew he'd hit a nerve. He took no pleasure in that, and was in fact deeply distressed by it, but couldn't seem to stop himself from asking the one question he instinctively understood that she wouldn't want to answer. "I know this man isn't your husband anymore, but that doesn't make him any less a daddy. Why isn't he here, Peggy? Why isn't he with his babies?"

Her knuckles whitened against the doorjamb. She stared straight ahead, into the hallway. "I don't want to discuss this with you."

Every nuance of her body language was warning him off, and Travis knew it. But he couldn't stop himself, couldn't keep from pressing forward, pushing himself into something that logic insisted was none of his business while his heart insisted otherwise. "A man has a right to be with his children. I'm betting you agree with that, or you wouldn't be so anxious to send pictures. Unless, of course, you're just being mean-spirited, showing the poor sot what he lost by leaving you.''

She spun around, her lips white, her cheeks flushed with indignation. "How dare you imply that I'd do something so vile?"

Travis's heart sank. "It's true, then. The rotten louse walked out on you."

Her eyes brightened, shifted away. "It wasn't like that. Clyde cared about me. He just...he just wasn't ready for children, that's all."

Oddly enough, Travis could relate to that. The responsibility, the loss of freedom. Hell, the thought of having children made his own palms sweat. What he couldn't understand, and what he'd never understand, is how any man could abandon a woman like Peggy. She was every man's fantasy rolled up in an incredibly beautiful package of sweetness and spirit, of generosity and courage, with eyes bright as a frisky colt's and a smile that could melt stone.

And there was the vulnerability, the telltale quiver of her defiant chin that expressed more eloquently than words how deeply wounded she'd been by her husband's betrayal, a betrayal that Travis had been only too willing to throw in her face. He sucked a quick breath, hooked his thumbs in his belt to keep from reaching out for her. "I'm sorry. Sue Anne always says my habit of poking my nose into other people's business will get me shot someday."

She lifted her chin even higher. "Sue Anne is right. Fortunately for you, I'm unarmed."

"Yes'm." He felt as if someone had tied a weight to his heart and dumped it into his stomach. "I suppose you'd like me to go now."

"Yes."

Defeated, Travis issued a curt nod and retrieved his hat from its resting place atop the antiquated television that sat in the corner on a shaky, foldout TV tray. He tugged on the Stetson and paused at the front door. "G'night, Peggy."

"Good night, Travis." She waited until he opened the screen before adding, "Is six-thirty too late?"

"Ma'am?"

"For dinner tomorrow. I can make it earlier if you'd prefer."

"No, ma'am, six-thirty is just fine."

She issued a brusque nod, then disappeared into the hall-way, but not before Travis saw the slightest trace of a smile tug the corner of her pretty mouth. He'd just been given a reprieve, a second chance. He planned to make the most of it.

Seven

"Jessica, is that you?" Peggy pushed her shopping cart to the edge of the aisle, then waved at the slender blonde hovering in the produce aisle and glowering at a melon as if wishing it dead. "Over here."

At the sound of her name, Jessica Hanson scowled, visibly annoyed by the interruption. When she spotted Peggy, she relaxed, even managed a surprised smile. After tossing a wary glance over her shoulder, she made her way toward the aisle where Peggy was waiting. "I barely recognized you. You look so different."

Peggy could have said the same of Jessica, whose trademark blond ponytail had been scissored into a pseudo-gamin cut that was less than flattering. "So do you. You, ah, have a new hairstyle."

The woman issued a pained sigh as she flicked her fingers through her feathery do. "Yeah. Looks like it was buzzed with a weed whacker, doesn't it?"

Actually, it did. "Of course not. It's quite, um, chic."

"Always the diplomat, hmm? Oh, well. It'll grow." She shrugged as if to wave the entire matter away with a flick of the wrist and changed the subject with a wicked grin. "You're certainly looking svelte, at least in comparison to the last time I saw you."

"Which was when I resembled a penguin that had swallowed a watermelon, right?" Peggy stepped aside, proudly revealing the red-haired infants nested in plastic carriers that took up most of the shopping cart. "Meet the water-melons."

"Oh, Peggy, they're, uh…"

"Red and wrinkly?" Peggy shrugged at Jessica's know-ing chuckle. "I've been told that they'll look less like little primates as they grow."

"It takes a while for baby cuteness to take hold," Jessica agreed. The pleasure in her blue eyes quickly dimmed in a cloud of guilt. She bit her lip, her gaze jittering away. "I heard that you'd had the babies. I've been meaning to call—"

"It's okay," Peggy assured her. "I've been pretty busy myself."

Jessica shrugged as she shifted slightly. Her eyes snapped with the same peculiar anger she'd displayed with the hapless melons, along with something else that Peggy couldn't quite identify. It could have been a touch of fear, but before Peggy could hone in, the expression faded as Jessica focused on the twins. "How old are they?"

"Let's see, today is Wednesday, so that makes them ex-actly four days—" Peggy glanced at her watch "—one hour and thirty-three minutes old."

"Goodness, no wonder they're so tiny. You haven't had a chance to fatten them up." She reached out, hesitated. "May I touch them?"

"Of course. That's Virginia," Peggy said as the young woman stroked a tentative finger over the baby's soft scalp. "And this rumple-faced little slug is T.J." At the sound of his name, T.J. issued a fortuitous burp. Peggy rolled her eyes and feigned a sigh. "As you can see, he's all male."

Jessica actually giggled, which was so out of character for the feisty woman that Peggy hiked a brow. "You must be so proud," she gushed. "I'll bet Clyde is about to burst. Except for that red hair, T.J. looks just like him."

At the sound of her ex-husband's name, Peggy's smile

stiffened as if it had been thumbtacked in place. She knew, of course, that it was perfectly normal for Jessica to comment about Clyde. They'd worked together at Squaw Creek Lodge, where Clyde had been a temporary ski instructor. When he'd fallen ill on a payday, Peggy had picked up her husband's check from Jessica, who was the lodge bookkeeper.

The two women had seen each other from time to time, and might have become friends if Peggy hadn't withdrawn from everyone who served as a painful reminder of how she'd failed in her marriage, failed in her life. Now, however, Peggy faced an implied question that was innocently issued, yet nonetheless heartbreaking. She deliberately kept her voice light, her expression neutral. "Clyde hasn't seen the twins yet."

Jessica pursed her lips and laid a comforting hand on Peggy's shoulder. "I'm sorry. I knew Clyde left town because the two of you had been having problems, but I assumed that with the babies and all—"

Peggy interrupted. "He'll be back any day now."

"Of course he will." Jessica patted her shoulder, then withdrew her hand and gave a sage stare. "Any day now."

"He's working at Yosemite," Peggy blurted, stung by the pity in her friend's eyes.

"Really?"

"Campground counselor. It's perfect for him, you know. All that beautiful landscape to inspire his art, and he's quite good with people, so the entire situation is perfect, absolutely perfect." Peggy knew she was babbling but couldn't seem to reel in her traitorous tongue.

The job really was perfect for Clyde. It was perfect for Peggy, too, which is why they'd applied for it as a couple more than a year ago. She'd been deeply hurt to discover that he'd taken it on his own. It was like a final death blow to the plans they'd made together. And to their marriage.

Suddenly compelled to rearrange T.J.'s blanket, Peggy avoided Jessica's empathetic gaze. "I left a message for Clyde on Sunday, telling him about the twins. It would take him a day or so to arrange for time off, of course, but he could be on his way back as we speak."

Jessica nodded as if she actually believed that. "Maybe he had trouble getting up the mountain. Not all of the roads have been completely cleared."

Peggy forced a smile and ignored the fact that Clyde had failed to return her call even though the town telephones were working perfectly. "The storm did leave quite a mess," she acknowledged, sobered by sad memories. "It's been a terrible week for Grand Springs. First the blackout, then the mayor's heart attack—"

"Hmm..." Jessica's gaze narrowed, and she issued a short snort of disgust. "If that's what you want to call it."

"What do you mean?"

Jessica's eyes flashed blue fire. "Olivia was a friend of yours, wasn't she?"

"I liked her, I admired her. She was very kind to me." Peggy fought a surge of emotion and lost. Her voice quivered. "Yes, she was a friend of mine. Her death was a terrible shock. No one realized that she was ill."

"She wasn't ill," Jessica stated.

"Excuse me?"

"Olivia Stuart wasn't ill."

"But her heart—"

"It wasn't her heart that killed her—" Jessica swore under her breath and covered her mouth.

Peggy rocked back on her heels, then steadied herself on a display case. "What are you talking about? I was in the emergency room. I heard the staff saying that Olivia died of a massive coronary."

The woman shrugged and glanced away, her blank eyes focused somewhere into infinity. "Yeah, well, doctors don't know everything. They just think they do."

Then Jessica Hanson turned, left her partially filled shopping cart in the produce aisle and walked out of the store.

"Am I late?"

"Nope, you're right on time." Peggy opened the screen door, allowing Travis to enter, which he did rather hesitantly. He looked positively smashing in beige brushed denims that cupped his slim hips like the proverbial glove and were set off by a polished belt buckle embossed with the icon of a bucking horse. His pearl-buttoned, western-style shirt, woven in muted earth tones, was tightly tailored to enhance an undeniably well-muscled chest, and a cream-colored suede Stetson completed the ensemble, which Peggy judged to be the cowboy equivalent of Sunday-go-to-meeting duds.

Travis was looking good, all right, and he smelled even better. His scent was earthy, with a hint of spice and a dash of musk. It was masculine, powerful, and so intensely alluring that she found herself inhaling deeply enough that her head spun.

She licked her lips, took a step back, then emptied her lungs all at once. It took a moment for her to realize that there was something a bit peculiar about his stance. She cocked her head, regarding him. "What are you holding behind your back?"

A dimple creased his freshly shaved cheek, sending an odd tingle down Peggy's spine. "It's a surprise."

"I don't like surprises."

"You'll like this one." Travis pivoted sideways as she tried to peek behind him. "Close your eyes."

"No way. The last time a male told me to close my eyes, I found myself kissing his pet hound." She sidestepped, craned her neck and muttered as he twisted around to block her view. "I spent the rest of the evening scrubbing dog germs off my mouth and vowing vengeance."

"And did you get it? Vengeance, that is."

"Hmm? Oh, yes. I told his mother where he hid his nudie magazines." Peggy smiled sweetly. "We were both twelve at the time."

"Ah." Travis whipped sideways as she made a grab for his arm. "Well, I promise there are no hound dogs behind my back."

"I don't care if you have six bishops and the pope back there. I'm not closing my eyes."

He sighed. "Spoilsport."

"I've been called worse." Peggy gasped as he extended two colorful, flat boxes. "Why, they're crib mobiles! How wonderful!"

"When you wind them up, they spin around and play music. Do you like them?"

"Oh, they're great. Look, little airplanes for T.J. and bright butterflies for Virginia. How perfect. Thank you so much." She pressed the boxes to her chest, then eyed his other arm, which was still hidden behind his back. For some strange reason, she was suddenly as excited as a kid on Christmas. "You've got something else, haven't you?"

"Maybe," Travis said with a smug grin. "Close your eyes."

"No."

"In that case, I'd better put this back in the truck—"

"Wait." She snagged his arm as he took a step backward. "Oh, all right, but I'm warning you, if anything cold and wet hits my face, you're a dead man." She gave him her best narrowed stare, then shut her eyes and tapped an impatient foot. "Well? I'm waiting."

"Uh-huh. Just another second or two...okay. Now you can look."

Peggy opened her eyes and stared in shock at a huge gift box complete with gold ribbon and a massive, fluffy bow. "Ohmigosh, what is that?"

"Open it and find out." He slipped the mobiles out of her hands, then extended the large box. "Go on, now. It's not going to unwrap itself."

"I don't know what to say."

Travis was beaming. "You can't say anything until you know what it is."

Peggy held the gift reverently, too moved to speak. She licked her lips and, to her horror, heard herself giggle in delight a moment before she ripped off the ribbon and opened the box. As she parted the crisp tissue, her breath rushed out all at once. It was an exquisite, lace-trimmed robe, in a rich royal blue velour. "Oh."

Travis watched anxiously. "It might be a little big. The salesclerk said that robes should fit kind of loose and such, but you can take it back if it doesn't suit you."

"It's exquisite." Peggy stroked the soft fabric lovingly. "I've never had anything so beautiful." She looked up in awe, almost in shock. "You didn't have to do this."

"I thought you might, you know, find some use for it." He shrugged, fidgeted with the mobile boxes and angled a nervous glance. "It's not too personal, is it? Sue Anne said she thought it'd be okay—"

"It's perfect." Peggy turned to dab moisture from her eyes, touched to the core by his thoughtfulness. "I love it, Travis. Thank you."

His shoulders instantly relaxed. "Great. Let's eat."

Two hours later, Peggy was wiping down the kitchen counters, relieved that dinner had gone well and her pot roast hadn't been dry. Travis, who'd insisted on helping with the dishes, had made a beeline for the twins' room the moment he heard a telltale squeak indicating that at least one of the babies was awake. Peggy had been glad of the reprieve and a few isolated moments to gather her thoughts.

Travis had been different tonight. Rather, her reaction to him had been different. She'd been intensely aware of him, not just as a person but as a male-type person. That had taken her by surprise, because she couldn't recall the last time she'd actually been so attracted to a member of the opposite sex. Even when she'd met Clyde, who'd followed her out of the college lecture hall and brazenly introduced himself as the man she was going to marry, Peggy had been basically unmoved by his physical attributes.

Clyde Saxon was good-looking, of course, in a toothy, all-American kind of way. Eventually, her body had issued a positive reaction, but that had evolved slowly, over a period of weeks. Truthfully, she hadn't found herself thinking of Clyde in a sexual way until she'd realized that she was falling in love with him.

Certainly she wasn't in love with Travis Stockwell. Good heavens, she barely knew him. Yet her body reacted as if *it* knew him. In a sense it did, because in the sweetness of slumber, Peggy and Travis knew each other intimately. No reality she'd ever experienced could match the wild passion of those incredibly vivid dreams that left her shaken, restless, filled with strange longings.

A shout from the nursery startled her. "Peggy!"

She dropped the sponge, spun around.

"Peggy, come quick— Oof!"

A dull thud had her sprinting through the living room. She skidded down the hallway, saw Travis sprawled on the nursery floor, one leg dangling over the upturned diaper pail. "Travis, my God—"

He swiveled around and kicked the pail with his foot. "Danged thing tripped me."

Peggy was already by the cribs, anxiously checking the babies. They seemed fine. By the time she looked back over her shoulder, Travis was on his feet, dusting his pants. "What on earth happened?"

He swung the pail up with one hand and pushed it back into place. "Ginny grinned at me."

"She what?"

"She grinned." Eyes glowing with excitement, his Texas twang took over. "I was tickling her belly and such, like you do with young'uns, when she just whacked them li'l arms and gave me the fattest grin I ever did see! I was running to get you when this here varmint—" he shot a scowl at the pail "—got in my way."

Peggy puffed her cheeks, blew out a breath and gazed down at the bright-eyed infant, who appeared to be staring at the colorful mobile Travis had installed at the head of her crib. "I hate to burst your bubble, Travis, but she probably just needs to be burped."

Travis frowned. "You saying I don't know a grin when I see one?"

"At this age, a grin and a grimace look pretty much the same." Peggy turned toward T.J., who was now awake and expressing extreme displeasure at the disturbance. She rubbed his tummy, murmuring softly. "Sh, sweetums, the excitement's all over. You can go back to sleep now."

He let out a cantankerous wail, startling his sister, who also began to fuss.

Travis was immediately on the case, leaning over the crib to awkwardly stroke a gentle fingertip over the baby's tiny shoulder. "Hey there, darling, your mama didn't mean no disrespect. All you got to do is grin again, just to prove you can." Virginia hiccuped, blinked, then fell silent. "That's my girl. Come on, now, squinch up those little cheeks and give us a big old smile."

Peggy cuddled T.J. against her shoulder and peered into Virginia's crib. The infant's forehead was furrowed, her wispy brows pleated into a definite frown. "Sorry, cowboy, but that doesn't look like a smile to me."

Travis shot Peggy a withering look. "She's thinking it over, that's all."

"Ah." Peggy shifted T.J., rubbing his warm little back with her palm. "Well, while we're waiting for this monumental decision, why don't you try burping her, just to humor me."

Blinking, Travis glanced down into the crib. "I don't know what that means, but it sounds kind of disgusting."

"Only if she spits curdled milk on that pretty shirt of yours. Use that towel hanging on the crib slats."

He dutifully picked up the towel, stared at it as if he'd never seen one before. "What am I supposed to do with it?"

"Lay it over your shoulder," Peggy explained patiently. "Then pick her up and pat her back, like this." When she used T.J. to demonstrate the suggested technique, Travis went absolutely white.

"Oh, no, I'm not gonna do that. No way, uh-uh." He tossed the towel as if it had burned him, then backed up so quickly he almost tripped over the diaper pail again. "I'd probably break her or something."

"Babies are tougher than they look. Just use one hand to support her head—"

"Excuse me," he blurted, then spun around and rushed down the hall. The slam of the bathroom door was followed by a rush of running water.

Peggy sighed. After returning T.J. to his crib and tending to her daughter, she found Travis in the living room, slumped on the sofa. The television was on, but he didn't appear to be watching it.

He angled a woeful glance at her as she entered the room. She sat beside him, regarding him thoughtfully. "Is it good?"

"Uh, is what good?"

"The movie," she added, nodding at the screen.

"Oh, yeah." Travis swallowed hard, wishing his hands would stop shaking. The mere suggestion that he take that fragile infant into his big, clumsy paws had evoked a flashback of the delivery, when T.J. had squirted out of his hands and danged near bounced off the cab floor.

The sad fact was that Travis had absolutely no experience with babies because, well, he'd never fancied them much. They'd always seemed so needy and delicate. The little critters weren't good for much, not until they were old enough to straddle a horse. Until then, all babies did was eat and cry and fill their diapers. Who needed that? Travis sure didn't.

At least, he'd never needed it before, and he sure as heck never wanted it. When his nephews were little, he'd pretty much ignored them, which had been easy enough since he'd been gone most of the time, out riding the circuit. As he recalled, he'd only shown up once or twice during their first years, so to his mind, they'd grown pretty fast. Soon as they were toddling around on their own two feet, Travis had taken a liking to them. But they'd never evoked the kind of feelings he had for Ginny and T.J.

That confused Travis, and it scared him. Because the twins weren't the only ones for whom he had unsettled emotions.

"Travis?" Beside him, Peggy cocked her head, looking up with big green eyes so clear a man could see the reflection of his own soul.

He swallowed hard and responded with as much dignity as he could muster. "Huh?"

"I asked what the movie is about."

It took a moment, what with the strawberry scent of that sweet hair tickling his nose, and her sitting so close that he could feel the flex of her thighs right through his jeans.

"Oh. The movie. It's about—" he slipped a quick glance at the screen "—racing."

Her brows puckered. She looked at the television, chuckled and shook her head. "That's a car commercial."

"Oh, sure. I knew that." He shifted and stretched his arm across the back of the sofa. "The movie is, ah…" He held his breath, then exhaled all at once when John Wayne suddenly galloped across the screen wearing a cavalry uniform. "It's a western."

She smiled as if she hadn't noticed his triumphant crow, or the bead of sweat gathered on his upper lip. "I love westerns." Then she issued a sigh that wrapped around his heart like tie wire, and snuggled down until her shoulder pressed sweetly against the side of his chest.

A fission of electricity jittered along Travis's ribs, warming his entire body with erotic heat. His fingers danced nervously along the cushions, then slipped over the edge to dangle above her shoulder. He waited for the protest. There was none, so he shifted slightly, allowing his arm to encircle her in a quiet embrace.

When she unexpectedly laid her head on his shoulder, the thrill made him giddy. He sat stiffly, afraid that any sudden move would startle her. His mind, however, was a boggle. Should he pull her closer? Try to kiss her? No, it was too soon. Maybe he should just sit tight, let her make the next move.

The next move toward what? She'd just had two babies. What in hell was wrong with him, thinking such things?

Still, she *had* laid her head on his shoulder and was snuggled up against him like a hungry tick on a fat dog. Even as the thought occurred to Travis, Peggy's body melted against him, her breathing deepened.

The thrill that had so electrified his senses instantly dissipated. Peggy wasn't the least bit interested in initiating a romantic liaison. She was sound asleep.

* * *

Peggy awoke with a jolt, her eyes darting through the early morning light. She blinked, listened and heard it again, the tiny distressed wail emanating from the twins' room. Struggling to sit up, she plucked at the strange covering that was holding her down. It was her grandmother's crocheted afghan, which was supposed to be neatly folded on the living room lounge chair.

Why was it in her bedroom? Even more perplexing, why was she lying beneath it fully clothed?

Mystified, she swung her legs over the edge of the mattress, rubbed her eyes and allowed the events of last night into her foggy brain. The last thing she remembered was settling down on the sofa to watch an old movie.

With Travis.

Peggy moaned, embarrassed to realize that she must have fallen asleep. Poor Travis. He hadn't even had his dessert, a custard pie she'd baked especially in his honor. Even worse, he'd probably been deeply insulted.

"Face it, Peggy-girl," she muttered aloud. "A gracious hostess does not snore in the presence of guests."

Spearing her fingers through her tangled hair, she glanced back at the afghan. A clue. The afghan had been in the living room. Peggy had been in the living room. Now both were in the bedroom, and the only available person who'd been large enough to accomplish that feat had been Travis.

He'd actually put her to bed.

Oh, Lord. If humiliation was poison, she'd have died on the spot. What must he think of her? But along with embarrassment, a warm sweetness flowed through her veins as she imagined him lifting her into his arms, laying her gently on the bed, fussing to smooth the coverlet over her sleeping form. She felt a twinge of regret that she hadn't been awake to enjoy the delicious luxury of being so well coddled.

A second wail joined the first, reminding her that both babies were now awake and quite ready for breakfast. "Mommy's coming," she mumbled, then shuffled to the nursery, stifling a yawn.

The morning routine was conducted smoothly, and with the efficiency born of practice. Feeding times had been halved when Peggy had discovered that with the help of a few well-placed pillows, she could nurse both babies at once. The twins seemed pleased by the arrangement, and mommy didn't have to suffer the stress of listening to one hungry baby scream while she was busy with the other.

Even with the streamlining of certain functions, however, motherhood was a time-consuming and exhausting business. By the time the twins had been fed, bathed and dressed, a saffron sun had risen from early morning gray to clear, blue daylight. Peggy poured a cup of instant coffee and had just settled down to watch the late morning news on television when a special bulletin sent chills down her spine.

"According to inside sources, the Grand Springs police department has requested an autopsy on Mayor Olivia Stuart's body. Results are expected to be made public by tomorrow morning. Miss Stuart was pronounced dead on Friday evening. Cause of death was listed as a heart attack. The coroner refused comment, and a police spokesman indicated only that the case was under further consideration, though our sources indicate that homicide is suspected.

"In other news…"

Coffee splashed over the mug rim, burning Peggy's thigh. She set the mug down quickly, staring at the screen in disbelief.

Possible homicide.

That meant that Jessica Hanson must have been right.

Maybe Olivia hadn't had a heart attack at all. Maybe she'd been murdered. *Murdered.*

Peggy was sickened by the thought. Who on earth would want to hurt Olivia? Everyone liked her. Of course, not everyone agreed with her politics. The strip-mine controversy had become a volatile issue over the past months, but even with the peculiar circumstance of the mayor's last word, Peggy couldn't believe that anyone would stoop to murder over a stupid lump of coal.

But now it seemed that someone had wanted Olivia dead.

Peggy was chilled to the bone wondering how Jessica Hanson could have possibly known about the murder when the supporting evidence had only surfaced in the past few hours.

The answer seemed obvious. And it was chilling.

Eight

Sue Anne plopped a heaping bowl of greens on the patio table, then scraped a disgruntled glance across the tree-shaded yard. "Look at them, four grown men hunkered over those babies like ticks on a hound."

Peggy, who'd just emerged from the Conway kitchen carrying a pot of German potato salad, smiled at the cooing group gathered around the double stroller where the twins were supposedly napping. "T.J. and Virginia have gotten used to being the center of attention."

"Humph. The only thing those tadpoles are used to is the shock of seeing an ugly, grinning face every time they open their eyes."

"I think it's kind of sweet," Peggy said, arranging the hot potato salad on a patio table bulging with goodies. The twins were a month old now, and Peggy was secretly pleased that Travis and the Conway men continued to shower her babies with attention. In a sense, they were joint father figures, for which she was deeply grateful.

The role-playing was just temporary, of course. Clyde would eventually come around to take over his position as permanent, full-time father. Peggy believed that with a fervency born of desperation despite the indisputable fact that he hadn't responded to either the pictures she'd sent or to her many pleading letters.

"Travis said there have been folks looking at the duplex."

"Hmm?" Peggy blinked up, momentarily bewildered.

"Folks looking at the duplex," Sue Anne repeated, adjusting her tight T-shirt over hips that were a tad too large. "Figured you might be having new neighbors soon."

"Oh, that." Peggy shrugged, propping a hip against the picnic table. "I doubt it. They haven't even started repairing the storm damage, except to board up the windows. There have been a few real estate agents sniffing around, though, so I hope the management company is getting ready to make the place habitable. It would be nice to have neighbors again."

But Sue Anne wasn't listening. She reared up and emitted a piercing whistle. "Hey! You guys stop fussing with them babies, hear? They need their rest." She folded her arms and flopped into a chair. "Men. Sometimes I wonder why we bother with 'em."

Peggy agreed under her breath and allowed her mind to wander back to her ex-husband. With memories came anger, seething resentment that a failure of birth control had led to abandonment, betrayal and a disillusionment that shattered any love she'd had for Clyde. But her feelings for him were ambivalent, because without him, she wouldn't have her precious babies, babies who deserved the nurturing love of both a mother and a father.

So she swallowed anger with optimism, and prayed each sunrise would herald the day Clyde would decide to accept his parental responsibilities for the sake of their children. But each morning passed quickly, quietly, until lengthening shadows slipped into silent sunsets, smothering darkness. Hope faded into despair, then surged with the dawn, a cycle that had taken a physical and emotional toll Peggy refused to acknowledge. To do so would concede futility, failure.

Because Peggy's mother had made that concession under similar circumstance. It had broken the poor woman's heart and her spirit, left her an embittered shell, unwilling to trust, unable to love. She'd been there physically for her daughter, but her emotional wounds continued to bleed, and as soon as her only child had mastered the skills necessary for survival, she'd given in to the despair. The day after Peggy's college graduation, her mother's broken heart simply stopped beating.

And Peggy had been alone.

"Hey, what a grip!" Peggy glanced up as Travis's head popped out of the male huddle. "T.J. grabbed my finger," he hollered, elbowing Ted to provide Peggy a clear view. The infant, nested in the double stroller beside his snoozing sister, was indeed clutching the digit in question. Travis was clearly thrilled. "Man, the kid's got real power. If that's not the grip of a born bull rider, I'll eat my boots."

Jimmy, crouched in front of the stroller, acknowledged that with a definitive nod. "Yep, he's a tough one, all right."

"Sh," Danny hissed, skewering his startled father with a hard stare. "You're going to wake Ginny up—" An irritated wail had him rolling his eyes. "Aw, now look what you've done." The boy bent over the stroller, his hands fussing with the blanket. "Hush, sweet thing, your Uncle Danny's here."

Ginny shrieked.

"Typical female reaction," Ted drawled, "to the sight of your ugly face."

"Oh, yeah?" Danny slid his brother a sly glance. "So which one of us has a date tonight, hmm?"

"In your dreams, geek man."

"Marta McKnight must like geeks."

Ted's jaw drooped. "That big-eyed brunette from the Dairy Freeze?"

"The one and only." Danny blew on his fingertips and slicked back his hair. "Said she appreciated a sensitive, intelligent man after all the muscle-bound jerks who've been hounding her." Danny glanced up, feigning innocence when Ted narrowed his eyes. "Oops. I flat forgot that you asked her out last week. Turned you down, didn't she?"

Ted hooked his arm around his brother's head and wrestled him to the ground. As the boys tussled around the grass, grunting and exchanging rough scalp noogies, a clearly disgusted Travis swung the stroller away from the sibling battle. "Fine example you're setting for the young'uns," he muttered.

Jimmy merely straightened, scratched his armpit, then ambled over to retrieve a beer from the ice cooler.

Sue Anne also ignored the melee, calling out to her husband, "You'd best be getting that grill lit. These burgers aren't going to cook themselves."

Jimmy nodded, wiped his mouth with the back of his hand and amiably followed his wife into the kitchen while their sons continued to wrestle in the grass.

Peggy smiled and leaned against the table, musing how her life had changed since the blackout. Then again, life had changed for just about everyone in Grand Springs. Residents had faced adversity with courage, making great strides in rebuilding the town they loved.

Beyond the physical hardships, however, citizens still mourned the loss of their mayor. Olivia Stuart had been the linchpin of city government, earning admiration and grudging respect even from those who disagreed with her politics. The town had been deeply saddened by her death, but had accepted it. What the town hadn't been able to accept, and what had divided much of its citizenry, was the shocking discovery that Olivia had been murdered.

Peggy's own turmoil had been deepened by Jessica Hanson's revelation the day before the terrible news was made public. Only when she'd seen her friend in the company of Stone Richardson, a homicide detective whom Peggy had met during contract negotiations with the police union, was she convinced that Jessica's information must have come from sources within the department rather than a nefarious, firsthand knowledge of the crime.

Still, the frenzy of speculation and suspicion following that gruesome discovery pitted neighbor against neighbor, friend against friend. It was, Peggy thought, a sad legacy for the woman so committed to maintaining quality of life in the town she loved so dearly.

But if the town's outlook was bleak, Peggy's had brightened considerably. Her friendship with Sue Anne had blossomed, and the Conways had become a second family. As for Travis, well, her relationship with Travis was confusing. Every time he showed up, her heart beat a little faster. When he left, she felt empty, as if an integral part of her had been surgically removed. Deep down, she secretly believed that she'd never see him again, that each time he walked out the door would be the last.

And yet he always returned, dropping by almost every day with small gifts for the twins, or a bag of groceries and a hungry expression. They had shared so much over the weeks, both quiet times and hysterical moments, such as their midnight rush to the hospital when Virginia developed severe heat rash, and their adventure with an overflowing sink that forced Travis, who barely knew the difference between a pipe wrench and pliers, to perform sink surgery. Unfortunately, he'd forgotten to turn off the water first, resulting in a flood of near biblical proportions.

They still laughed about the incident—or, more precisely, Peggy still laughed about it. Travis simply reddened around the earlobes, muttering that if the good Lord had wanted cowboys to fix pipes, he wouldn't have created plumbers.

"What're you grinning about, woman?"

Peggy glanced up as Travis wheeled the stroller onto the patio. "Fond memories. You really are quite adorable with water dripping off your nose."

He yanked down his hat and swore softly. "You're never going to let me forget that, are you?"

"Nope, never. Too bad I was out of film."

"There is a God," Travis muttered, eyeing the scrumptious repast laid out on the patio table. "When are we going to eat, anyway? I'm so hungry I could chew the horns off a Brahman."

Peggy patted his hand, which was protectively curled around the stroller handle. An odd tingle tickled her palm where her skin touched his. "Soon," she assured him, withdrawing her hand. The tingling continued. "Sue Anne's giving Jimmy last-minute grill instructions as we speak."

Judging by his puckered brows, that news didn't appease him. "Shucks, if Sue Anne's wound up with one of her lectures, we won't be having supper until it's danged near time for fireworks."

"Oh, well." Peggy reached to straighten a toppled salt shaker and knocked a serving spoon off the table. She knelt to retrieve it, stood too fast and steadied herself on the table until her head stopped spinning. She'd been feeling weak all day. That, coupled with a vaguely familiar chest tightness reminiscent of stress-induced asthma from her childhood, was unnerving, although Peggy managed to convince herself that the heat and shift in wind conditions had merely caused a flareup in the allergies that occasionally plagued her with headaches and general malaise.

When the dizziness passed, she wiped her moist brow and issued a thin smile. "Even if we miss tonight's event, there'll be another Fourth of July next year. We'll catch it then."

Travis, who'd been too busy watching the babies to notice Peggy's dizzy spell, was clearly distressed by the prospect. "We can't miss fireworks," he insisted. "I promised the twins. Told 'em all about the big booms and how there'd be pretty colors all over the sky. They're looking forward to it.''

Peggy wasn't the least bit certain that the babies would be particularly impressed, especially by the "big booms," but she was most definitely amused by Travis's insistence that they'd be disappointed, primarily because she knew that he sincerely believed it. Travis was absolutely convinced that T.J. and Virginia were the most brilliant babies on the face of the earth, possessing the geniuslike ability to understand every word said in their presence.

Which is why he'd nearly come to blows with a big-mouthed redneck who'd used inappropriate language to express displeasure with the length of the checkout line. It was the last time Peggy had allowed Travis to accompany her to the grocery store.

"It's okay, darling," Travis murmured as Virginia started to fuss. "You're going to see fireworks tonight even if I have to starve to get you there."

Peggy emitted an exaggerated sigh. "Such selfless generosity cannot go unrewarded. Here—" she forked a fat, steaming potato chunk out of the bowl and held it up to his mouth "—try this."

"Mmm." His eyes lit up as he chewed. "Tangy. Good."

"I'm overwhelmed by the praise."

"Real good." He whipped the fork out of her hand and helped himself. "Tastes kind of bacony."

"There's bacon in it, along with vinegar, sugar and a handful of secret spices. It's an old family recipe, handed down to my Irish grandmother from her German uncle." She held up a palm when he eyed her strangely. "Trust me, the genealogy is too complex to explain."

Travis shrugged, scooped up another man-size bite and nearly choked on it when T.J. emitted a squeaky sneeze. Travis coughed, swallowed, wiggled a finger at the stroller. "Did you hear that? He *sneezed*."

"Umm, yes, I heard it."

Instantly Travis crouched beside the stroller and laid a worried hand on the baby's head. "He feels warm."

"I imagine so. It's ninety degrees out here."

"But he's all drooly, too."

Peggy was already reaching for the towel tucked over the stroller handle. "Babies drool, Travis. It's one of the few things they do really well." She dabbed T.J.'s chin, and he instantly turned a greedy mouth toward the towel.

Travis was delighted. "Look at that! What a smart little duffer."

"For trying to suck on a towel?"

"For letting you know he's hungry," Travis explained patiently. "Most babies would just lie there and cry."

"He's certainly been known to do that."

"But he's figured out a better way. That takes real brain-power." Grinning like a proud papa, Travis rubbed his index finger on T.J.'s palm, then let out a hoot when the baby grabbed hold. "Man, isn't that something? He's near strong enough to pull himself right out of that stroller."

"He can't even lift his head, Travis."

"I'll bet he could if he wanted to."

Suddenly too weary to respond, Peggy sat on a nearby chair and fanned herself with her hand. It really was hot. She wondered if she should take the babies inside.

But Travis, still squatting beside the stroller, had launched into a discussion about the significance of Independence Day with the twins, both of whom appeared to be watching him intently. "And so every year, we celebrate with fireworks to re-create the night when all those bombs were 'bursting in air' so America could be a free, independent nation. Pretty cool, huh?"

Virginia whacked her little fists as if agreeing, which tickled Travis immensely. Then, with an expression of exquisite joy and pure love, he brushed a knuckle over the

infant's furry little scalp. "That's my girl," he whispered
so softly that Peggy could barely hear.

But she did hear. And the wall around her heart was
cracking.

"I don't understand." Travis stepped through the threshold, shifted T.J.'s carrier, and pushed the front door shut
with his boot heel. "I explained all about the booms and
such. Just can't figure why they got so perturbed."

Ducking a shoulder, Peggy shrugged off the diaper bag
strap and lowering the stuffed vinyl case onto the sofa. She
placed Ginny's carrier on the coffee table, biting back a
smile as she unfastened the little harness and scooped the
warm little body into her arms. "Don't take it personally,
Travis. Babies are notorious for disliking loud noises."

"Aw, it wasn't all that loud," he grumbled, situating
T.J.'s carrier beside the now-empty one from which his
sister had just been removed. Nested in the padded interior,
the baby dozed peacefully, his button nose poised above a
butterfly of blue plastic. T.J. jerked slightly as Travis expertly wiggled the pacifier to break suction, then eased it
from between the infant's quivering gums. "They didn't
even look at all those pretty lights."

Peggy cradled her daughter and skipped a loving kiss
across her fuzzy crown. "I wouldn't hold that against them.
It's kind of difficult to see pretty lights when you're wailing
so hard that your eyes are glued shut."

Travis, who still refused to handle the infants unless they
were safely nestled in a protective carrier or stroller, made
no attempt to remove the sleeping baby boy. Instead, he
tucked the moist pacifier in the diaper bag, then sat glumly
on the sofa, staring at his knees. "I thought they'd have
fun."

"If it makes you feel any better, everyone else had fun.
Watching you flit from baby to screaming baby, wringing

your hands and begging for divine intervention in no less than three languages was the highlight of our evening.''

He narrowed his eyes. ''Why, yes, as a matter of fact, being the donkey-butt of y'all's entertainment just pleases me no end.''

''Good.'' She slipped a sly grin over her shoulder and shifted Virginia in her arms. ''Now that we've settled that, I think it's time for beddie-bye. These two have had quite enough excitement for one night.''

As Peggy carried her wide-awake daughter into the nursery, she heard Travis issue a woeful sigh. A moment later, he entered the babies' room toting T.J., carrier and all. He placed the carrier in the vacant crib, automatically pulled a fresh diaper out of a package on a nearby dresser and passed it over to Peggy, who already had her hand out.

Travis had never actually diapered a baby but had watched the procedure often enough to have the routine down pat, and handed over the powder can and tube of heat-rash cream in the proper order. When Peggy handed the items back, he dug a fresh pair of pink baby pajamas out of the dresser drawer. A few minutes later, the efficient duo repeated the entire procedure with T.J., who slept through the changing process with admirable determination.

''There you go, sweet girl,'' Peggy murmured, placing the pink-bowed Texas elephant beside the bright-eyed baby girl. ''Sleep tight.'' Virginia yawned on cue and focused on the stuffed elephant that had become her favorite nighttime companion. As her baby eyelids slipped into snooze-mode, Peggy turned off the lamp, flipped on the soft orange night-light, and eased out of the room with a relieved sigh. ''That ought to hold them for an hour or two.''

In the hallway, Travis scowled at his boots, scuffing a piece of carpet lint with his toe. ''Can't figure why they wouldn't watch those pretty lights.''

''Oh, gracious, forget the silly fireworks, will you? But

speaking of watching things..." She hurried into the living room to root through the stuffed diaper bag. "I know it's in here. I distinctly remember— Aha!"

Travis ambled into the living room and peered over her shoulder. "What are you looking for?"

"This," she said, wiggling a black videotape case. "The grand finale of our evening's entertainment."

"A movie?"

"More or less." She popped it into the VCR, grinning madly. "Sue Anne loaned it to me. Said I'd get a kick out of it."

A wary glint darkened his gaze. "Sue Anne, huh?"

"Yep." Peggy snagged his arm, ushering him to the sofa. "Sit." When he hesitated, she placed flattened palms on his chest, giving a gentle push. He plopped backward onto the cushions. "Wait there."

Fairly bursting with excitement, Peggy dashed into the kitchen, then returned with a bowl of potato chips and two cans of soda. "Refreshments," she announced, placing the bowl on the coffee table. She slapped a cold can into his palm, kicked off her canvas deck shoes and wiggled her bare toes. "Aah. Now this—" she scooped up the remote control and punched a button with her thumb "—is gonna be great."

The screen flickered with color and movement. A cheering crowd, brilliant sunlight spilling into an empty arena. The camera zoomed, focused on a metal gate, behind which an irritated horse tossed its magnificent head in challenge. A cowboy straddled the fence, eyed the beast with blatant trepidation, then yanked down his hat and prepared to mount.

Travis moaned.

"Go-o-o, Travis!" Peggy cheered as she gave a raised-fist salute to the screen. "Ride 'em, cowboy!"

"I'll kill her," he muttered, covering his eyes. "My sister is dead meat."

"Ooooh." Peggy leaned forward, completely engrossed in the videotaped action. "Isn't the horse supposed to wait until the gate opens before he does that? Geez, I didn't realize you could jump that high, Travis. Umm, ripped your pants wide open. And in front of all those people, too." She made a tsking sound with her tongue. "How embarrassing."

Travis slumped forward, dropping his head into his hands.

Peggy, enjoying herself immensely, popped a chip into her mouth and settled back into the cushions. "At least you got back on," she said between chews. "Good for you. Now the horse respects you."

Giving up, Travis heaved a sigh, slouching back on the sofa. He glowered at the screen. "That's Juggernaut, baddest bronc on the circuit. Only time I ever saw that horse smile was after he'd crushed a cowboy into sawdust."

"Horses don't smile."

"That one does." Travis bit into a potato chip Peggy held in front of his mouth, then wiped the crumbs away with the back of his hand. "Just watch."

She did, bending forward, her gaze glued to the television. On screen, Travis had eased himself back onto the snorting animal and was wrapping a lariat of some sort around his right hand. "What are you doing, bonding with the saddle?"

"In bareback, the horse wears a holding harness, not a saddle. You've got to wrap your hand up tight or you'll loose your grip on the upswing and shoot into the stands like a human missile." He popped the soda can top and took a deep swig. "Juggernaut comes out like a Brahman, one big leap to the left, then circles right while his rear is kicking air. Hell of a ride."

A cowboy wearing floppy chaps dropped off the fence, grabbed the gate's pull rope with both gloved hands and tensely waited for the rider's nod. When he finally got it, he yanked the gate open, scurried up the fence as the bronc exploded from the chute.

Peggy winced as Travis's head jerked backward, then flopped forward with such force that his chin smashed into his chest. "Ouch. That's gotta hurt."

Travis shrugged. "Not as much as the landing."

"Why do you keep grabbing that poor animal's neck with your feet?"

"That's called spurring. You've got to lay your back to the wall, keep your feet above the point of the bronc's shoulders and keep working him to get points."

"Well, no wonder the poor horse is so irritable. I think he'd give a smoother ride if you treated him with a bit more respect."

"He's not supposed to give a smooth ride. The bigger he bucks, the higher you score—"

Peggy gasped as the taped image of Travis suddenly somersaulted in the air and hit the ground with a crushing thud.

Travis flinched. "Unless that happens."

Covering her mouth with her hand, Peggy watched the crumpled form rise painfully, dust off and glare at the prancing animal that was snorting a victory lap around the ring. "Actually, that horse does seem to be pretty pleased with himself."

"Told you."

"I wouldn't go so far as to say he's smiling. Smirking, maybe." She squinted at the screen, watching Travis limp back toward the fence, ego bruised and torn pants flapping in the breeze. "You know, you might consider switching to navy blue underwear. Those white briefs stand out like a neon fanny flag."

He gave her a withering look. "Thanks for the pointer."

"Don't mention it. Rodeos look like great fun. I'd love to see one sometime." She popped another chip into her mouth and washed it down with a swallow of soda as the tape segued into another segment. "The arena looks different."

"That's another rodeo. Danny got a video editor for Christmas a while back, and spliced together televised footage. The first piece you saw was filmed in Salinas, about six years ago. This one is—" he leaned forward, studying the film as the camera panned around an indoor arena flagged with advertisements and strewn with a thick layer of sawdust "—Austin, I think. An event where top-ten contenders were invited to put on a demonstration for charity."

"You were in the top ten?"

"Only in saddle bronc. I wasn't a contender in bareback until a couple of years ago, and I've never made finals in bull riding. But I will."

"No doubt." She watched the screen, utterly fascinated. "I'm really impressed."

"Why?"

"Heck, you're practically a champion. I'd say that's impressive."

"Fact is—" He paused to bite off half of the chip she held up for him and chewed a moment before continuing. "Fact is, I topped saddle bronc points two years running." He cleared his throat and rubbed a thumb over the embossed silver belt buckle.

"You actually won the championship?"

A humble shrug didn't match the proud gleam in his eye. "A couple of times. 'Course, I was healthy then."

"Wow." She flopped back, bowled over by the revelation. "Imagine that. I'm actually sharing potato chips with a world champion."

Travis plucked a fat chip from the bowl and held it up to her lips. "Guess that makes you a champion's lady."

Their eyes met, held. "Am I your lady, Travis?"

He didn't answer right away, but his eyes softened, glowing with amber lights. "If you want to be."

Without taking her gaze from his, she nibbled the edge of the chip, allowing her lips to brush his fingertips. A quiver ran down his arm. His jaw twitched. Emboldened, she scraped her teeth along the crispy ridges, until he eased the entire chip into her mouth. She chewed slowly, provocatively, then deliberately moistened her lips with the tip of her tongue. She knew the gesture was erotic, enticing. She meant it to be, because Travis's gaze was riveted on her mouth, on the sensual circle of her tongue slipping in and out, in and out.

In a rational moment, Peggy would have been horrified by such brazen behavior, but this wasn't rational. Peggy wasn't rational. She was awash with sensation, a fluid, flexing warmth that drowned her inhibitions in a flood of deep yearning, desperate desire.

Travis sucked a quick breath. He flicked the corner of her mouth with his fingertip, as if brushing away crumbs. Before Peggy could consider the consequence of her actions, she instinctively turned toward his touch and licked the salt from his fingers.

He shuddered so violently that the couch creaked, then cupped her face between his palms, questioning her silently. She responded by parting her lips and raising her chin. Her heart raced, pounding her rib cage with such painful intensity she feared it would burst. She knew he was going to kiss her, knew her world would change when he did. Yet she wanted him, welcomed him, opened her scarred heart to him, trusting he would cherish it as no other man had.

Travis lowered his head, his eyes still searching hers. He

paused painfully, so close she could feel the warm condensation of his breath, smell its salty tang.

Panicked that he would withdraw, she clutched his shirt, tangling her fingers in the fabric. At the same time, her mouth sought his, found it, took it greedily.

His response was instantaneous and explosive. Muscles rippled, tightened. She was crushed in an embrace that thrilled her with intensity at the same time she was unnerved by its power. Every inch of her body reacted to him, to the convulsive flare of emotion erupting from her innermost core.

Travis wasn't simply kissing her. He was making love to her with his mouth, with his hands, with the rhythmic ripple of muscle and bone vibrating from the very depth of his body and his soul. Strong fingers tangled in her hair. His tongue teased, his lips tasted, absorbed each nuance of her mouth, her throat, the pulsing sweetness at the curve of her shoulders, until her blood blazed with a desire beyond anything she'd ever experienced.

Then, with startled abruptness, explosive power was replaced by exquisite tenderness as Travis cupped her face between his palms, gently nuzzling her lips, her eyelids, tracing her brow with delicate kisses. He laid his cheek against her forehead, shivered, then pulled away slowly, as if exercising monumental control.

He swallowed hard. "I shouldn't have done that. I had no right."

Peggy smiled, tracing the line of his twitching jaw with her fingers. "I think a champion has a right to kiss his lady, don't you?"

"I'm not a champion anymore."

Peggy saw the sadness creep into his eyes, and her heart ached for him. Sue Anne had told her about the disastrous injury that took Travis off the circuit, shattering his hopes of saving enough for the down payment on a ranch outside of Lubbock that he'd been yearning to buy.

Although Sue Anne hadn't actually said that Travis would be unable to rodeo in the future, she'd certainly implied as much. Peggy could only imagine how devastated Travis must have been, not only to have his dream of being a ranch owner indefinitely postponed, but also being forced to give up the rodeo, which had been part of his life since he'd been a boy.

From Peggy's perspective, Travis seemed to have accepted his fate stoically. Changing careers wasn't easy, yet he'd made the transition from cowboy to cabdriver without losing his optimism, or the easy charm that had attracted her from the first moment she'd laid eyes on him.

Well, perhaps not the very first moment, since she'd been somewhat preoccupied at the time, but she'd certainly taken note of him when he showed up at the hospital and she'd experienced the full impact of those humorous, brown eyes and that crazy, lopsided grin.

The memory evoked a smile, which Travis apparently misunderstood. His brows puckered with worry. "Did you hear me, Peggy? I said I'm not a champion anymore."

She pressed a fingertip to his lips, silencing him. "You'll always be a champion, Travis. You're *my* champion."

A grateful smile crinkled the corners of his eyes. He lifted her hand to his lips, sweetly kissed her palm.

If happiness was fatal, Peggy would have died on the spot.

Nine

Peggy hunched over the handwritten ledger, correlating the scrawled ink figures and the colorful columns on the computerized spreadsheet. Grasping the electronic mouse, she expertly clicked, scrolled, compared, until a mismatched total caught her eye. "Here it is."

Sue Anne swiveled away from the dispatch center and propelled her wheeled steno chair over to the computer desk where Peggy was working. "You found the error?"

"This debit entry was keypunched as a credit, that's all. I'll just reverse the sign—" her fingers clicked over the keyboard "—and *voila!* The books balance."

"Girl, you're a certified genius."

"Actually, accounting isn't particularly difficult once you get the hang of it," Peggy mumbled, studying a rather bizarre note on the expenditures column of Conway Cab's internal ledger. She would have asked about it if Travis hadn't burst through the door, his eyes rounded in shock.

"The twins are in the living room," he blurted. "Danny's feeding them white stuff out of *a bottle!*"

Sue Anne gave her brother a wry stare. "Hello to you, too."

Ignoring his sister, Travis crossed the room in two strides, slipped a proprietary arm around Peggy's shoulder and brushed a kiss on her cheek. "Hi, honey," he murmured against her skin. "So, what's with this bottle business?"

"It's formula," Peggy said without glancing up from the

monitor. "They're growing so fast, the doctor suggested a supplement. If they do well on it, I'll be able to wean them in a month or so."

Travis was clearly horrified. "Wean them? They're only eight weeks old."

"Wean them off breast milk," Peggy explained. "Words cannot express how excited I am by the prospect of actually wearing a bra without flaps, and since I must eventually venture into the world to earn a living, it would be nice if I didn't have to worry about wet spots on the lapel of my power suit."

"It does kind of spoil the administrative image," Sue Anne agreed.

Travis, flushing to his hairline, was clearly flustered by the open discussion of such an intimately female matter. He cleared his throat, wiped a forearm across his brow and quickly changed the subject. "So, how did things go at city hall?"

Peggy and Sue Anne exchanged a telling look. "Not wonderful," she admitted. "My job is no more."

He frowned. "They fired you?"

"Technically, they downsized me out of existence but the result is the same." Peggy sighed and folded her arms. Her savings was nearly drained, and although her maternity leave officially ended next week, she'd been so busy looking for good day care that she hadn't even considered the possibility that her job wouldn't be waiting. "I was counting on that paycheck," she murmured. "Fortunately, Sue Anne popped up out of nowhere and saved my life."

Travis slid his sister a skeptical stare. "How'n heck did she do that?"

Sue Anne paused for a leisurely sip of cola, smacked her lips and flashed a smug grin. "I hired her."

"You *what?*"

Clearly pleased by her brother's reaction, Sue Anne

stretched like a lazy feline, purring with self-indulgent pride. "I hired Peggy to help out with the books."

"Why on earth would you do that?"

Taking umbrage at his tone, Peggy snapped her head around. "I didn't exactly drop off a turnip truck, you know. I have a degree in business administration, a minor in finance, and I happen to be quite adroit with the nuances of at least ten of the most widely utilized computerized spreadsheet programs."

"Uh, sure, honey, sure." Travis withdrew instantly, although his peculiar expression made Peggy regret the pompous recitation of her résumé. "Just kind of took me by surprise, that's all."

She touched his arm, an affectionate gesture that had become second nature to her. In the month since they'd shared that first explosive kiss, she and Travis had been inseparable. There had been many more kisses, some achingly sweet, some desperate with need for something more intimate, a need that grew stronger, deeper by the day.

Peggy knew this man, knew every furrow of his brow, every twitch of his rugged jaw. He was plainly perturbed. "You don't mind, do you? I mean, it's only temporary, until Sue Anne gets the hang of this new computerized system."

"Why should I mind? It isn't my company." Despite the muttered assurance, Travis stepped back, avoiding Peggy's stunned gaze as she found herself stroking thin air. Her hand dropped away while Travis scratched the side of his neck and moved to the leather sofa. "You two just go on with your business."

Peggy regarded him thoughtfully, trying to identify the odd glint in his eye. He didn't seem angry—just, well, hurt. Which didn't make sense to Peggy, although she realized that this wasn't the time to question him.

Sue Anne had left her swivel chair and was anxiously

peering over Peggy's shoulder. "So, have you found any other screwups? On the ledger, that is."

"Hmm? Oh." She refocused on the page she'd scrutinized earlier. "Actually, I was just wondering what 'fiol' means."

Sue Anne eyed the entry in question and chuckled. "That stands for 'figure it out later,' kind of my own personal shorthand when I'm not sure what account to use. Usually I let the CPA sort things out."

"I see."

"Why are you frowning?"

"No reason, I guess." Peggy tapped a fingernail on the page. "It's just that this entry is a check written from the company to your personal account."

"We needed some extra cash for an insurance payment, that's all. Hell, we own the damned company."

"Oh, you haven't done anything wrong," Peggy added quickly. "And I'm sure that in the past your CPA has shifted this type of entry into the proper area before completing your annual financial reports. Unfortunately, the computer won't be quite as forgiving, and by writing the check off as an expense, you've set yourselves up as vendors to your own company. At the end of the year, the computer will spit out an automatic 1099 form, showing the amount as personal income."

Sue Anne's eyes went blank for a moment, then widened in comprehension. "You mean we'll have to pay taxes on it?"

"The way it stands now, Uncle Sam will think so."

"But that isn't right. We've already paid taxes on it once, and besides, that money is just payback for what we've already put in."

"I know. Don't worry, we can fix it."

"How?"

"By making certain that it's properly posted. For example, you and Jimmy used personal funds to start the company. That money is now shown as an outstanding loan on the cab company's books, so whenever you transfer funds from the company to your personal account, the check should be shown as a payment on the loan. That way the company's debt is reduced and you won't be sending a red flag to the IRS on taxes that you really don't owe."

Sue Anne closed her mouth, fanned her face with her hand and issued an exaggerated sigh of relief. "Like I said, the woman's a genius, right, kid?"

Travis's blank stare sent chills down Peggy's spine. "Right," he murmured. "A genius."

Then he leapt up from the couch as if his butt was on fire, pivoted smartly and strode silently out of the room.

Travis tested the lasso, spun a sloppy loop over his head, then flicked his wrist toward a black barbecue grill at the edge of the patio. He roped it easily, then tightened the loop. Not a bad throw, he thought, although it felt a bit rusty. If the barbecue had been sprinting across the yard the results would no doubt have been different.

He was definitely out of practice, a situation he'd have to remedy if he expected Cassidy Sloane to partner up with him for team roping and steer wrestling next season. Not only was Cassidy a top-notch roper, he owned a stable full of excellent working mounts, a real plus for Travis, who'd never been able to afford the expense of training and transporting his own horses.

The way Travis figured, qualifying for two additional events would provide an opportunity to pull in extra winnings, money he needed if he was ever going to save up enough for that hunk of ranch land outside Lubbock. He'd been eyeing the property for years, imagining how it would look with a thousand head of prime beef grazing the flatlands. His beef. His land.

Hell, he'd even own his own stable of top-notch working horses, just like Cassidy Sloane.

Then Travis would be more than a broken-down cowboy. He'd be a rancher, a landowner. He'd have something to offer—

"Whoa, you got him, partner."

Travis glanced up as Peggy crossed the patio and nodded at the rope loop he'd just pulled from the grill. "Danged thing near got plumb away," she drawled, mimicking his accent. "But you showed the varmint a thing or two."

Smiling, Travis hooked his thumb through the open loop, draping the remainder of the rope into a loose coil. "I'm real good at roping things that can't get away."

She spread her arms, grinning in challenge. "Prove it."

After a moment's hesitation, Travis shrugged, shifting the knot in his palm. "You asked for it," he murmured, swishing the lasso over his head. He aimed, flicked his arm forward and gave the rope a sharp tug as the loop settled around her shoulders.

She squealed and clapped her hands. "Now, that's talent. I guess you're not just another pretty face, cowboy."

He ambled forward, recoiling the rope tail as he moved toward the spot where Peggy was eyeing him the way a hungry horse eyes a fresh bucket of oats.

Lord, but she was beautiful, with all those perky little freckles and a smile brighter than sunlight. It was enough to make a grown man weep.

"Guess you've got me," she murmured as he reached down to loosen the knot around her chest.

"Guess I do." He swallowed hard as his knuckles accidentally brushed her breasts. He loosened the rope quickly, removing his hand from the danger zone, but not before he saw the tremor vibrate her body, noted the sensual darkening of her eyes. She wanted him, he realized, and his heart line-danced down his ribs. Because he wanted her, too, more than he'd ever wanted anything or anybody in his entire life.

It wasn't the first time Travis wanted what he couldn't have. But it was the first time it had ever hurt so bad.

"Is something wrong?" Peggy ducked down, allowing Travis to lift the loosened loop over her head. "You look so, I don't know, pensive, I guess."

He tried for a smile, but his cheeks felt like sun-dried leather. Because he couldn't help himself, he reached out to brush a knuckle along her cheek. "Just a bit tuckered, that's all."

She cocked her head, studying him, then stepped forward to slip her arms beneath the worn leather vest he favored to encircle his waist and massage the tight muscles above the dip of his jeans. "Are you sure that's all?"

The gentle kneading of soft palms against his back twisted his stomach, tightened his groin, made his heart ache with need. He swallowed hard and stared over the top of her head, but was aware of her worried eyes focused on his face.

Peggy regarded him thoughtfully. "A few minutes ago, when you were in the office, you seemed upset. Are you angry that I'm working with Sue Anne?"

"No," he said honestly. "Sue Anne's been having nothing but trouble since the company books went on that computer. She needs the help, and I'm glad you can give it to her. If it helps you out, too, that's even better."

Peggy nodded, but a quick glance downward convinced Travis that her eyes weren't buying it.

The words formed before Travis had a chance to think them through. "I didn't realize you knew so much about figures and such."

That seemed to surprise her. She took a step back and craned her neck to look up at him. "Does that bother you?"

"No," he lied. "Why should it?"

"It shouldn't."

"Well, there you go." He brushed a chaste kiss across her forehead, feeling like a first-class heel. Petty insecurities were bad enough—lying about them was even worse.

The problem was that although Travis knew Peggy was an educated woman—she'd mentioned having met her good-for-nothing louse of an ex-husband at college—he'd never actually realized what that meant for their relationship. Now he did, and it scared the liver out of him. After all, what could a useless horse jockey with nothing more impressive than a high school diploma possibly have to offer a bright, educated woman like Peggy Saxon?

To Travis, the answer was crystal clear. And it damn near broke his heart.

Peggy leaned over the counter, waiting for the room to stop swimming. Her legs felt like rubber, her arms like lead. With some effort, she opened an overhead cabinet to retrieve a bottle of allergy pills. Even though the medication wasn't as effective as her usual prescription, the doctor felt it was safer for nursing mothers. The pills had eased her watery eyes and chest tightness, but had done absolutely nothing to alleviate her headaches, dizzy spells or the annoying muscle weakness that had struck with increasing frequency over the past few weeks.

A low-grade fever also added to her misery, along with a queasiness that suggested she'd come down with some kind of flu bug. That was particularly upsetting, because she feared the virus could be passed to the twins. The pediatrician thought that a remote possibility since breast feeding provided the added benefit of strengthening an infant's immune system. But Peggy still fretted.

Hoping the antihistamine would stay down long enough to do some good, Peggy swallowed the pill dry, then felt her way along the wall to her bedroom and collapsed on the bed. She lay there exhausted, mustering up a modicum of gratitude that Travis wouldn't be dropping by tonight.

It wasn't that she didn't want to see him; she simply didn't want him to see her all weak and woozy.

Peggy paused by the front window, drawn by a strange vehicle at the curb. She saw a real estate logo on the passenger door, one of several such vehicles that had cruised the area in the past weeks. Good news, she decided. Clearly the neighboring duplex was in the process of being sized up by potential rental agencies. It would be nice to have people close by, although she no longer felt a gnawing need to have neighbors. She had friends now.

She had Travis.

Even when they weren't together, Travis was on Peggy's mind. She thought of him constantly, even at the most inopportune times. Yesterday, a scrumptious daydream about Travis walking the twins to kindergarten on their first day of school had been rudely interrupted by the honking of traffic behind her. Judging by the gestures offered by other drivers, the light must have been green for quite a while.

Peggy should have been embarrassed; instead, she'd been patently annoyed by the intrusion. It had been, after all, a particularly wonderful image, one that touched on the deepest hopes she harbored for her babies—that they grow up with a father who cherished them as much as she'd wanted her own father to cherish her.

If she'd dissected the daydream rationally, she'd have wondered why her mind insisted on placing Travis in the role of father instead of Clyde, whom she still believed would choose an active role in parenting their children.

But thoughts of Travis didn't make Peggy feel particularly rational. They made her feel warm and fuzzy and secure. Most important, they made her feel loved.

Travis was peering into the refrigerator when Sue Anne sidled into the kitchen. "So," she said, grinning madly.

"Saw you and Peggy in the backyard this afternoon, all kissy-wissy and lovey-dovey."

Slamming the fridge door, he shot his sister a killing look. "I don't much cotton to being spied on."

The caustic remark was lost on Sue Anne, who merely winked as Jimmy ambled through the door, then turned her attention back to her brother. "And to think I was fixing to give up."

Travis spotted a pretzel bag on the counter and snagged it. "Give up on what?" he asked, dipping his hand inside the cellophane.

"On you, kid. I'd figured you for a mustang too wild to be broke," Sue Anne said, ignoring her husband's warning stare. "Then you come a'trotting out with a bit in your mouth, all trussed and harnessed and saddled up smart. Who'd a'thunk it, hmm?"

Crunching pretzels, Travis angled a curious glance from his grinning sister to her clearly distressed husband, who puffed his cheeks and issued a pained sigh. "Y'know, Sue Anne, sometimes you're harder to follow than a drunken sidewinder. I don't have a clue what you're yammering about."

"She ain't yammering about nothing," Jimmy muttered, grabbing his wife's arm. "Just likes the sound of her own voice."

"Turn me loose, fool." Sue Anne scowled at her husband until he released her, tossing up his hands as she pivoted around to elbow her brother in the ribs. "So, when's it gonna be? Spring's always good, but judging by the way Peggy was looking at you today, I don't figure she'll be wanting to wait that long."

"Wait that long for what?"

Lost in thought, Sue Anne blinked at her brother as if she'd forgotten he was there. "A wedding, what else?"

Travis choked on a pretzel. Jimmy moaned.

Sue Anne didn't notice. "It'll take time to put things together, but we'll manage somehow. Worse case, I suppose y'all could elope—"

"Elope?" The word squirted out between coughing fits that left Travis beet red and pounding on his own chest. He finally took a wheezing breath and gave his sister a horrified stare. "Are you out of your ever-loving mind?" Before she could respond, Travis spun and stomped out of the room.

Sue Anne's smile faded as her her wary gaze flicked to her husband. "What did I—" she flinched as the front door slammed "—say?"

Jimmy scoured her with a look. "Talking marriage around a man who don't even want to be in love is about as bright as stealing raw meat from a badger."

The truth sank in quickly, sank to the pit of Sue Anne's soul. She knew her husband was right. The one thing on earth that terrified her brother more than death itself was the fear of falling in love; or more precisely, of losing someone he loved.

Travis stoutly maintained that he couldn't remember their mother, but Sue Anne remembered. She remembered when Mama died, and she remembered her little brother's stoic refusal to accept that his beloved mommy wouldn't be coming back. Sue Anne remembered the pitiful retching sobs, the agonized little eyes that begged to understand, yet couldn't.

And she remembered the blank stare in those same eyes, all that was left when her brother's tears finally dried into a vacuous expression that conveyed more eloquently than words that he'd never, ever allow himself to feel such pain again.

That fear of loss had kept Travis on the move over the years, never committing, never letting anyone get too close, always on the run from a fear he refused to acknowledge, a pain he could never forget.

Somehow Peggy Saxon had managed to slow Travis down long enough to penetrate his protective shield. Shoot, the thickheaded fool hadn't even known what was happening until Sue Anne opened her big mouth.

Now Sue Anne sagged against the counter, shaken by the realization of what she'd done. Jimmy slipped his arm around her shoulders, offering quiet consolation. Neither spoke. It wasn't necessary. By this time tomorrow, Travis would be gone. And they both knew it.

It was barely dawn when Travis exited the doughnut shop carrying coffee in a disposable foam cup. As was his routine, he walked up the street toward the spot where he'd parked the cab, passing the same shops he passed every morning. Usually he ignored the window displays, opting to focus on the panoramic sunrise inching over the mountains. Today, however, a flash of white caught his eye, and he found himself staring into the boutique window. What he saw took his breath away.

A red-haired window mannequin displayed a floor-length gown of lustrous white satin. It wasn't a wedding dress, but it could have been. Travis was mesmerized. In his mind, a flowing veil appeared, obscuring the mannequin face, and a streaming bouquet of white roses dripped from the sculpted hands.

A bride.

A wedding.

A lifetime commitment.

Travis convulsively squeezed the paper cup, then leapt back, cursing as hot coffee bubbled over his hand. Hell, he couldn't even think straight anymore. He didn't need this...this frustration, this mental torture. Why the devil was he doing this to himself? His ribs were long healed.

He should have been back on the circuit weeks ago instead of piloting a creaking heap of painted metal and getting softer by the day.

Disgusted, he dumped the coffee out, tossed the wadded cup in a trash can and strode up the street, planning to drop the cab off at the Conway's garage and tell his sister where to forward his paycheck. It wouldn't be a shock to her. He'd only agreed to help out for a few weeks until he'd recovered enough to rodeo. Well, he'd recovered, and he was suddenly chomping at the bit to hit the road.

Just as Travis reached the taxi, a man stepped out of the drugstore doorway, strode toward the curb and raised his palm. "Hey, cabbie."

Travis glanced over the cab roof. "Sorry, out of service."

The man's gaze narrowed, his thin shoulder twitching beneath a faded gray T-shirt that had seen better days. His eyes jittered toward the street, focusing on a beige four-by-four that cruised past. "Gotta get to Sixth and Magnolia, man. My mom's waiting for this medicine." He held up a brown paper bag. "She's real sick, you know?"

Travis hesitated, then shrugged. One last fare wouldn't kill him. "Okay, hop in." He slid into the driver's seat, popped the door locks and watched in the rearview mirror as the fare climbed inside.

The fellow settled in, met Travis's gaze in the mirror and smiled. "Thanks, man."

"No problem." Travis flipped the ignition, turned on the meter and pulled away from the curb. "Sixth and Magnolia, right?"

"Yeah." The customer perched forward, staring intently out the windshield as Travis drove about a quarter mile down the road. As they approached an intersection, he spoke suddenly. "Turn left at the light."

"Hmm?" Travis frowned as he glanced in the mirror.

"That's the long way, mister. We'll get there faster by using Sixth."

"The street's all torn up," the man told him. "Still making storm repairs."

"I was up that way a few days ago. There wasn't any construction work going on."

"Just started yesterday." The guy sat ramrod straight, watching anxiously as Travis made the left turn and accelerated down the narrow, curving street that led to the outskirts of town and beyond.

Travis hadn't been out this way very often, but if memory served, there was a cutoff a ways up that led over to Magnolia. He didn't know exactly where the road intersected the street they were on, but wasn't too worried about it. The fellow in the back seat clearly knew where he wanted to go and how to get there, so Travis just cruised along until the scenery of scattered structures evolved into a lush wall of forest.

Up ahead, a familiar dirt road veered to the right. Behind him, the paper bag crinkled.

"Pull over."

Travis touched a cautious toe to the brake. "This is Virginia Road, mister. It doesn't go anywhere near—"

"I said, pull over." The passenger leapt forward, growling low in his throat. "Now!"

A wisp of air brushed his ear. Travis knew without looking that there was a gun pointed at his head.

Ten

Travis jammed the brake, jerked the wheel. There was a deafening blast. A barb of fire scuffed his brow. Glass shattered. His ears roared. The acrid stench of gunpowder stung his nostrils, burned his lungs.

Vaguely aware that the robber had been thrown against the right passenger door, Travis whipped the steering wheel left, sending the cab into an uncontrolled spin. He saw the ditch, saw the massive oak looming straight ahead.

Then he saw nothing.

"Sh, little man, Mommy's here." Bleary-eyed and exhausted, Peggy scooped the howling infant out of his crib, nestling him against her shoulder. "Goodness, we certainly have developed our lungs, haven't we?"

T.J. sniffed, blinked, gave a shuddering hiccup, then screwed up his face and belted out his displeasure.

Swallowing panic, Peggy continued to murmur softly and pat the sobbing infant's back. He'd been awake half the night, crying inconsolably, only partially relieved by her feeble attempts to comfort him.

Over the past two months there had been many such nights; this one had been the worst. Or at least, it seemed worse to Peggy, who felt the final vestiges of strength seeping out through the base of her throbbing skull.

Forcing her wobbly legs into motion, she carried T.J. to a creaky wooden rocker by the nursery window. The smooth motion usually soothed the cranky babies, providing the added benefit of calming their harried mom, as well. Thankfully, this morning was no exception. After a few moments, T.J.'s head grew heavy against her shoulder, and his shuddering sobs dissipated.

Limp with relief, Peggy laid her cheek against his soft scalp and closed her eyes.

The doorbell awakened her. Disoriented and half-asleep, Peggy sat up with a start, clutching T.J. so tightly that she nearly wakened him, too. The bell rang again, followed by an insistent pounding on the front door. She rose shakily, laid her sleepy son in his crib, then hurried to answer the door.

"Oh, God." She tottered backward, pressing a hand to her mouth. "Oh, good Lord, Travis, you're hurt."

Travis entered without ceremony but didn't remove his hat as was his usual custom. "It's nothing. Can I borrow your phone?" The question was purely perfunctory, since he was already limping toward it.

Peggy gathered her wits long enough to close the front door. "What happened?"

"Some jerk tried to rob me," he muttered, snatching up the receiver. "I wrapped the cab around a tree. When I came to, the thieving jackass was gone, and the two-way radio was smashed into rubble. There's blood in the back seat, though, so I figure he's not feeling much better than I am."

Peggy steadied herself on the sofa, licked her lips. "Your head is bleeding."

That seemed to startle him, but not much. He touched the oozing wound over his brow, flinched slightly, then shrugged. "The bullet must have grazed me."

"The bullet?" Peggy's legs gave out. She sat heavily, clutching her throat, fighting for breath. "Oh, God, you could have been killed."

"If I ever get my hands on that sniveling two-bit coward,

he'll wish to hell I had been." Travis dialed, rubbed his temple, then straightened and got right to the point. "Yeah, Sue Anne, unit six is smashed in a ditch at the corner of Virginia and Pine. I'm at Peggy's. The cab needs a tow. I need a cop."

Turning away, he lowered his voice, presumably to keep Peggy from hearing the gruesome details of the harrowing incident he relayed to his sister. Still, Peggy wobbled forward, wringing her hands and honing in on every terrifying word.

Her fingers were numb. Her heart raced. The metallic taste of fear flooded her mouth. The thought of what could have happened to Travis was frightening enough, but the grim expression in his eyes horrified her. The softness was gone, replaced by a hard-edged fury that chilled her to the marrow.

He hung up, flexing his fingers over the phone as he swung a glance toward the hallway. "Twins okay?"

"They're fine," she whispered, pushing herself to her feet. She reached out to him. "Let me tend to that—"

He turned away and pulled his hat down to conceal the injury. "No need."

"But the wound should be cleaned."

"It's just a scratch, woman. Quit harping." Before the words were out of his mouth, regret was pouring into his eyes. He covered his face with his palms and heaved a shuddering sigh. "I'm sorry. It's not your fault I'm such a damned fool."

"You're not to blame for what happened, Travis."

His eyes flashed. "You think Jimmy would've been caught flat-footed like that? Or even Ted?" He issued a disgusted snort. "Hell, either one of 'em would've taken one look at that stupid paper bag and smelled a gun. But not me, and you know why?"

"Travis—"

"Because I'd rather clean septic tanks than drive a damned cab. I hate it. Sometimes I even hate my sister for going into the business, for guilt-tripping me into working for her even though she knew I'd figure a way to screw up. I always do. But you didn't know that, did you? You didn't know that everything I touch turns to dirt, that the dumbest beast on the circuit has more common sense."

"That's not true, Travis. You're a highly intelligent man. You had a college scholarship, for goodness' sake."

"But I didn't use it." His face contorted, not in anger but in pain and a frustration so explosive that Peggy could actually feel the emanating vibration. "I was too danged stupid to think about the future, to think about what I'd do when I was too old, too crippled to sit a horse. There's a powerful difference between having brains and being smart enough to use them."

"Why are you doing this, Travis? Why are you putting yourself down?"

His shoulders shuddered, sagged forward. "You need to know who I am."

"I *know* who you are, Travis Stockwell. You're the kindest, most decent man I've ever met."

"I'm a failure."

"I don't believe that."

"Believe it." His eyes hardened, and he clenched his fists at his sides. "I was such a disappointment to my daddy that he up and drank himself to death. There's nothing on earth I'm good at, except spending eight seconds on the back of an animal even madder and dumber than me."

"Don't say that. The rodeo was good to you, yes, but just because you can't ride anymore doesn't mean there aren't other things you're just as good at. You're an intelligent man. You just haven't given yourself a chance—"

"What makes you think I can't ride anymore?"

"Sue Anne told me about your injuries. I just assumed—'' She bit off the words as he slowly shook his head.

''Just a few broken ribs, bruised innards. Doc cleared me to hit the circuit weeks ago.'' He issued a derisive grunt. ''It may not be much to brag on, but I've got a few good years before I'm ready for the bone yard.''

Peggy licked her lips, absently rubbing her head. ''I don't understand. I thought you were happy in Grand Springs. I thought you cared about Sue Anne and Jimmy, cared about their company.''

''I do.'' Travis shifted, jammed a fist on his hip. He rolled his head, massaged the back of his neck and stared at the ceiling as if seeking a divine message. Finally he sighed and met her gaze. ''Driving a cab isn't for me, Peggy. Never has been. I only do it now and again to help out, pull in some extra fares during the off-season, or when I'm on the mend.''

''I see.'' Icy fingers of comprehension squeezed the base of her spine. ''So this has all been just a temporary respite.''

It took a moment for him to answer. ''Rodeo is what I do, Peggy. It's the only thing I *can* do.'' He glanced away. ''At least for a while, until I get enough money put by to make something out of myself.''

If Peggy hadn't been so shaken, she might have recognized the wistful plea in his eyes and responded to it. But she didn't see, didn't respond, was too shattered by the realization that Travis had never really given up rodeo, never would. He was a man for whom the whisper of the road was more powerful than any woman. Travis Stockwell was a wanderer, an adventurer, just like her father. Just like Clyde.

To Travis, her silence spoke volumes. He pivoted on his heel and strode toward the front door.

Peggy snapped out of her mental fog long enough to snag his arm as he passed. "Wait."

His jaw twitched, then slackened. He met her gaze, held it deeply. Lifting his hand, he tenderly brushed a curl from her face, then stroked his thumb over her cheek. "You look tired, honey. Go back to bed. Get some rest."

"Please don't leave."

His eyes reddened, grew moist. "I have to."

Before Peggy could stop him, he yanked the front door open just as a police cruiser pulled up at the curb. Travis stepped over the threshold, hesitated, then swung around, pulled her into his arms and kissed her so sweetly that her heart nearly stopped.

She stumbled when he released her, and she had to grab the doorjamb for support. When the squad car drove off with Travis inside, Peggy had the horrible sensation that she might never see him again.

"He's okay, hon. Shook him up a bit. Bruised that big ol' cowboy ego of his, but my brother's taken worse falls. He always dusts himself off and climbs back in the saddle."

Peggy shifted the phone, trying to take Sue Anne's encouragement to heart, but there was a tight edge to the woman's voice that played right into Peggy's worst fears. "But Travis looked so, I don't know, so distraught. I've never seen him like that. He kept talking about being a failure, and how he'd let everybody down. He even said something about being responsible for his father's death."

"He said that?"

"Yes. He thinks his father drank so much because he was disappointed in him."

Silence hung heavily on the line. When Sue Anne finally spoke, her voice shook with anger. "Even dead, the rotten louse is still ruining his son's life."

Peggy was shocked by the venom in her voice. "How can you say that? He was your father."

"He was a sperm donor," Sue Anne spit back. "Being a father takes a danged sight more than that. Silas Stockwell didn't care a lick about anyone except himself. Travis tried the best he could to take care of that man. Set to mowing lawns when he was barely seven, moved up to paper routes, stocking grocery shelves, whatever work a kid could find. All he got for his trouble was a pack of misery from a drunken lout who swiped every penny Travis earned, then gave him the back of his hand because it was never enough. Even lying on his deathbed with Travis tending his every need, there was never a thank-you, never a kind word for his own son. Silas flat sucked the life out of that poor boy. Made him feel worthless."

Peggy's fingers cramped around the telephone. Tears stung her eyes, slid down her cheeks. She couldn't imagine a father inflicting such cruelty; she couldn't imagine a son surviving it. Yet Travis *had* survived. He'd grown into a caring man, with a gentle heart and a strong, nurturing soul.

"Travis has gone beyond that," she said, struggling with a voice that threatened to crack. "He cares about people. A man can't care about others without caring about himself, too."

Sue Anne sighed. Peggy could picture her leaning back in the dispatch chair, raking her fingers through that poorly cut bob and pursing her lips in frustration. "Travis has always had a big heart, but the scars run deep. My brother's a smart man, but even smart men can be kind of dumb when it comes to the stuff that really scares them."

"What is it that scares Travis?"

"Letting people down," Sue Anne said quietly. "Especially people he loves. He can't keep himself from caring about folks because he's just naturally softhearted and such, but he works real hard at not caring *too* much. That way, he won't get hurt so bad when it's over.''

Peggy's stomach twisted. "So what Travis and I had—our friendship—it's over?"

"My brother is confused," Sue Anne said kindly. "Deep down, he knows what he wants. I think he's just afraid to go after it for fear things won't, you know, work out. Give him some space, hon. Maybe he'll come around this time."

A nauseous surge had Peggy clutching her stomach. She struggled with it, fought it off. "What do you mean, 'this time?'"

A sharp rustle filtered over the line, as if Sue Anne was restlessly shifting papers across the dispatch desk. "Travis has roped in his heart a time or two."

"His heart?" Peggy licked her lips, felt faint. "I think you've misunderstood my concern. Travis and I are...well, friends."

"Uh-huh."

"I don't need a man in my life."

"Of course you don't."

"And even if I wanted a man, which I most certainly do not, why on earth would I choose one whose boots twitched every time he saw a road map?"

"I don't guess you would, assuming you had a choice."

"What's that supposed to mean?"

Sue Anne's shrug was practically audible. "When it comes to love, we don't always have a say in the matter."

Peggy jolted upright, felt the hairs on her nape rise. "I didn't say anything about love."

"You didn't have to," Sue Anne replied sadly. "It's as plain as the nose on your face, and on my brother's too, I'm afraid."

Closing her eyes, Peggy swallowed hard and fought a new surge of tears. Sue Anne believed that Travis was in love with her, but the realization brought no joy. Instead, it brought paralyzing fear. For the first time, Peggy felt as if she truly understood Travis, and she knew that to understand him was to lose him forever.

She moistened her lips, tried to speak, then tried again. ''Sue Anne?''

''Hmm?''

''You don't think Travis will come back, do you.''

Silence stretched like death. ''No, hon,'' Sue Anne said finally. ''I don't figure he will.''

Red dust billowed beneath pounding hooves. Lassos hummed, swirling a swath through thick, humid air. Windblown grit scuffed his face, clawed his eyes. Travis squinted through the crimson cloud, focused only on his stampeding target and the steady drone of the whirling loop above his head.

The rider beside him stood in the stirrups, flashed forward, then hauled his speeding mount up short. A rope loop sailed out, settled over the steer's horns. Travis dropped his lasso to the side, flicked it at the animal's heels, simultaneously jerked the reins and yanked up the lasso. The steer, with Cassidy Sloane's rope still tangled around its horns, kicked away from Travis's sloppy throw and spun to face its harassers.

Cassidy swore, touched his heels to his horse's flank. The animal responded instantly, jiggling sideways as the steer lowered its head to charge.

Spurring his own mount back into position, Travis hauled in his empty rope, thumbed open the loop and flicked a hurried toss that snagged only one of the young steer's heels. He clicked his tongue and lifted the reins. His horse executed a smart pivot and backed up until the trussed steer was stretched out on the ground, safely immobilized and ready for branding.

Theoretically, that is, since the animal in question was

already marked with Cassidy Sloane's Lazy S. This had been a practice run, one of many that Travis had insisted upon over the past hour. As badly as this run had ended, it had been better than most. At least this time he'd roped one of the danged steer's legs. A disqualification, of course, but not complete humiliation.

Cassidy shifted in his saddle and used the tip of his finger to poke back a well-worn Stetson. He pursed his lips, managing a bland expression, but his black eyes sparkled with blatant amusement. "Looks like you're a mite out of practice."

Travis flipped a leg over his mount's head and slipped to the ground. "Hell," he muttered, eyeing his sloppy handiwork. "More'n a mite. I'm rustier than an old barn nail." The unhappy steer rolled its eyes, snorting as if in agreement. Travis heaved a sigh, loosened the tied ankle and flipped off the front loop as the annoyed animal scrambled to its feet.

Travis gave it an affectionate slap on the rump, then the steer bolted across the pasture to join the impressive herd grazing as far as the eye could see. He turned away, recoiled his rope, tried to keep his eyes from wandering the vast spread that always sent a stab of envy into his heart. It wasn't that Travis begrudged his friend's success, he just wanted a little piece of it for himself.

To his mind, Cassidy Sloane had everything Travis had ever wanted in life—a loving family, a successful ranch, the respect of peers and neighbors. Folks considered Cassidy a hard worker, trustworthy and fair, with more than his share of good, old-fashioned common sense. Naturally, a man like Cassidy Sloane never would have been caught flat-footed by a twitchy cab thief.

And he would have known there was a damned gun in the bag.

Frustrated by the memory of this morning's fiasco,

Travis pivoted sharply and hung the coiled rope on his saddle. "Let's cut another one."

Cassidy issued a grunt, rolling the reins lightly in his gloved palm. "Think we've worried them enough for one day. Besides, I'm getting hungry. How about you?"

Disappointed, Travis gave a limp shrug. "I could eat." He scuffed a pebble with his boot toe as he squinted at the grazing herd. And sighed.

"You've been out of the saddle for nearly three months," Cassidy told him. "It's going to take a while to work out the kinks."

Travis swung back onto his mount and wiped his forehead with the back of his hand. "I don't have 'a while.'"

"What's the rush?"

"I'll have to double up for the rest of the season to make up for what I've already missed."

"How'n the devil are you going to do that, enter each event twice?"

It was the opening Travis had been waiting for. "That's against the rules. But—" he reached into his back pocket, where a creased flyer was sandwiched between the folds of his wallet "—there's no rule says you can't enter twice as many events." He plucked out the flyer, shook it open and held it out to Cassidy, who'd laid the reins against his big gelding's neck, urging the animal forward.

"What's this?"

"The latest schedule on the pro rodeo tour," Travis said, slipping the wallet back into his pocket. "Look at the circled section."

Cassidy scanned the sheet and shrugged. "So there's a Cowboy Jamboree outside of Cheyenne next week."

"Only a couple hundred miles from here. You'd be back Sunday night." Avoiding his friend's startled gaze, Travis made a production of plucking a fresh bag of pumpkin seeds out of his shirt pocket. "Unless you had a mind to head on up to Kalispell with me for the Pro Open later this month. Big purses up there. Top finishers all take a share.'' He popped a couple of seeds in his mouth and held the bag out to Cassidy, who waved it away.

The big man crossed his forearms over the saddle horn, staring at Travis as if expecting him to sprout horns and moo. "Let me get this straight. You want me to rodeo with you?"

"Just for team roping.'' Travis glanced away and tucked the cellophane bag back in his shirt. "Maybe steer wrestling.''

Cassidy's eyes narrowed into black slits. "Do I look like a complete idiot?''

"Now that you mention it—'' Travis caught the flyer Cassidy thrust at him, then jammed it back into his pocket. "Aw, c'mon, all I need is a hazer to run the steer straight. I'll do the takedown. You won't even get your boots dusty, and you'll get thirty percent of the winnings. Fair enough?''

But Cassidy's big gelding was already cresting the hill, heading back toward the ranch house.

Travis turned, urging his horse into a trot. "Okay, you win,'' he muttered, easing alongside Cassidy's mount. "Forty percent. Damned generous considering you've never ridden the circuit in your life.''

"I plan to keep it that way.''

"Hell, Sloane, you love the rodeo.''

"I love fried chicken, too, but that doesn't mean I'm going to roll myself in flour and jump in a pan.'' He ducked under an oak branch, angling a glance toward his glum companion. "What's this all about, anyway?''

Travis feigned a nonchalant shrug and focused on a twisted hunk of barbed wire in a mended section of fence they were passing. He'd been too embarrassed to tell Cassidy about this morning's robbery and how he'd left his sister's cab wrapped around an oak tree. He hadn't men-

tioned Peggy and the twins, either. Real men didn't talk
about things like emotions and relationships and how a pair
of flashing green eyes could turn masculine innards into a
quivering heap of jelly.

Nope, real men talked about real-man stuff, like the high
price of cattle feed and what brand of pickup truck was
tough enough to handle a real man's work.

"Travis?"

"Hmm?"

"I said, what's this all about?"

Travis snagged a twig off a low-hanging branch, guided
his horse around another one, then cut toward the barren
rise that led to the Sloane house. "Just looking for a little
extra action. After what you said at the saloon a few weeks
back, I figured you'd like a piece of it, that's all."

Cassidy angled a wary glance over his shoulder. "What
exactly did I say?"

"Nothing much." Tossing the twig away, Travis pulled
off his right glove with his teeth, tucked it in his vest, then
repeated the process with the left glove while Cassidy
glowered impatiently. "Only that you'd married too young
and wished you'd had a chance to hit the circuit for a few
years before settling down."

Cassidy dragged his hat down and slouched forward in
the saddle. "I was drunk."

"On two beers?"

"Whatever I said, forget it. I got a ranch to run, a family
to feed."

Travis swallowed resentment at the reminder. "How's
Victoria doing? You know, after her little cave adventure."

"She's fine."

The terse reply was issued tightly, with a twitch at the
jawline that gave Travis pause. "Must have been scared,
though, poor little squirt. Tough thing to have happened."

"It shouldn't have happened," Cassidy snapped. "It

wouldn't have happened if her mother had been watching her proper.''

"Karen?" Travis frowned, scratched his head. "I heard she was working the ER that day. All the town doctors were called in on account of the storm and all.''

"Yeah, doctors were called in. Mothers stayed at home with their kids. Guess it depends on priorities." He shook his head as he muttered under his breath. "Never marry a smart woman, Travis. Nothing's ever good enough for her.''

"Whoa, partner, this is Karen you're talking about. Sure, she's a doctor, but she's also the mother of your child, your wife and the woman you love.''

Cassidy shifted the reins in his hand, gazing down the hill toward the sprawling, structured center of the Lazy S ranch. The tightness in his jaw eased, and an indefinable sadness crawled into his dark eyes. "Love sucks you in," he said quietly. "You think everything will be wonderful when you put the ring on her finger, but that's when she starts to change.''

Before Travis could even begin to digest the significance of that statement or the sadness behind it, Cassidy clicked his tongue, spurred his mount and shot down the grassy slope toward the house. Travis reined his horse, holding the impatient animal at the crest of the hill so he could watch the scene unfolding below.

A pigtailed girl zipped out of the house and dashed across the yard to greet her father. Cassidy dismounted, caught the excited child and swung her in the air. A woman stepped onto the porch, hovering there as if blessing the sight of loving family unity.

And it was one heck of a sight. Even from Travis's vantage point high on the hill, the scene could have been pulled straight out of a Norman Rockwell painting. He wondered if little Victoria knew how lucky she was, growing up with a dad who loved her. T.J. and Ginny would never know what that was like, not as long as Peggy believed that good-for-nothing ex-husband of hers was going to suddenly grow a heart and decide to be a real father to those babies. That flat-out wasn't going to happen. A man who'd walk out on a woman like Peggy couldn't be trusted any further than a Brahman bull could be flung from a slingshot.

Peggy deserved a real man to love and care for her. The twins deserved a real father.

In his mind's eye, Travis imagined himself in Cassidy's place, riding in from his own range to his own beautiful home, with a pair of exuberant, red-haired youngsters dashing out to greet him. Hell, he could even picture Peggy posed on the porch holding strawberry-rhubarb pie, the kind with sugary sparkles all over the crust. It was paradise.

A fool's paradise.

Because what you saw wasn't necessarily what you got. There was trouble in the Sloane household, an invisible river of darkness flowing beneath the surface calm.

Never marry a smart woman, Travis. Nothing's ever good enough for her.

Those words made Travis's blood run cold. Peggy Saxon was a smart woman. Even if she wasn't the genius Sue Anne thought her to be, she was still too good for a broken-down cowboy who'd never amounted to a hill of beans in his entire life, and probably never would. Travis had wanted to be like Cassidy Sloane, a man who'd made something out of himself, who had something to offer. If a guy like Cassidy couldn't make marriage work, there wasn't a snowball's chance for Travis, and he was six kinds of a fool for even thinking about it.

Trouble was, he couldn't help but think about it, and when he did, his heart felt like it had been tied with barbed wire. Luckily, Travis knew how to deal with the pain, the sense of loss. He'd been doing it all his life.

* * *

By sundown, Travis was back in his pickup truck, speeding toward Cheyenne. In a few days, a week at most, Peggy Saxon would be nothing more than a sweet memory. A few laughs, a few beers, then on to the next town, the next livestock draw, the next roaring crowd. It wasn't all Travis wanted, but it was all he could have.

It was the cowboy way.

The heat was stifling. Even the darkness couldn't soften the oppressive layer of choking humidity that made Peggy's hair stick to her wet face, cling to her nape like soggy cotton. It drove her crazy. The heat drove her crazy.

The silence drove her crazy.

She adjusted the nursery fan, then touched Ginny's soft cheek. It was warm, but not sweaty; neither was T.J.'s. Both babies were sleeping peacefully. They hadn't noticed that the room was spinning.

Fighting another nauseous surge, Peggy felt her way along the wall, stumbled to the living room and clung to the sofa, swaying.

Travis.

The voice in her mind was hoarse, desperate. She knew he wouldn't answer, couldn't answer.

Peggy knew he was gone.

Thirsty. God, she was so thirsty. She hadn't been able to keep anything down all day, not even water. But her mouth was so dry that her tongue felt like suede. It stuck to her teeth like Velcro.

Peggy gripped the sofa cushion, closed her eyes, hoping to orient herself. The vertigo eased slightly, giving her a modicum of hope that she could make it to the kitchen. She was so damned thirsty.

The kitchen light was on, so she focused on the doorway, which resembled a brightly lit tunnel that was happy, cheerful and inviting. She tottered forward one step, then another. The tunnel tilted.

Peggy knew she was falling. She cried out first in fear, then in pain as something exploded inside her head.

Travis!

It was her final thought before the tunnel completely disappeared and she floated into a netherworld of blackness.

Eleven

Travis slouched over the counter and fiddled with a limp French fry, using it to draw designs in the ketchup that flooded one side of his plate. He remembered that Peggy didn't like ketchup on her French fries. She ate the danged things dry. A man just couldn't have serious feelings about a woman who didn't know how to eat French fries.

Worst part was that she'd probably raise those babies to eat French fries wrong, too. That'd be a real shame, especially for T.J. The little wrangler needed someone to teach him real-man stuff, like how to whack the ketchup bottle with a flat palm instead of a fist so the contents wouldn't glug out all at once. And then there was the fine art of chomping down a burger in four bites or less. None of this nibbling around the edge stuff. Girls nibbled. Men gobbled. Belching was optional.

It wasn't that Peggy wouldn't be a good mother to those babies. She was a wonderful mama. The best. Patient and tender, all cooey and kissy. Travis didn't have a doubt in the world that those sweet babies would be well-loved and happy. It's just that there were girl manners and boy manners, and Travis hated the idea that T.J. would grow up not knowing the difference.

Travis pushed away his plate, eyeing his own half-eaten burger with disdain. It looked, well, it looked nibbled. Pitiful, just pitiful. Ordinarily he was a three-bite-man and proud of it. Tonight his stomach wasn't up to the challenge.

Maybe it was the peculiar sense of apprehension that had been plaguing him. He'd had trouble concentrating, had even missed a turnoff and found himself heading toward Nebraska. It had taken an extra hour to backtrack. Now he'd be lucky if he made it to Cheyenne by morning.

Travis took a final gulp of cold coffee, then tossed a two-buck tip on the counter and went to the diner's cash register to pay his bill. The cashier greeted him with a lukewarm smile, waiting while he eyed the array of gum and mints displayed in the glass counter case.

"Got any pumpkin seeds?" he asked, handing over a twenty.

She accepted the currency and gave the display a disinterested glance. "We've got sunflower seeds."

"I don't want sunflower seeds."

"We've got gum."

"I don't want gum. I want pumpkin seeds."

She plopped his change on the counter. "Well, cowboy, you can't have 'em if we don't got 'em. How about a breath mint?"

He narrowed his eyes. "How about some antacids?" he said loudly enough to startle some patrons that had just entered the establishment. "I could use 'em about now."

The patrons did a U-turn and left.

Travis barely noticed, nor did he pay attention to the infuriated cashier's dark scowl. He was completely overwhelmed by a soft buzz in his skull and the chill skittering down his spine. He shifted, glanced over his shoulder, saw nothing but his own reflection in the diner's glass door.

Then he felt it again, a whispered uneasiness, unfocused but intensely compelling. His shoulder tingled as if touched. And he could have sworn he heard someone call his name.

"Why did you leave me, Daddy?"

"I had to."

"Didn't you love me anymore?"

"I loved you."

"Then why did you go away?"

"I thought you'd be better off."

His face was blurred, features obscured by a cloudy vapor. But Peggy could hear his voice and knew without doubt who he was. "But I cried, Daddy, and so did Mommy. We were so sad without you."

"I know." The vapor grew thicker, more opaque. "I'm sorry. I'm so sorry...."

"Daddy?" As Peggy reached out, empty mist swirled around her fingers. "Daddy, please come back. I'll be a good girl, I promise. I promise, Daddy."

A wail emanated from beyond the cloudy wall, a cranky, frightened sound that pierced her very soul. She clawed forward, only to find herself lost in the mist. The cry intensified, more desperate now, more terrified. She had to find the source. She had to.

She had to.

Travis pulled up to the curb, letting his truck idle a moment before turning off the ignition. He didn't have a clue why he was here, or what he was going to do. All he knew is that he'd left the diner heading south, back toward Grand Springs. Now he was parked in front of Peggy's duplex, wondering why the kitchen light was on at three o'clock in the morning.

At the risk of once again finding himself staring down the business end of a police revolver, he exited the truck and went to have a look-see. Of course, the twins couldn't tell time, and he knew their hungry little bellies didn't much care if the sun was up or not. Still, he couldn't shake the sensation that he really ought to check things out.

He considered peeking in the back window, a notion

quickly discarded when he remembered how frightened Peggy had been the last time he'd slunk around her house like some kind of perverted peeper. Instead, he strode up the front walk. By the time he reached the porch, he could hear the twins crying. He listened a moment, waiting for the change in pitch or intensity that confirmed they were being tended. The cries continued unabated, desperate, choking little wails that went straight through his heart.

"Peggy?" He tapped on the door, waited, then pounded it with his fist. "Peggy, it's Travis. Open the door."

Nothing. No lilting voice, no flurry of footsteps. Only silence.

A quick twist of the knob confirmed that the door was locked, so he sprinted around back, rushed through the gate and found the kitchen door locked, too. In a sickening rush of déjà vu, he took a step back, booted it open and dashed inside.

What he saw nearly stopped his heart. "Oh, God. Peggy." He knelt beside her crumpled form, frantically massaging her chalky cheeks. "Peggy, honey, wake up. You've got to wake up, honey, you got to."

She moaned. He nearly wept with relief. At least she was alive.

"Babies," she murmured, rolling her head. "My babies."

"They're fine, honey, just fine." At least, he hoped they were. "I'll, ah, be right back."

Travis sprinted down the hallway, into the nursery where both babies were still wailing. He skidded to Ginny's crib. The pathetic little thing was beet red, flailing her hands and kicking madly. A wet stain on the mattress hinted to at least one of her problems.

Travis awkwardly patted her rigid tummy. "There, there, darling." She sucked a startled sob, blinked expectantly up at him, then screwed up her face and wailed even louder.

Travis wrung his hands, muttering. He grabbed the pink pacifier at the foot of the crib and wiggled it inside the baby's open mouth. Instantly, she clamped her gums together and startled to suckle.

"One down," he mumbled, then headed toward T.J., who was just as red-faced as his sister and twice as loud. Frantic, Travis searched the crib for the blue pacifier, finally spotting it on the floor by the dresser. He scooped up the precious piece of plastic, sprinted into the bathroom to scrub it off with hot, soapy water. By the time he'd managed to dash back and pop the clean pacifier into T.J.'s greedy little mouth, Ginny was crying again.

He ran to her crib, retrieved the pink pacifier, which had slipped away and fallen under her ear. When he tried to reinsert the rubbery nipple, she turned her face away, yowling in protest. "I know it's not exactly what you had in mind, but it's the best I can do. Make believe it's Mommy, okay, darling?"

Ginny stared up, heaved a resigned shudder and accepted the pacifier.

Travis exhaled all at once. "That's my girl."

With his heart pounding, he retrieved a wet washcloth from the bathroom, then lurched back down the hall and knelt to sponge Peggy's pale face.

She moaned again. "You do love me," she whispered without opening her eyes. "I knew you did. I knew it."

A lump the size of Wyoming wedged in Travis's throat. He wanted to speak, hell, he wanted to holler that yes, yes, he loved her. But those words had never touched his tongue before, and he couldn't form them now.

Her lips moved. "I love you, too, Daddy."

Every drop of moisture instantly evaporated from Travis's mouth. Peggy didn't love him. Hell, she didn't even know who he was. She was delirious, dangerously sick and out of her mind with fever. There was only one thing to do.

So Travis did it.

The first awareness Peggy had was of an uncomfortable tightness pressing the bridge of her nose and the hiss of oxygen being fed into the mask. She blinked at the light, squinted at the blurred form leaning over her. It was a woman with short blond hair and a gentle smile. "Easy, now. You're going to be fine."

"Where am I?" The question came out slurred, muffled by the mask, but the female EMT didn't seem to notice.

"In an ambulance," she replied.

An ambulance? The answer was confirmed by a jarring bounce as the vehicle sped along a bumpy road. Peggy lifted a weak hand and grasped the female medic's wrist. "My babies..."

"Your babies are fine," the woman said, loosely grasping Peggy's wrist and pressing a thumb against the pulsing vein. "Your friend is taking care of them."

"My friend?"

"Umm." The medic studied her watch, then smiled and placed Peggy's hand back onto the cot. "You had us worried for a while, but your pulse is much stronger and your blood pressure has stabilized."

"I don't have any friends," Peggy blurted.

"Well, you certainly have one. He probably saved your life."

"He?" Disoriented as she was, Peggy took a moment to clear her fuzzy mind.

The medic chuckled. "Very much a 'he.' Big brown eyes, shoulders to die for, and hips that look so good in jeans it ought to be illegal."

Peggy moaned. "Oh, God. Travis." She yanked at the

mask, tried to sit up, fought the medic's attempt to calm
her. "Please, I have to get back, I have to go home."

"Sh, you're going to be fine."

"You don't understand. Travis can't take care of the
twins. He doesn't know how, he's even afraid to pick them
up." Peggy fought against the woman's restraining hands.
"Please, you have to take me back...aah!" A burning sensation shifted Peggy's attention, and she stared in horror at
the tube jutting from her taped arm. A fluid bag was suspended above her head, dripping clear liquid into the tube.

Memories slid through her mind, fuzzy images of the
lighted kitchen, the tilting tunnel door. She remembered the
feel of rough carpet against her cheek, the desperate cries
of her babies. How long had she been unconscious? How
long had her babies lain there, crying with hunger, with
fear?

Reality hit like a sledge. If Travis hadn't come back, it
might have been days before anyone found them.

But he *had* come back, and he'd saved their lives. Again.

"You've got to come over," Travis shouted into the telephone. "Ginny's all wet and T.J.'s crying, and they're both
hungry as vultures, and I've got to get to the hospital to
see about Peggy, and—"

"Peggy's in the ER," Sue Anne said. "I just called.
She's awake and alert, and the doctors are examining her
now."

"I've got to get there," Travis insisted.

"What you've got to do is take care of those babies."

"Me? I don't know anything about babies."

"You've spent every spare minute with them for the past
eight weeks. I figure you've picked up a tip or two."

"That's different." Travis raked his hair, dragging the
telephone toward the hallway until the cord went taut. He
swore.

"Humph, nice language in front of those babes."

"The twins are in the nursery. I'm in the living room.
The blasted cord is too short." He spun around, clutching
the phone in one hand and the receiver in the other. "Sue
Anne, please, I'm begging you. I'll wash every cab in the
fleet with a cotton swab and drive night shift for a year.
Hell, I'll even do your laundry. Just come over!"

She was silent a moment. "Does that include ironing?"

"Sue Anne!"

A chuckle filtered through the line. "Sorry, kid, much
as I love to take advantage of panic-based generosity, I
can't leave the dispatch center."

"Danny can take over."

"He'll be in Denver for the rest of the week. College
registration—" A telephone rang on Sue Anne's end of the
line. "Hold on," she muttered to Travis, then answered
what he presumed to be the dispatch center's call-out
phone, which was a separate line for Conway Cab custom-
ers. He heard his sister speak briefly, repeat an address on
the west side of town. There was a ripping noise, as if she'd
torn a sheet of paper from a pad. A moment later, he heard
her on the two-way radio, relaying the information.

Travis checked his watch and groaned. It was 6:00 a.m.,
and the day shift was just pulling out. Where had the time
gone? The three hours since he'd first arrived had flown by
in chaos, and Lord only knew how long it had been since
those poor babies had anything to eat. They'd dozed off for
a spell after he'd given them the pacifiers, but they were
awake now and sounded hungry enough to suck off the
wallpaper.

"Travis?"

He tightened his grip on the receiver. "Yeah?"

"Things are getting busy here. Listen, do you still carry
that portable two-way in your truck?"

"Sure, but why...?"

"If you use it to patch into the dispatch center, I might be able to give you a few pointers while you're caring for the kids."

"Oh. Yeah. Great." Travis dashed toward the front door, and would have made it if he hadn't been carrying the telephone. The cord tightened, yanking the phone body out of his hand. The instrument bounced across the floor. He dove for it, retrieved the phone and lost the receiver, which skidded under the sofa.

Frantic now, Travis grabbed the curly cord and dragged it out hand over fist, hollering, "Sue Anne, Sue Anne? I can't get through the front door. The cord's not long enough—"

"Hang up, Travis."

"Huh?"

A long-suffering sigh made him wince. "Hang up the telephone, brilliant brother of mine, then go get the two-way out of your truck and use it to contact the dispatch center."

He frowned and rubbed his forehead, feeling like a damned fool. "I knew that."

Sue Anne chuckled. "Sure you did."

There was a click. The line went dead. Sue Anne had broken the connection, leaving Travis utterly alone with two hungry infants and a heart full of fear.

"Am I going to die?"

Dr. Amanda Jennings smiled and patted Peggy's hand. "Of course not. We're going to take very good care of you."

"But you don't know what's wrong with me."

"Not yet," she conceded. "But we'll run some blood tests, take a couple of X rays—"

"X rays?"

"You've got a nasty lump on your head. The paramedic

report indicates that you probably struck the kitchen table when you fainted.''

Peggy bit her lip and turned away so the doctor wouldn't see the tears form. For the first time, she realized how vulnerable her babies were. If anything happened to her, they'd be raised by strangers, alone and unloved. The thought made her nauseous. That couldn't happen. She wouldn't let it happen. ''Could someone please call my ex-husband? I have an emergency number.''

''I'll see to it myself,'' Dr. Jennings replied kindly. She jotted the number on a blue scratch pad on the bed table, tore off the sheet and clipped it on Peggy's chart. Then she gave Peggy a reassuring pat and disappeared between the folds of the drawn bed drape.

Peggy lay there, watching life-giving fluid drip into her veins and feeling more terrified than she had since the day she'd watched her father walk out of her life. At least she'd still had a mother to love and nurture her. One parent wasn't enough, but it was better than none, which is exactly what her beloved babies would face if they lost their mother.

With her fingers tangled in the bedclothes she fought panic, reminding herself that even if the worst happened to her the twins still had a father. Clyde wouldn't abandon his children to foster care. He'd come through for them. She knew he would.

She knew it.

''Oh, Lord.'' Travis grabbed a towel, flapping it at the billowing white cloud.

The radio strapped to his belt crackled. ''What's going on?''

Travis continued flapping with one hand and poked the send button with the other. ''A mite too much powder,'' he muttered. ''Got it under control.''

T.J. sneezed and whacked his little fists. The poor, red-headed little thing looked like a sugar-dusted carrot cake. Travis used a corner of the towel to clear white powder from the baby's face, but his fuzzy little scalp was coated with the stuff. A problem for later, Travis decided. He tossed the towel aside, fastened the diaper's sticky tabs, anchored the tiny pajama snaps and heaved a relieved sigh. Behind him, Ginny, who'd already been changed and diapered, had given up trying to get milk out of the pacifier and was wailing her little heart out.

Travis brushed his palms together and hit the radio switch. "They're both clean and dry," he announced. "Now what?"

"Well, what's the first thing you want when you step out of your morning shower?"

His heart sank. "I don't suppose you're talking about a cup of strong, black coffee."

"Not unless you suck it through a nipple."

"Oh, for crying out loud—"

"Which is possible, I suppose, considering how many times I dropped you on your head when you were little. Accidentally, of course, even if you were a whiny little twerp who made my life miserable."

"Dang it, Sue Anne, quit giving me grief and tell me what the devil I'm supposed to do here."

"Does the word *formula* ring any bells?"

The image of Danny feeding T.J. white stuff out of a bottle came to mind. Travis sighed. "I don't know how to make it."

"Check the fridge," Sue Anne suggested cheerfully. "My guess is that Peggy has a few bottles already made up and waiting."

The mere thought gave him hope. He spun on his heel, dashed to the kitchen and yanked open the refrigerator. Relief made him limp. "Oh, yeah. Oh, thank you, Lord."

"Travis?"

"Umm?" He poked the radio send button, steadied his voice. "There's four bottles in here." A distressed wail floated from the nursery. "Geez, Sue Anne, the babies are getting all perturbed."

"Warm the bottles."

"Okay." He snatched up two of the bottles, kicked the fridge door shut, then looked frantically around the room. "How?"

The radio remained stubbornly silent.

"*How?*" Travis shouted at thin air. "There isn't a microwave. Do I put them in the oven, tuck them under my armpits, *what?*"

The radio crackled. "Okay, I assume that by now you've got a bottle in each hand and are too rattled to hit the send button, which suits me fine because hearing a grown man snivel makes my teeth itch. So just keep your mouth shut and listen. First, put a couple inches of water in a saucepan."

Travis's frenzied gaze swept the room and settled on the cabinet where he thought Peggy kept her cookware. He dashed over, clunking a bottle against the knob.

"Put the bottles down, Travis, *then* open the cupboard."

He straightened, staring down at the radio.

His sister's amused voice floated from black plastic. "No, there's not a camera in there, m'dear. I just know you. Now, get your fanny in gear and heat up that dadgummed water before those poor babes are old enough to climb out of their cribs and do it themselves."

Muttering, he set the bottles on the counter, retrieved a saucepan and continued to follow his sister's eerily clairvoyant instructions until the bottles had been warmed. At Sue Anne's insistence, he tested the contents on his wrist, howled in pain, then held his wrist and both bottles under the faucet to cool them.

When the formula was as close to lukewarm as Travis could manage, he hurried back to the nursery, where he stood in the center of the room, clutching the precious bottles and staring from one wailing infant to the other. "Which one do I feed first?"

The radio was silent. Frustrated, he shifted both bottles to one hand and reached for the button at his hip. "They're both screaming, Sue Anne."

She sighed. "You've got two hands, don't you?"

"Yeah, but I can't reach both cribs at the same time. My arms aren't long enough."

"Then, I guess you'll have to move one of them, won't you?"

His heart plummeted toward his boots. "You mean...?" His frantic gaze spun from one cranky infant to the other. "Oh, Lordy, I can't, Sue Anne, I just can't. They're squirming and squawking, wiggling like a pair of hooked worms. I'll drop them for sure."

"Oh, for crying out loud, Travis, get a grip. You can flatten a thousand-pound steer with your bare hands. I figure you can handle a tiny baby that doesn't weigh more than a bag of flour."

"A bag of flour doesn't wiggle!"

The radio buzzed, crackled. "Okay, let's try this. Picture the look on Peggy's face when she finds out you let those babies starve because you were too chicken to pick 'em up."

Travis felt the blood drain to his toes. "Right."

He set the bottles on the dresser, flexed his fingers, then slipped his hands beneath T.J.'s warm little body and lifted.

Peggy tried to shift up on an elbow, but dizziness forced her to lie back, helpless in the hands of the efficient technicians who were cheerfully guiding the gurney down the hall. "Where are you taking me?"

"X ray," replied the male nurse, angling a flippant grin. "We're going to make sure that thunk on your noggin didn't shake anything loose."

Peggy closed her eyes a moment, frustrated and feeling lost. "My head is fine," she muttered. "It's everything else that's spinning. What's wrong with me, anyway?"

"We won't know until the blood tests come back, but you certainly look a lot perkier than you did a few hours ago."

"Only if your definition of *perky* includes the sensation of having been wrung out like a wet rag. I don't feel quite as weak, though." She eyed the bag of dripping liquid that had been her constant companion since the ambulance trip. "What's in there, anyway?"

The male nurse winked. "All kinds of magic stuff."

The female nurse gave her colleague a withering look. "She's a patient, not a fool." Ignoring the man's embarrassed flush, she patted Peggy's hand. "Forgive him, dear. He tends to treat all patients as if they were recalcitrant children. The bag contains a saline fluid solution. You were extremely dehydrated."

"Oh." Peggy would have asked more questions had her attention not been captured by the large glass window they were passing. "Wait...please."

The gurney slowed, then stopped in front of the hospital nursery. Peggy focused on two Plexiglas bassinets in the front row. They were empty now, but almost nine weeks ago, they'd cradled her own precious babies. The memory made her ache with loneliness. She missed them so. She told herself that they were all right, that Travis had probably called Sue Anne over to care for them.

They'd be fine, just fine.

So why was she crying?

As she turned away, movement caught her eye, and she focused on the incubator at the far side of the room. She twisted to her side as the gurney began to move. "That baby in the incubator, isn't it the same one that was here during the blackout?"

The female nurse followed her gaze and heaved a sad sigh. "Yes, that's Christopher. The good news is that he's doing splendidly and will be ready to go home soon. The bad news is that he has no home. His mother still hasn't been found."

Peggy was horrified. "You mean that poor child has no one to care for him?"

"Oh, I wouldn't say that. In fact, I doubt there's a baby on the face of the earth who has more care than our Christopher. We all adore him." She leaned down and whispered, "To tell you the truth, the staff has grown so attached to him that I'm not sure they'll ever let the little guy leave. He certainly doesn't lack love and attention."

It wasn't enough, Peggy thought as the gurney was rolled toward the elevator. Little Christopher deserved a mother's nurturing love. All babies deserved that, just as they deserved fathers to provide role models of a strong, caring male.

But her babies didn't have a caring father. They had only Clyde.

Still, Peggy was hopeful. She knew Dr. Jennings would explain the situation to Clyde and inform him that if anything happened to Peggy, the twins would be shuttled off to foster care unless he returned to Grand Springs and exercised his parental responsibility.

But later that morning, after the X ray's had been completed and Peggy had been returned to her room, she awoke to find Dr. Jennings standing beside her bed with a blue scratch sheet in her hand, pity in her eyes. Peggy knew then that Clyde had refused.

Twelve

Travis bent like a human safety pin, his aching elbow levered over the crib's lowered side slat. At the business end of the bottles he held were two sticky, sucking, milk-splattered infants, lying side by side in Ginny's crib. Rubber nipples, Travis had discovered, tended to squirt un-controllably when tipped toward greedy, biting little mouths.

Initially, he'd withdrawn the bottles, launched into a face-wiping frenzy that had the twins shrieking and whip-ping their heads in a desperate attempt to recapture the delivering mechanism of their much-needed meal.

Eventually, Travis had given up his quest for cleanliness, wishing nothing more than to simply survive the sloppy process before his stooped spine cracked under the strain. It may not be the most practical posture from which to play Mr. Mom, but since the formula was nearly gone, it had clearly worked well enough to resolve the basic crisis.

In fact, T.J.'s bottle was empty. The baby continued to suck happily, which didn't bother Travis one whit. Ginny still had some formula left, so he didn't see any need to take her brother's bottle away. After all, the little guy was enjoying himself, and it didn't seem fair to penalize T.J. just because the masculine milk-sucking apparatus was just naturally more powerful than the puny pucker of a baby girl.

Of course, Travis had expected Virginia to feed more demurely than her brother. She was a nibbler, after all,

weet and delicate and ultimately feminine, just like her
mama. That's how it was supposed to be.

But T.J. was a rough-and-tumble boy child, a no-
onsense gulping gobbler. There wasn't a doubt in Travis's
mind that his namesake was destined to be a three-bite
urger man.

Travis couldn't have been prouder.

The radio on his belt crackled. "What's going on?" Sue
Anne asked. "Are they still eating?"

Travis rested the empty bottle on T.J.'s tummy and
eached for the transmission switch. "Ginny's almost
done," Travis told his sister, then couldn't resist adding,
"T.J. finished up a few minutes ago."

"Good." Sue Anne paused. "By the way, you do know
nough to take the bottle away as soon as it's empty so
hey don't get air in their tummies, right?"

"Uh, sure, everyone knows that." Horrified, Travis re-
lized that T.J. had probably siphoned enough air to float
a blimp. As he snatched the bottle away, the nipple snapped
rom startled infant's mouth with a noisy pop. "Okay, Gin-
y's done, too," he muttered, setting both bottles on the
resser. "Breakfast is officially over."

"Don't forget to burp them."

Travis glared at the radio. "I'm not a complete idiot. I
now what to do."

Actually, he didn't, but the thinly veiled amusement in
ue Anne's voice was beginning to grate on his nerves. He
ubbed his forehead, tried to jog his memory. Peggy always
reast-fed the babies in private, so Travis hadn't actually
itnessed the post-meal burping process. He had, however,
een a similar activity that consisted of holding the infant
pright at the shoulder and patting the baby's back until
e anticipated result was obtained. It seemed easy enough
hen Peggy did it.

But the mere thought of holding a fragile infant against

his big, bony chest gave Travis palpitations. What if h
patted too hard and broke something? What if a bobblin
little head flopped backward? What if…?

T.J. let out a massive wail. Travis wrung his hands, the
gently touched the baby's tummy. It was rock hard an
swollen like a balloon. There was no choice now.

Mumbling to himself, Travis slipped one rigid hand un
der T.J.'s sticky, powder-gummed little head, and the othe
hand beneath his diapered, pajama-clad bottom, then too
a deep breath and lifted.

The baby stopped crying, bobbled his little head aroun
and stared at Travis as if he was also shocked by this un
expected development. "Okay, partner." Travis shifte
awkwardly, managing a couple of tentative pats betwee
the tiny shoulders. "Do your stuff."

T. J. gurgled, kind of grinned. They smiled a lot now
and not a gassy-type grimace, either. They'd plumped u
real pretty over the past couple of months and had learne
to sprout honest-to-goodness life-is-swell, happy-to-see-yo
grins. Travis loved the little critters so much it hurt.

But he still didn't know squat about doing for them, an
propping such a tiny warm body against his own bon
shoulder was just about the scariest thing Travis had eve
done in his life.

He took a shaky breath and turned his head to check th
burping progress. It wasn't going well. T.J. was just lyin
there, blinking. Milk oozed from his open mouth.

Figuring that changing the gravitation pull might help
tad, Travis arched his own body backward so the bab
wouldn't fall off what seemed to be an exceptionally pre
carious perch, then patted a little faster. T.J. drooled hap
pily.

Frantic now, Travis bowed his poor spine backward unt
blood rushed to his head. He patted, he rubbed, then h
tested a gentle bouncing technique. It worked only too wel

The burp was so loud it sounded like an exploding football. There was a relieved hiss of escaping air. Travis figured that was good. Along with it, however, came a substantial portion of curdled milk.

That wasn't so good.

"Oh, man, oh, geez..." Snapping upright, Travis hastily returned T.J. to the crib, snatched up a towel, mopped the baby's gooey face and soggy pajamas, then turned the towel to his own soaked shirt.

"Sue Anne!" Frantically poking the send button, he blurted, "T.J. barfed all over the place. It's in his hair, all over his face. His clothes are all sour and stinky. He's a mess, Sue Anne, a total mess. And...and..." Travis stared in horror as T.J. clenched his little fists, went red in the face. "Oh, no, buddy, don't do that, please, please don't do that."

A foul aroma drifted up. T.J. blinked happily.

Travis slumped against the crib. "Ah, sis? We've got an emergency here."

Her voice tightened. "What kind of emergency?"

"The, uh, bath kind." Travis raked his sticky fingers through his hair. "I'll give you a million dollars if you'll come over and clean these critters up."

The radio was silent a moment, and when Sue Anne spoke again, her voice was quivering with laughter. "The baby shampoo is on the dresser, Travis. Use the kitchen sink, not the tub. Make sure the water's just tepid, not hot. Oh, and don't drown them. Peggy would take a dim view of that. Dispatch out."

"Out?" Travis lurched forward, snatched the radio from his belt and screamed into the speaker. "Oh, no, you don't. Come back here, Sue Anne. Don't you dare sign off on me, don't you *dare*. Sue Anne!" He strangled the radio, shook it, tried to squeeze the life out of it.

Finally he tossed it aside, hung his head and trudged of
to fill the kitchen sink.

There was nothing on earth as terrifying as a naked baby

With stiff arms, Travis suspended T.J. over the sink a
if the child was a leaky watermelon. Swallowing hard
Travis stared into his namesake's wise little eyes. "Yo
understand that I've got to do this, partner. It's for you
own good."

T.J. gurgled, then whacked a fist against his fat littl
tummy.

"It'd be a whole lot easier if you wouldn't, you know
wiggle so much."

The baby seemed tickled by the notion, then blew
wreath of spit bubbles. Travis sighed and lowered him int
four inches of lukewarm water. T.J. seemed delighted. H
emitted a joyful shriek, churned his chubby legs, smacke
the water and gasped as he splashed himself in the face.

Travis awkwardly swished the baby around as if rinsin
out grubby socks. He realized he'd have to do better tha
that—heaven only knew what kind of disgusting goo wa
lurking beneath those fat little chin folds—but in order t
do the soap thing, he'd have to let go of the baby with
least one hand. That was a frightening prospect.

Clearly it must be done, however, and even a brain-dea
cowboy could figure out that the bottom part of a baby wa
more logistically submersible than the top. Travis splaye
his hand to support T.J.'s upper torso and cautiously lath
ered the infant, who instantly became as slippery as a pigle
in a mud hole.

Somehow Travis managed to swizzle the little guy of
only to be thwarted by the crust of milk-moistened powde
coating the baby's scalp. The hair thing would be tricky.
took a couple of test runs before Travis figured out how t

drizzle water from a washcloth so that the shampoo bubbles ran back into the sink instead of down the baby's face.

After what seemed a small eternity, T.J. was ready to be dried, dusted and dressed, a feat no less monumental than the bathing process itself.

Eventually a squeaky-clean T.J. cooed happily in the net playpen that had been a gift from the Conways.

One down, one to go.

The second time around, things proceeded a bit more smoothly. First of all, Ginny wasn't quite as, well, grungy as her brother. She was, however, even more enthusiastic about bathing. The baby girl squealed with delight, kicking and splashing with such exuberance that she managed to soak not only Travis, but half the kitchen.

Eventually she, too, was clean, dry, freshly dressed and nested in the playpen. "There you go, darling," Travis murmured, using the soft bristled brush to sweep short feathers of red hair into a delicate swirl. "Just like your mama does it."

Ginny chewed on her fist, seeming pleased by his efforts.

Travis blew out a breath, pressed his knuckles into the throbbing muscles of his lower back and stretched his torso, trying to relieve the ache. He was soaked to the skin and hadn't been this tired since he'd entered five rodeo events in one afternoon.

At least the babies were tidy, which was more than he could say for the kitchen. It looked like it had been water bombed. The floor was swamped, as were the counters. Soapy bubbles dripped from the overhead cabinets and oozed down the walls. All in all, Travis figured it would take the rest of the morning just to mop the place down.

Unless, of course, he just sat back and let it air dry....

He issued a pained sigh, eyed muddy boot prints on what had been spotless linoleum, then lumbered to the broom closet.

* * *

Peggy fiddled with the button. The foot of the mattress hummed upward. She fiddled with the second button and was relieved to feel her shoulders lift. As soon as the bed had positioned her into a sitting position, she stared at the empty walls, the vacant bed beside her. She longed for a roommate, someone to talk to. The room didn't even have a telephone. She'd asked for one and been told that telephones had been removed in all but private rooms because the constant ringing annoyed other patients and interrupted the recuperation process.

There was a public telephone in the hall. Peggy was just about desperate enough to yank out the IV needle and go use it to find out what was happening with her babies. What if Travis had simply given up, handed them over to social services and taken off?

That's what her own father would have done, and although she refused to acknowledge it aloud, Peggy secretly suspected that it's also what Clyde would have done. Assuming, of course, that he ever got close enough to his children to walk out in the first place, a possibility that grew more remote by the day.

Logic told her that Travis would never do such a thing, but Peggy had been wrong about men before. In fact, when it came to the male of the species, it seemed that Peggy had never been right. If she had a talent in this world, it was for consistently being in the wrong place at the wrong time and placing trust in the wrong people. Peggy Saxon was the hands-down champ of being wrong, wrong, wrong.

Trusting Clyde Saxon had been the biggest mistake of her life. How could she trust anyone now? How could she trust Travis?

Peggy had no choice but to trust him; he had her children. So she lay there, weak and helpless, and told herself that Travis wouldn't betray her trust. And prayed that for once in her life she was right.

Travis's back felt like it had been stomped by a Brahman. Kitchen cleanup had indeed taken the entire morning, but the danged floor shone like polished leather and there was nary a soap bubble in sight. Not a bad day's work, he decided, feeling enormously pleased with himself.

This parent-thing wasn't so tough, after all.

Travis's satisfied gaze swept the shiny room, landing on the refrigerator. His stomach growled. He'd just opened the fridge door and set his sights on a bowl of tuna salad when Ginny started to fuss.

He glanced over his shoulder, frowning. "What's the matter, darling? You don't need another change, do you?"

She hunched her shoulders, twisted on the playpen floor and issued a cranky wail.

Travis tossed a final longing glance at the tuna salad, then closed the fridge and ambled over to check the diaper situation. Things were thankfully dry, so he was at a loss as to what the baby needed. He tried the pacifier. She spit it out and gave him a reproachful stare. Her chin quivered.

"Aw, c'mon, sweetie pie, tell Uncle Travis what you want."

She fussed, squeaked and issued a cranky cry. T.J. joined in with a loud me-too wail that had Travis grabbing for his two-way. "Sue Anne? Are you there? Dang it, Sue Anne, I know you hear me."

The speaker hissed. "So, how goes it, baby-sitting brother of mine?"

"They're crying again," he shouted, covering one ear to block out a small portion of the twins' lusty screams. "They're all clean, and they don't need changing, and they won't take their pacifiers... what do they want, Sue Anne, what am I supposed to do now?"

"Hmm, they do sound a bit perturbed."

"Huh?" He turned away, pressed the radio to his ear. "What did you say?"

"Look at the clock, Travis."

He frowned, did as he was told. "Yeah, so?"

"It's almost noon." She waited a beat before adding, "Lunch time, bro'. They're hungry."

Travis dropped the radio, stared at the gaping pair of cavernous little mouths and realized that he had to start the whole thing all over again.

He could have wept.

The more Peggy fretted about past mistakes, the more concerned she became about the here-and-now. Her heart ached. She missed her babies and was desperately worried about them.

And right outside her door was a telephone.

Peggy swung her legs over the mattress, waited for a wave of weakness to pass, then focused on the tangle of tubes extending from the taped splint on her arm to plastic bags suspended from a metal hanger attached to the bed. If she unhooked the bags from that hanger, maybe she could carry them and—

A swish of movement by the open door caught her eye.

She turned, saw nothing but an empty doorway. Still, someone had been there. Or something.

A shadow fell across the threshold. She saw the brim of a hat, a pair of blinking eyes. The eyes darted left, right, settled on Peggy. They crinkled at the corners, then withdrew.

Peggy leaned forward, wondering if she was dreaming. "Travis?"

He stepped into the doorway, his head swiveling to check both directions of the hall before he reached out for something that was just beyond Peggy's view. A moment later, he swung the object around, wheeling it into the room.

Peggy clutched her throat, overcome with emotion.

The twins were nested in the double stroller, all gussied up in matching apple-green jumpsuits. Ginny wore an elasticized headband with a fluffy white bow. T.J.'s sparse hair had been neatly parted and slicked back in a decidedly masculine style. Both babies were wide-awake and seemingly quite interested in their new surroundings.

Travis poked his head back into the hall for a final look, then closed the door, jammed his hands in his pockets and gave her a sheepish grin. "They, uh, don't allow babies in the patient wards. Some kind of dumb hospital rule."

All she could do was nod.

Travis glanced down at her bare feet dangling over the floor. He frowned. "Going somewhere?"

"I, ah—" She cleared the lump from her throat. "The telephone. I was going to call you."

His gaze slipped to her bandaged arm, then traveled up the dripping tubes to the fluid bags. He went pale. "Lordy, they've got you trussed like a thrown steer."

"It looks worse than it is."

"So you're okay? I mean, they've got you all fixed up?"

She glanced away. "Not exactly. They don't know what's wrong yet."

"Oh." He was silent a moment, then his voice took on an optimistic tone that only quivered a little. "Well, doctoring takes time. Once they figure things out, you'll be good as new."

"I know," she whispered, although she didn't know at all. She was scared to death, but certainly didn't want Travis to see that, so she managed what she hoped was a convincing smile. "The twins look adorable. Sue Anne did a wonderful job."

"Sue Anne didn't do squat," Travis muttered, tossing

his Stetson on the vacant bed. "Except cackle over the radio while I was getting peed on."

Peggy felt a draft on her tongue, closed her mouth and was as startled by the concept that Travis could actually have handled the twins as she was by the fact that he was now kneeling beside the bed. "You took care of them...all by yourself?"

"I did my best," he murmured, gently lifting her feet, guiding them back under the covers. He fluffed her pillow. "Sure are hungry little devils."

"You *fed* them?"

He looked stung. "Did you think I'd let 'em starve?"

"Well, no, not on purpose." She moistened her lips. "I mean, you found the formula?"

"Yep, and ah, well..." He scratched his ear, casting a glance down at the stroller. "Thing is, they kind of went through all of it you had made, what with breakfast and lunch and all, and I figured, well, what with it being near supper time, I figured they might be craving—" he tugged at his shirt collar, drawing Peggy's attention to a stiff milk stain on his shoulder "—well, you know."

She looked from his spotted shirt to his tousled hair, which poked up in sticky spirals dusted with some kind of white powder. "Would you like me to feed them?"

Before the words were out of her mouth, Travis had whipped T.J. out of the stroller and plopped him into Peggy's arms. "If it wouldn't be too much trouble," he said, fairly melting with relief.

Peggy hugged T.J.'s warm little body, rubbed her cheek against his silky skin and fought tears of sheer joy. "You picked him up," she murmured. "You actually picked him up. I can't believe it."

"Well, I asked 'em to crawl into the stroller on their own, but they couldn't quite manage it." As if to prove the point, Travis scooped Ginny up and tucked her into the crook of his arm. Granted, his movements were a bit awkward, and there was no mistaking the stark terror in his eyes. He smoothed the front of her little jumpsuit, adjusted the elastic bow. "See there, darling, I promised Mommy was going to fix your supper. Cowboys always keep their promises."

Ginny gazed up adoringly.

Travis's eyes crinkled. He brushed a tender knuckle across the baby's cheek.

Peggy watched the loving interaction between Travis and her daughter with awe, and infinite wonder. The contrast of male strength tempered by tender compassion, of worn blue jeans and tiny frills, of boots and baby powder and milk-stained plaid was so overwhelming that her heart ached at the sight.

So this was fatherhood. This was what she had missed, what her children would miss. This was love.

Travis smiled at Ginny, gazing sweetly down at her little face as if he'd forgotten where he was until Peggy coughed the lump from her throat. He glanced up, blushing to the roots of his stiff powdered hair. "Oh, uh, I figured I'd just, umm, kind of keep Ginny company until you're ready for her."

Peggy moistened her lips and shifted T.J. in her arms. "I'm ready for her now."

"You do them both at once?"

"It saves quite a bit of time."

"Well, yeah, sure, I reckon it would." For a moment, Travis was oddly hesitant to relinquish the precious bundle. He gazed into Ginny's face for a moment, felt an odd tug inside his chest, then gentled cradled the baby girl in the crook of her mother's free arm.

Peggy smiled her thanks, which made Travis's heart twitch. She turned her attention to the babies, rotated her shoulders, and somehow managed to free her hands from beneath the two squirming infants. Travis realized that she was loosening her clothing, preparing to breast-feed. He knew he should look away, but he was so intensely fascinated by the process that he continued to stare rudely.

Peggy didn't seem to notice and wasn't the least bit self-conscious about the nursing procedure. Oddly enough, neither was Travis. It seemed so natural, so nurturing, that he was transformed inside, overcome with wonder. This was motherhood, he realized. This was the purest form of love.

This was what he had missed in his life.

For the first time since he was a child, Travis saw the image of his own mother in his mind's eye. He remembered her gentle smile, the softness of her hands, the melodic tinkle of her laughter as she'd scooped him into her arms.

Then he remembered whispered voices outside his darkened room the night she died. He remembered his screams and his tears and the pain in his chest that wouldn't go away.

He had loved his mother so much. So very, very much.

"Travis?"

He blinked, saw the twins sucking greedily and looked at Peggy in bewilderment.

There was concern in her eyes. "You look a little odd. Are you all right?"

"Yeah, great. Never better." He glanced down at the twins and felt his cheeks relax into a smile. There was nothing sexual about breast-feeding, he realized, and was vastly relieved. All you could see was a swell of freckled skin above the babies' fat little cheeks. He'd secretly wondered if the process would, well, arouse him. It didn't. It did, however, fascinate him and cause a peculiar, rather pleasant billowing sensation inside his chest. "They sure look happy."

She laughed then, a melodic, tinkling sound that sent shivers down Travis's spine. "I'd be happy, too, if I'd just spent an entire morning being pampered and fussed over by a handsome cowboy.''

"I didn't do much—'' He widened his eyes. Whoa. Did she say "handsome"? Was it possible that Peggy Saxon, who was prettier than a buckskin filly in a field of starflowers, could actually consider a bowlegged cowboy with a crooked chin to be handsome?

Before Travis could fully digest the implications of that shocking statement, Dr. Amanda Jennings pushed open the door and strode into the room. "Well, well, what have we here?"

Travis whipped a blanket out of the stroller and used it as a modesty shield. The gesture was instinctive, protective, and apparently amusing, since Dr. Jennings concealed a broad smile behind her hand and Peggy burst into laughter.

"I think she's seen this before," Peggy said between chuckles. "She *is* a doctor."

"Oh. Sure." Feeling more than a little stupid, Travis lowered the blanket, twisted it behind his back and wished the ground would swallow him whole.

Still grinning, Dr. Jennings opened the clipboard chart. "The lab results are in," she said cheerfully. "You're a very lucky lady."

Travis heard a low hiss and realized that Peggy had exhaled all at once. "I'm all right, then?"

"You certainly will be, with proper treatment." Softening the ambiguous response with a smile, Dr. Jennings flipped the chart closed and crossed the room. "You're mildly anemic and there's evidence of an upper respiratory infection, neither of which are serious by themselves. When coupled with exhaustion and dehydration, however, the effect could have been quite damaging if we hadn't caught it in time."

"But she'll be okay, right, Doc?"

Dr. Jennings glanced up, smiling curiously. "I believe

so. We'll treat the anemia with iron supplements, the infection with antibiotics." She turned her attention back to Peggy. "I'm most concerned about how dehydrated you were."

"What caused it?" Peggy asked.

"A combination of things. The infection upset your stomach, so you weren't able to keep liquids down. That, combined with hot weather, breast-feeding and the antihistamine tablets you were taking for your allergies, led to a very serious fluid loss."

"I'm feeling better now," Peggy insisted, a bit desperately, Travis thought. "I've been drinking water like crazy, and I'm not the least bit queasy anymore."

"That's good."

"So, when can I go home?"

Dr. Jennings frowned. "I'd like to keep an eye on you for a while. There's also the matter of a mild concussion. Nothing serious, but you should be closely observed for a few days in case other symptoms develop. Meanwhile, we'll start the antibiotic—"

"A few days!" Peggy's eyes went wild. "Oh, no, I can't. You don't understand, I have to take care of my babies...." She shifted her frantic gaze to Travis. "Tell her, Travis, tell her I can't stay here."

Jolted, Travis touched his chest with his thumb. "Me? Uh, well, thing is, if the doctor thinks you need to be in the hospital, then that's where you need to be."

Peggy sagged back as if she'd been kicked.

Meanwhile, Dr. Jennings had leaned over the bed and was cooing at the feeding babies. "My, you two have grown so fat and sassy since I last saw you." She angled an empathetic glance at Peggy, who'd paled three shades and seemed ready to cry. "I'm sorry. I know how much you want to go home, but until you've gained some strength I can't in good conscience allow you to return to the same situation that made you ill in the first place. You need rest, Peggy, lots of it."

Travis stepped forward. "If she had someone to, uh, take care of things, would that make a difference?"

The doctor straightened, regarding him with mild amusement. "If Ms. Saxon is all alone, caring for the demands of two infants, she can't possibly get the bed rest she needs."

"She won't be alone."

Peggy's head snapped around. "Travis!"

"I'll be there day and night, long as it takes." He avoided Peggy's shocked stare, focusing instead on the doctor. "So, can she go home, or what?"

Dr. Jennings pursed her lips and tapped a fingernail on the chart's metal sheath. "Babies take a lot of work, Mr. Stockwell. Are you up to the challenge?"

"Yes'm." He nearly swallowed his Adam's apple. Something deep in his brain screamed that he was crazy, that he should take it all back, say he'd made a mistake, and run straight to Cheyenne without so much as a backward glance. He should do all of those things, and he should do them *now.*

Only it was too late.

"I imagine you are at that," Dr. Jennings murmured, regarding him thoughtfully. He didn't much care for the devilish gleam in her eye. "All right, then. If she's still doing well tomorrow, I'll sign the release."

"Tomorrow?" The light in Peggy's eyes almost made Travis's terror worthwhile. Almost.

Travis wasn't exactly sure what he'd gotten himself into, but had the sinking feeling that he'd just skidded onto a one-way road and was staring at headlights. He didn't have a clue where that road was leading. He only knew that life would be a heck of a lot different when he got there.

Thirteen

The happy squeal was distant, a pleasant intrusion into her midafternoon slumber. Peggy sighed, jogged herself awake and indulged in a luxurious stretch. Although half-asleep, she listened with a mother's heart, acutely aware of the tiniest sound emanating from the nursery. She recognized a high-pitched, playful squeak from T.J., who always woke up cheery and ready to roll. The cranky, hey-things-are-a-little-damp-down-there fuss was pure Virginia, who was less enthusiastic about the awakening process but was considerably more bright-eyed than her brother as the day progressed.

Peggy sat up, massaged her mussed hair and stifled a yawn. It had been three days since she left the hospital, three glorious days of pampered bliss. Travis hadn't let her lift so much as a finger. He'd prepared all her meals and served them on a bed tray. He'd set the kitchen clock timer for her medications, watching like a persnickety eagle while she swallowed each and every pill. He cared for the twins like a doting papa, brought them to Peggy for daytime meals and staggered from his sofa bed to take care of night feedings himself. He'd even learned how to mix formula.

Pretty heady stuff for a woman who'd never had a man so much as pour her a cup of coffee.

Even now, he was probably on his way to the nursery to check on the twins. She cocked her head, listening for the familiar scuff of boot heels on carpet. All she heard was baby noise.

Frowning, she left the comfort of her bed, shuffled down the hallway and peered into the living room. A neat pile of bedclothes was folded beside the sofa, topped with a pillow.

"Travis?" Silence tightened her stomach. "Travis, are you in the kitchen?"

She hurried into the living room and skimmed a quick glance through the window. Her heart sank like a stone when she saw the empty curb. Travis's truck was gone.

He was gone.

Sheer terror iced her bones, numbed her shaking hands. Her mind warred with itself, logic arguing that Travis wouldn't just leave without a word, emotion screaming that of course he would, because he was a man and men did that kind of thing all the time.

But this was Travis. Travis, her very best friend, the man who made her heart flutter with joy simply by entering the room, the man who had become as important to Peggy as her own children. He was different, special. He was...he was...

A diesel engine clattered outside, hummed closer, then abruptly fell silent. Peggy froze, staring at the front door. It burst open.

Travis rushed in with a laundry basket tucked under one arm and a grocery bag in the other. His eyes widened when he saw her. "Oh, Lordy, you're awake." He kicked the door shut behind him and tipped sideways to release a fist-ful of mail on the lamp table. "I'm sorry, honey, I figured I'd be back sooner, but those danged laundromat machines are slower than snail spit."

It took a moment for the euphoric buoyancy to reach Peggy's lungs and fill them with air. All she could say was "You're back."

Travis dropped the heaping basket on the sofa and frowned toward the hall, where a variety of squeaks and squeals was becoming more insistent. "The twins are

awake, too? Dang. Nap time is getting shorter every day."
He shifted the grocery bag and gave Peggy a reproachful
stare. "What are you doing out of bed, woman?"

Peggy fingered a fluffy little jumpsuit that smelled like
soapy lemons. "You did laundry," she murmured. "I can't
believe you actually did laundry."

He seemed taken aback by her blatant amazement.
"Shoot, I've been washing clothes since I was knee-high
to a hunting hound. A body doesn't need a whole lot of
brainpower to shove stuff in a machine and push a few
buttons. I, ah—" he scratched his ear, glanced away
"—used the gentle cycle for your, umm, delicates and
such. They seemed to come out okay."

"I'm sure they did." She laid the jumpsuit back on the
jumbled pile, sobered by the reminder that Travis had been
forced to take care of household chores since childhood.
"Thank you."

He shrugged, sidling toward the kitchen. "You go on
back to bed now, y'hear? I'll bring your lunch in directly."
As he spoke, his gaze dropped to the grocery bag, and he
shifted it to his other arm, almost as if he was trying to
conceal it.

Or perhaps its contents.

Curiosity just naturally brought out the devil in Peggy.
She moseyed closer. "Whatcha got in there, hmm?"

"You know, stuff." He turned away and hustled into the
kitchen.

Peggy followed. "What kind of stuff?" When he turned
his back, blocking her view, she tried to peek over his
shoulder. "Ooh, more juice and a whole gallon of milk."

"Nursing mothers need lots of milk," Travis muttered,
shifting his position to conceal the open bag. He retrieved
a container of formula mix, several cans of soup and tuna,
a loaf of bread and a package of chicken breasts. "High

protein, low fat,'' he explained, setting the package on the table. ''Thought I'd grill some up for supper.''

''How nice of you to notice that I'm in need of a low-fat diet.'' When his stoic expression crumpled, Peggy took pity on him. ''I'm just teasing,'' she assured him with a happy laugh. ''Grilled chicken sounds wonderful.''

Relief in his eyes turned into glowing guilt as he pushed the bag away, took hold of her elbow and tried to usher her out of the kitchen. ''Tell you what, if you don't want to go back to bed, why don't you just sit yourself on the sofa and watch TV for a spell. I'll fix lunch as soon as I get the young'uns up.''

Peggy stubbornly refused to budge. Hoisting up on tiptoes, she tried to peer into the grocery bag. ''What else is in there?''

''Nothing much.''

''Cookies? I love cookies.''

''You do?'' He shifted an unhappy glance at the bag. ''I'll go get some after lunch, okay?''

''Chocolate chip?''

''Sure, honey, anything you want, just go on into the— Aw, doggone it, Peggy.''

Having snatched the bag, Peggy peeked inside and laughed. ''A box of cat food?''

He frowned and whipped it out of her hand. ''We ran out.''

''Oh, my goodness, I forgot all about that poor stray. You've been feeding him, haven't you? And after he almost got you arrested, too.''

''Little guy gets hungry, just like any other critter.'' Flushing to his earlobes, Travis ripped open the box, went to the back porch and poured a healthy dollop of kibble on the kitty plate. He stuck two fingers in his mouth and whistled. A moment later, a blur of orange-striped fur shot across the porch.

Peggy tiptoed over, peered through the screen door and was stunned to observe the cat in question enjoying its supper while Travis stroked the animal's back.

"I couldn't find the stuff you're used to," Travis told it. "This is supposed to have fish in it. You like fish, don't you?"

The animal crunched contentedly and pushed its rump up for a scratch.

"How did you do that?" Peggy asked. "I've been trying to coax him into petting range for months."

At the sound of her voice, the cat stiffened and shot a look over its shoulder.

"It's okay," Travis said. "She's a friend."

The animal's wide yellow eyes regarded Peggy warily and gave Travis a trusting blink, then it returned to its dinner, pausing only to lap water out of a large bowl. A large, familiar bowl.

"Is that...?" Peggy leaned forward, wiggling an accusing finger. "Ohmigosh, that's my good serving bowl."

Travis licked his lips. "It's been real hot outside."

"What has that got to do with the fact that a piece of my best china is studded with cat hair?"

"Um, well, thing is, those plastic cereal things you use are so puny that he was drinking 'em dry in no time. Water stays cooler in a deep bowl, you know? Tastes better, too."

She shook her head, tried not to smile. "A softhearted cowboy. What am I going to do with you?" When he tucked his thumbs in his belt and hung his head, Peggy sighed. "Do you think water would taste as good to him out of a stainless-steel mixing bowl?"

Travis brightened. "Yes'm, I reckon it would."

"Powder."

Peggy, having just finished with the product in question, slipped a sideways glance at Travis, who was hunched over

T.J.'s crib, then slapped the powder can into his outstretched palm. Turning back to her own diapering project, she fastened the tabs, guided her daughter's kicking feet into the legs of a Sugar-n-Spice jumpsuit and hurriedly snapped the garment front.

"I win," she announced, scooping Ginny out of the crib.

Travis tossed a harried look over his shoulder. "That's not fair. Boy babies have, uh, complicated equipment that needs tending. Takes time."

"To powder a little spout?" Peggy chuckled, shaking her head. "Men are such braggarts, Ginny, always trying to convince us that wearing their sex on the outside is a good thing."

"It *is* a good thing," Travis mumbled, completing his task. "Menfolk are rightly proud of their personal gear."

"I guess they must be, considering the way they protect the poor little thingy with jock straps and athletic cups for any activity more strenuous than flipping a television remote."

"Anything worth having is worth protecting." Travis glanced over his shoulder and met Peggy's gaze. His eyes were dark, penetrating, smoldering with intensity. "Texans take care of their own."

A warm tingle slid down her spine. Travis wasn't talking about male anatomy, and they both knew it. He was talking about protecting family, people he cared about. He was talking about Peggy and the twins.

To Peggy, who'd spent her entire life longing for love and the emotional nourishment of a supportive circle of kin, the realization Travis actually cared about them, considered them as his own, touched her to tears. "Yes," she whispered. "Texans do."

They stood there for a long moment, eyes locked in mutual revelation, the air crackling with electric wonder. Feelings surged silently, sensations too powerful to articulate, too deep to ignore. Peggy was awed by the strength in Travis's eyes, the energy of resolve and conviction. But she saw something else, too, something that softened the shield around her heart and raised a lump of compassion in her throat. She saw his vulnerability.

She saw his secret fear.

It was the caring that frightened him, Peggy realized, the tug of conflicting emotion at war in a heart scarred by rejection and loss. She wanted to soothe that heart, to heal it, to nurture his soul, refresh his spirit, to give him the love that had been so cruelly withheld.

Because she *did* love him.

The realization shocked her to the core. Apparently that shock was reflected on her face, because Travis became visibly agitated. He turned away and scooped T.J. out of the crib. "Hey there, partner," he murmured, "ready for a wild ride to the playpen?"

T.J. pursed his lips, blew a gurgling bubble.

Travis smiled. "Okay, here we go. Today, we're going to be an airplane." With that, he cradled the baby tummy side down, growled low in his throat to emulate a revving jet engine and "flew" him all the way into the living room.

Peggy, who was still stunned by the revelation of her deep feelings for Travis, stood as if rooted to the nursery floor. When Ginny's little head bobbled at her shoulder, Peggy snapped from her trance, moistened her dry lips and carried her daughter into the hall.

Travis met her there, his eyes creased with concern. "Are you okay?" he asked, slipping Virginia out of her arms. "You look a mite peaked."

"I'm—" She coughed the squeak out of her voice to manage a thin smile. "Fine, thanks. Just fine."

He didn't seem convinced. "You should have gone back to bed after lunch."

"I don't want to go back to bed, Travis. There's nothing wrong with me. In fact, I feel better than I have in weeks."

He stepped aside, politely waiting for Peggy to traverse the hallway ahead of him. "Dr. Jennings said you oughtn't do too much too soon, else you might relapse or something."

"I'm not going to relapse," she insisted. "Besides, the doctor said I shouldn't do too much. She never said I shouldn't do anything at all."

Peggy sat on the sofa beside the basket of laundry and wiggled a finger wave at T.J., who appeared to be watching from the net-sided playpen on the far side of the room. He responded by whacking himself in the face. Peggy flinched, but the baby didn't appear particularly upset. In fact, his attention instantly shifted as Travis laid Ginny into the playpen. T.J. greeted his sister with an excited squeak, then focused on the musical toy Travis had wound up and placed between the twins.

Travis bent over the playpen, shaking a rattle above Ginny's curious little face, then he danced a stuffed toy through the air and was rewarded by drooling smiles and gurgles of pleasure.

Peggy watched, fascinated by the softness in Travis's eyes and the dimpled quirk of his smiling lips as he tickled the fat baby bellies. A liquid warmth spread through her veins, a paradoxical mingling of contentment and yearning that evoked an odd sense of, well, restless serenity. She was deeply happy, yet longed for something more... intimate.

The thought made her blush, as a familiar ache spread through her loins. And her gaze was riveted on Travis's tight, denim-clad rear.

Peggy wondered why she hadn't noticed how incredibly erotic Travis's body was, with wide, muscled shoulders tapering into lean, masculine hips. *Hips that look so good in*

jeans, it ought to be illegal. That's what the female paramedic had said, and she'd been right. Travis Stockwell was
downright gorgeous.

The effect was so sudden, so breathtaking, that Peggy
couldn't tear her gaze away. Travis straightened, turned and
was clearly startled to catch her staring at him with her
mouth ajar and lust in her eyes.

Horrified and embarrassed, she squirmed sideways,
bumped into the basket and instantly launched into a
clothes-folding frenzy. "You did a great job with the laundry," she chirped like a hyperactive canary. "Everything
is so fluffy and, ah, clean."

"Clean is good," Travis murmured, eyeing her
strangely. "The way I figure it, that's kind of why folks do
laundry in the first place."

"Yes, I suppose it is." Issuing what could only be cat-
egorized as an utterly insane giggle, Peggy flipped a tiny
T-shirt in half and flopped it on the coffee table. "Of
course, if dirty clothes ever come into fashion, think how
many quarters we could save? I mean, society would positively be drowning in quarters, don't you think?" Peggy
snatched up a towel, folded it sloppily and tossed it aside,
wishing her tongue would fall out before she said anything
else.

The wish was futile. "Which is probably why laundro-
mats were invented," she babbled brightly. "To control the
quarter population, and keep it from taking over the world.
Can you imagine what life would be like if it weren't for
all those hungry laundry machines? Why, we wouldn't be
able to step outside our doors without being devoured by
huge, man-eating mounds of voracious silver disks. What
a horrible way to go." She gave a short, maniacal laugh
and wiped her forehead. "Say, is it hot in here or what?"

Travis cocked his head, looking like a man on the brink
of panic. "I could open a window."

"I'd appreciate it." Peggy licked her lips, clamped her tongue between her teeth and silently vowed not to say another word until her brain stopped foaming.

Behind her, there was the rub of warped wood as Travis raised the window. A moment later, he joined Peggy on the sofa, slipped her a tentative look and retrieved a sock from the basket that was between them. "You want some juice or something? You seem kind of edgy."

Biting down on her tongue, Peggy smiled brightly, shook her head, snatched the sock out of Travis's hand and absently dug through the basket for one that matched.

There was no question about it, she decided. She had quite clearly lost her mind. Barely ten weeks after giving birth, she couldn't get her mind off of the behavior that had put her in a motherly way in the first place.

If only Travis wouldn't sit so close, or wear that wonderful, spicy fragrance that made a woman's head spin with unladylike thoughts.

If only he wouldn't look at her with that sexy gleam in eyes so dark a woman could get lost in them.

If only his lips weren't so invitingly masculine, so temptingly lush that it made a woman want to—

"Mate?"

"Exactly," Peggy murmured, then blinked, staring stupidly at the white cotton tube dangling in front of her nose. "Huh?"

Travis nodded at the sock clutched in her hand, the mate to the one he held out. "Isn't this what you're looking for?"

"Ah, yes. Thank you." Avoiding his curious gaze, she twisted the socks into a ball and tossed it on the table, where it rolled into the stack of mail Travis had brought in earlier. The sock ball jarred the telephone bill askew, revealing part of a handwritten envelope tucked further down the stack. Peggy yanked it out, staring at the familiar, sloppy scrawl.

"Peggy?" Travis's voice seemed a thousand miles away. "What is it, honey?"

When she didn't reply, he eased the envelope from her stiff fingers and saw there was no return address. A smoldering fury ignited in the pit of his stomach. "It's from Clyde, isn't it?"

Her face was deathly pale. She nodded.

The envelope made his fingers itch. Travis didn't know what was inside, but his gut told him it wasn't anything good. What if the spineless jerk had a change of heart and decided he wanted Peggy back? The thought made him ill.

Travis knew he was being selfish. Peggy had never made any bones about the fact that she wanted her ex-husband to be part of her life. Hell, she'd spent the past two months writing him, sending photographs, calling and leaving desperate messages. She wanted her children to have a father. Travis couldn't blame her for that.

He was, however, a man divided against himself. Part of him wanted Peggy to be happy, no matter what form that happiness took. But deep down, in a hidden place where Travis feared to tarry, was a niggling sense that *he* wanted to be the one to make her happy.

That wasn't fair, of course. It probably wasn't even possible. Nevertheless, Travis had never wanted anything in his life as much as he wanted to rip that letter into shreds, fling the pieces outside and let the wind carry them to Kansas.

Instead, he handed it back to Peggy, folded his arms and scowled.

Her fingers trembled as she opened the envelope, then unfolded a single sheet of yellow lined paper. Almost instantly her eyes glazed and reddened. A sheen of tears beaded her lower lashes, stained her chalk white cheeks.

Travis wanted to tell her that it didn't matter what the damned letter said, that everything was going to be all right. He wanted to touch her, to hold her, to gather her in his arms and caress away the pain and bring the spunky sparkle back to her dying eyes. Instead, he simply sat there like a charred lump in a cold campfire, saying nothing, doing nothing and hating himself for his cowardice.

Peggy stared at the paper long enough to have read it six times, then lowered it to her lap, smoothing the folds with an odd reverence. She moistened her lips, took a shuddering breath and stood. The yellow sheet fluttered to the floor. "I'm feeling a little tired," she murmured. "I think I'll lie down for a while."

"Sure, honey, sure." Travis rose and laid an awkward hand on her shoulder. "I, ah, I'll wake you when supper's done."

She stared into space. "I'm not very hungry."

"We'll eat later, then, when you're up to it." His hand slipped from her shoulder as she stepped away from the sofa and disappeared into the hall. A moment later, her bedroom door clicked shut.

Travis stood there, feeling helpless. Feeling useless.

He swore, flopped back onto the sofa and hunched forward with his elbows on his knees. His eyes fell on the yellow paper. He retrieved it, then read it with total disgust.

Apparently old Clyde had been spooked by the hospital's call, fearing he'd be legally forced to take financial responsibility for children that he'd never wanted and refused to acknowledge. The terse note indicated that Clyde was leaving his present location and would never contact Peggy again, then ended with a warning not to look for him, along with a veiled threat that she'd be sorry if she did.

Travis wadded the paper and flung it across the room. Damn Clyde Saxon, he thought bitterly, damn him to the fires of hell. Deep down, Travis could understand why a man wouldn't want to be tied down with children, especially since he'd felt the same way himself before T.J. and Ginny came into his life.

But what Travis couldn't understand, what he'd never, ever understand, was how any man could abandon his own family, once he did have one. Especially a family like Peggy and the twins. A wife like Peggy, who had so much love inside that she was fairly bursting with the need to give it.

Only, Peggy was pining to give all that love to a man who didn't appreciate her, a man who wasn't worth a single speck of the dust that clung to her sweet little shoes. It would take a complete fool not to realize that Peggy was still in love with her husband.

And that's what broke Travis's heart.

It was dark when Peggy heard the soft tap on her bedroom door. She sat silently on the bed, feeling strangely calm, almost detached. The past hour had been one of reflection and revelation. And of enlightenment.

There was a quiet click, and a thread of light sprayed through the room. "Honey...are you awake?"

At the sound of his voice, a gentle warmth flowed through her veins, awakening her spirit, soothing her troubled soul. "Yes, Travis, I'm awake."

The light spread wider as he stepped tentatively into the room. "I thought maybe I should put the chicken on."

She smiled at him, at the concern in his eyes, the sweetness of his expression. "You've worked hard enough today. I'll cook the chicken." She swung her legs over the bed and took a deep breath. "Just let me feed the twins first."

"They already had supper. I, ah, gave them a bottle and put them to bed." Travis took another awkward step into the room and squeezed his hands together. "They'll sleep through till morning. Well, almost morning."

Tears sprang to her eyes. Travis was so dear, so very precious. Peggy covered her mouth, stifling a grateful sob.

Apparently Travis misunderstood, because he leapt forward to kneel beside the bed and grasp her hands. "Don't cry, honey, please don't cry. It's going to be all right, I swear it is. I'll track that lily-livered varmint down and drag him back by the scruff of his cowardly neck. He'll do the right thing by you and those babies, I promise he will."

Stunned by his vehemence, Peggy could barely find her voice. "Are you talking about Clyde?"

"I'll get him back for you," Travis insisted. "I swear to God, I will—"

"I don't want him back."

"Even if I have to kick his sorry butt halfway across— Huh?" Travis sat back on his heels. "But the letter...you were all perturbed, and crying and such."

Peggy rubbed her eyes, shook her head. "Yes, I was hurt, but only because I've been so stubborn. Because I couldn't accept the thought that my children would grow up unloved and abandoned by their father, I convinced myself that Clyde would eventually accept his parental responsibilities. The letter made it crystal clear that I'd been deluding myself. I can't force Clyde to be a real father to our children."

Travis pursed his lips, balanced himself on one knee as he studied her wrist and gently stroked her delicate pulse with his thumb. "Yes, you can, Peggy. Or at least, the law can. It takes two people to bring children into the world, and both are responsible for them. A man can't just tip his hat and mosey off because he's not in the mood to be a daddy."

"In theory, that's true. Reality isn't as cut and dried. Oh, I could set legal bloodhounds on his trail, lay claim to his paychecks until he wises up and changes his name and social security number. But all I ever wanted was for him to love his children. No law can force him to do that.''

"People change, honey. Once I bring him back, once he sees how much you love him, then maybe—"

"Love him?'' Peggy's head snapped up. "How could I possibly love a man who wanted me to abort our children and walked out when I wouldn't? Good Lord, Travis, I don't love Clyde Saxon. I don't even like him."

Clearly rattled, Travis stared up in bewilderment, licked his lips, puckered his brow. "Then, why on earth have you been so all-fired up to get him back?"

"That's a good question.'' She sighed, wrapping her palms around one of his big, work-roughened hands. "I never actually wanted Clyde to be part of my life, but I'd hoped that he'd be a father to the kids. You know, birthday cards, Christmas presents, a weekend visit once in a while, just enough contact that my children didn't grow up feeling abandoned like...like..."

Travis finished the thought. "Like you did?" When she nodded, he continued to caress her wrist, each stroke of his callused thumb sending warm shivers up her arm. "Kids are pretty smart little critters, you know? They know when they're loved, and they can spot a fake a mile away. Honesty hurts, but in the long run, kids usually accept the way things are better than most grown-ups can."

Simple wisdom, eloquently expressed by a deceptively complex man. Peggy couldn't stop a fresh flow of tears.

He brushed them away, smoothed back a tangle of hair. "I'd give anything I have to take those tears away,'' he whispered. "It kills me to see you so unhappy."

"I'm not unhappy.'' A husky laugh bubbled from her throat as if to prove it. "In fact, I've never been happier in my life."

He was plainly mystified by her response. "Women sure have a peculiar way of showing such things."

"Yes, we do." She touched his face, stroked the roughened stubble of cheek and chin, saw his eyes widen in surprise. His hand stilled against her wrist, his thumb poised over the pulse as she used her free hand to trace the rugged outline of his jaw. "My mother always said that men and women were so different that she sometimes wondered if we were really all part of the same species. She told me that men didn't feel things the way women did, that they weren't capable of looking beyond their own needs. But she was wrong, Travis. She was wrong because she'd never met a man like you."

Unnerved, Travis shifted just enough that his raised knee brushed her outer thigh, then spun away as if singed. His Adam's apple twitched. "I'm nothing special."

"You're special to me," she whispered, feathering her fingertips through his hat-tousled hair. It was soft, gliding between her fingers like strands of fine silk. The sensation was incredibly erotic, intimate. She indulged her hunger for more, tracing the sturdy ridge of his brow, the sharp strength of his cheekbones, the sexy softness of his sculpted mouth.

A muscle below his ear quivered and his eyes glittered, reflecting sparse light with sensual intensity. Travis caught her stroking hand, brushed his lips across her palm. His eyes fluttered shut for a moment, and when he looked up at her, they were filled with need. "You're special to me, too, honey, but—" Travis took a shuddering breath, laid her hands gently on her lap. "But you're feeling kind of sad right now. It wouldn't be right for me to take advantage of that."

"Do I look sad?"

He gazed up and his jaw drooped.

"Well?" Peggy touched the zippered tab at the throat of her robe, lowered it slowly. "Do I?"

"You look—" he swallowed hard "—beautiful."

"Then, show me I'm beautiful." The robe gaped open, exposing bare skin, a hint of cleavage. "Show me I'm special." She leaned forward, clasped his dear face between her trembling palms, whispered against his lips. "I want to make love with you, Travis." Then she proved it with her kiss.

Fourteen

The kiss was explosive, a fiery release from weeks of denial and self-imposed restraint. Stars whirled through Peggy's mind, the fanciful fireworks of passionate poets and bawdy bards, a stunning surge of sensation blending desperate desire with aching sweetness.

She clung to him, pulled him closer, thrilled to his instant response. Travis rose up, lurched forward, pressed her back against the mattress. Their mouths were moist and frantic. Hands sought skin, frenzied fingers memorized the planes of face, the tangled texture of hair.

The kiss deepened, a burst of intimacy that sent liquid fire coursing through her veins, a molten heat of pure need that went beyond anything she'd ever experienced.

It was a rhapsody of the soul, the erotic essence of romantic novels and sensual sonnets, of girlhood dreams and grown-up desires, a peculiar paradox of carnal chastity that was incredibly potent, unbelievably powerful, utterly profound. She could have devoured him, consumed every succulent fiber of his goodness, his masculine power.

It was everything she'd ever yearned for, ever dreamed of.

And then it was over.

With a ragged gasp, Travis turned away, pushed himself upright. Peggy sucked air, opened her eyes and saw him stagger to a standing position beside the bed, swaying slightly and raking his hair. She propped up on her elbows, blinking blurred vision into focus. "Travis...?"

His face contorted, a hand extended in silent plea. "I'm sorry. I shouldn't have, I never meant to—" A shuddering sigh shook him to his boots. "I ought to be shot."

"What?" She struggled upright, sat on the edge of the mattress, trembling, craning her neck to look up. "I don't understand, Travis. Are you angry with me?"

"Angry? Oh, Lord, no, I—" He wiped his face with his hands, peered over his fingertips. "What I did wasn't right, wasn't right at all. Time was a man would be horse-whipped for taking such liberties with a lady."

If he hadn't been so genuinely distraught, Peggy would have had a hard time holding back a smile at the quaint euphemism. "You were born in the wrong century, Travis Stockwell. In this day and age, ladies have the right to be the seducer as well as seducee. Which, I might add, is exactly what was happening here." She stood, smoothed the shirt fabric that her grasping hands had wrinkled and angled a shy peek from beneath partially lowered lids. "I have to admit that I'm not exactly used to being the aggressor in these, um, situations."

Travis's eyes glazed. "Situations?"

"I was hoping to ravish you. Since we're discussing it instead of actually doing it, I plainly haven't succeeded."

It took a minute for the impact of her words to reach his eyes, which snapped wide open and stared in what could have been either disbelief or utter horror.

Suddenly besieged by embarrassed doubt, Peggy fidgeted with the front of his shirt, avoided his stunned stare and found her fingers dancing around the first snap. It was a turning point, she realized. If she lowered her hands, remained mute, Travis would retreat quietly and never speak of this again. It would always be there, of course, a silent, sexual yearning stretching the folds of their friendship, a friendship that Peggy cherished deeply and didn't want to lose.

But friendship wasn't enough. She wanted more, perhaps more than Travis was willing to provide. And there was desperate urgency in her need to share, to express, to give. Emotions surged forth with uncontrollable power, an unfathomable hunger to care for him, to nurture him. To love him.

She stared at the shirt snap, oddly fascinated by its pearlescent luster encircled by a glint of gleaming silver. A tug would release it. A tiny, gentle tug.

The soft metallic pop reverberated like thunder. Travis went rigid. For a moment, Peggy feared he'd stop her, but he didn't.

So she stared at the second snap.

Pop.

And the third.

Pop.

A ripple of smooth skin was exposed, slick and shining in the reflection of hallway light that sprayed into the darkened room. Peggy bit her lip, entranced by the muscular perfection, the masculine power, most of which was still concealed beneath the thin cotton. She fisted her fingers in the fabric, jerked the fasteners apart.

Pop, pop, pop.

Her breath caught in her throat, her gaze zeroed on the arrow of brown hair encircling his navel, slipping down into the waist of his low-slung jeans. Magnificent. She'd never considered the human body as a work of art, but Travis's was truly superb, an exquisite sculpture of muscle and bone, of animalistic power and aristocratic grace that weakened her knees, sent her heart racing in anticipation.

Gathering her courage, she laid her palms against his warm chest, felt the pounding of his heart through her fingertips. Her eyelids fluttered shut, allowing her to see with her touch, to absorb every nuance of polished contour, every subtle twitch beneath her seeking fingers.

Then he suddenly took hold of her wrists, held them away.

Startled, she looked up. Every trace of moisture evaporated from her mouth.

Travis gazed deep into her eyes with an expression she couldn't identify. It could have been desire; it could have been disapproval; it could even have been fear. "You don't have to do this, honey. You don't owe me anything."

"Is that what you think, that I'm trying to repay a debt?"

He shuffled, kept his grip firm. "Well, no, of course not, only—"

"Only it's not called prostitution unless there's an exchange of hard cash?"

Travis couldn't have looked more horrified. "I didn't mean that, I swear to—"

"Sh." When he released her, she laid a gentle finger against his lips. "I know you didn't." She moistened her lips, shored up her courage. "This is a big step. I understand that, and if you're not comfortable with a change in our relationship, well, I understand that, too." She tried for a bright smile. Failing that, she settled for staring at the floor, feeling like a complete and utter fool. "Timing has never been my strong suit."

"Peggy—"

"So, what should we do with that chicken? I can bake it, I suppose, and I can mash up some potatoes. I'm not too good with gravy, but—"

Travis caught her shoulders as she rose to her feet and tried to swing past him. She turned her head to conceal the sheen of humiliated tears. "But I might have some cream of chicken soup or something."

Embracing her gently, Travis cradled her in his arms. Melting against him was probably the wrong thing to do, but Peggy couldn't help herself. His warmth was so enticing, his tenderness so exquisite, that she automatically bur-

ied her face in the smooth curve of his shoulder. A relieved
shudder caught like a tiny sob. He whispered something—
she didn't know what—and brushed his lips across her ruffled hair.

"I do want you," he murmured quietly. "So bad that
every inch of me aches for you and my heart's near ready
to burst. I just want you to be sure that you won't regret
anything later. It'd kill me if we, you know, and then you
were sorry after." He slipped a knuckle under her chin,
urging her to look up at him. "All I want is for you to be
happy."

"You make me happy, Travis."

He caressed her cheek, absorbing the tears onto his fingertips, then lowered his mouth to hers. The kiss was sweet,
soft, so tender that it made her heart ache. She never realized how lush a man's lips could be, how honeyed and
gentle.

Travis tightened his embrace, and the kiss became more
urgent, more demanding. Peggy's body responded. Before
she realized what was happening, her arms had magically
slipped beneath his loosened clothing, and her hands
splayed over the firm, rolling muscles of his back.

The fire built more slowly this time, gently, without the
frenzy of fear that had exploded within them only moments
ago. Now there was time, time to explore and to savor, to
cherish the depth of love that remained unspoken, yet was
nonetheless real.

Peggy stepped back, tugged his shirt out of his jeans and
pushed it back to reveal lean shoulders, strong, corded bi-
ceps. He shrugged off the garment, let it puddle at his feet.
He brushed the bodice of her velour robe, the one he'd
given her only weeks ago. His fingertip traced the lace
opening, paused at the zipper tab that was poised at the dip
between her breasts.

He took a massive breath, let it out all at once. "Are

you sure it's, you know, okay? I mean, the twins are only ten weeks old. I don't want to hurt you or anything.''

"You won't hurt me." She took his hesitant hand, pinching the zipper tab between his index finger and thumb.

"Are you sure?"

"The doctor gave me the green light weeks ago." During her final postpartum exam. Peggy had thought the man insane to imply that she'd ever consider indulging in such activity again.

Boy, was she indulging.

The rasp of her robe zipper sent chills down her spine. She shivered, felt the soft fabric float away from her bare shoulders. A draft brushed her belly as the robe slithered down her torso, pooled at her feet.

At her feet.

Peggy's eyes flew open in panic. Nudity, she suddenly realized, was a fundamental expectation of sex. There she was, clad only in an unattractive flapped bra and sensible cotton panties, beneath which lurked a small tummy pouch and a road map of silvery stretch marks.

Since the twins' birth, her body had about as much sex appeal as an inflated balloon. She crossed her arms over her chest, tried to suck in her saggy belly. "Umm, it's chilly in here, don't you think?" It was hotter than a glazing oven. "We'd be cozier in bed, and—"

Travis gently uncrossed her arms, gazed lovingly at her slightly misshapen torso.

"Less exposed," she finished lamely.

"You're so beautiful," he murmured, caressing her waist with his fingertips. "So soft and sweet and kind of, well…"

"Squishy?"

He blinked. "Ah, truth is that I was thinking that your skin was velvety as a healthy mare's nose, but that didn't seem romantic enough. Cowboys aren't real poetic," he added apologetically.

Peggy smothered a smile, fought the urge to wrap herself in bedclothes. "I think it's very romantic."

He cocked his head, smiling. "Then, why do you have the wild-eyed look of a calf being branded?"

"Maybe because I feel like a darned cow." When his smile faded into a mystified frown, she angled a hateful glance at the light spilling in from the hall. "I'm a bit self-conscious at the moment. If we could just close the door—"

"Your body is beautiful," Travis whispered. A startled glance confirmed that he was gazing at her as if she was the most precious person on earth. "It's a woman's body, full and lush, and incredibly sexy." A gentle caress swept the bra straps over her shoulders, then he pinched the front fastener and the garment fluttered away.

Eyes glowing with appreciation, he tested the soft weight of her breasts, traced tiny blue veins with his fingertips. "Freckles," he murmured, clearly delighted with his discovery. "Freckles everywhere, all the way around them. I wondered about that...."

The words drifted away as he brushed his thumbs over the darkened tips, and she shivered with sensation. When he bent to kiss each nipple, her knees turned to water, and she grasped his shoulders to keep from collapsing. He pressed his face to her belly, nuzzled her warmth and expertly removed her panties.

Kneeling now, Travis continued to excite the delicate areas of her torso and inner thighs with his fluttering fingertips, his soft, stroking lips. "Red," he whispered against the fluff of auburn at the apex of her thighs. "Like an autumn forest." Then he parted her and tasted.

Peggy gasped, clutched at him and would have collapsed on the spot had he not been hugging her hips. It was so exquisite, so impossibly magnificent, that she couldn't suppress a cry of pure joy.

He loved her until she trembled with ecstasy, until her body shook with explosive release. Then he lowered her to the bed, whispering sweet words that filled her heart, her mind, yet were indistinguishable from the plethora of sensation that ignited her body into a conflagration of desire.

She felt the mattress dip as he sat to pull off his boots. There was a quiet thud, then another. He removed his jeans, tossed them aside and was crawling beside her when he suddenly frowned, turned away.

Confused, Peggy propped on one elbow, saw him rifling through the pockets of his discarded jeans. When he found what he sought, he dropped the garment, fiddled with something, then turned back and took her into his arms.

Peggy knew without looking that he was wearing a condom, and her heart swelled with love. She drew him to her, brushed her lips across his collarbone, felt the moist ricochet of her breath against his slickened skin. She was awash with feelings, with sound, smell, sensation, all blended into an incredible blur of exquisite sensitivity. Her mind whirled with silent whispers, soulful pleas.

Love me. Stay with me. Promise you'll never leave.

Travis laced his fingers with hers, gazed deeply into her eyes. "I'll always be here for you. Always."

I need you.

"I know, honey, I know."

Then he moved over her, into her, and swept her away with the sweet fire of his love.

Travis lay awake in the darkness, watching Peggy sleep. She was cuddled against him like a trusting puppy, with her sweet face nested against his chest. His arm was numb, but he'd have cut it off before he'd have disturbed her. She looked so peaceful, so sated and content. He loved the way her parted lips vibrated with each sleeping breath. She was everything he'd ever wanted in a woman, a lover, a mate.

A mate, a lifetime commitment. Once those words would have sent him sprinting for the highway, sweating like a horse rode hard and put away wet.

Funny, he mused, twirling a red curl around his finger. Not only was he still here, he'd actually made that commitment out loud.

Always.

That meant he'd never leave her, that he'd spend the rest of his life caring for Peggy and the babies, protecting them, making them happy.

The strangest part of all was that he wasn't frightened by that, nor did he fear the responsibility of taking on a ready-made family. In fact, he relished it, realized that there was nothing on earth he wanted more. Peggy and the twins needed him. For the first time in his life, Travis wasn't frightened by that. He actually felt up to the challenge.

Maybe it was time to settle down. Maybe it wasn't.

Not that it mattered. Travis couldn't back out now. He'd promised Peggy that he'd never abandon her, that he'd never leave.

A cowboy never breaks his promise.

Baby squeaks had barely evolved past the test stage when Peggy awakened. She cherished the moment, the warmth of Travis's smooth chest beneath her cheek, the rhythmic heave of his breath, the erotic scent of him and of her, mingled to create the unique fragrance of their lovemaking. Her happiness was a tangible entity, solid enough to grasp, to embrace, to fill the emptiness. She felt whole, complete.

Peggy rose slowly, taking care not to disturb her sleeping lover. *Lover.* What a beautiful word, possibly the most exquisite noun in the entire English language. She smiled, wishing she could touch his face, smooth his hair. But he needed rest, so she withdrew quietly, retrieved her robe from the floor and slipped it on.

Fearing he'd stumble over the discarded boots, she set them neatly at the foot of the bed, then gathered his shirt and jeans, folding them over a nearby chair. His wallet lay on the floor beside the bed. She retrieved it, along with a haphazardly creased sheet of paper. After placing the wallet on the chair with his clothing, she noticed an odd notation on the paper, a circled dollar amount along with the hand-written word *entry*.

A glance over her shoulder confirmed that Travis was still sleeping peacefully. She turned her attention back to the folded paper, weighing curiosity against the guilt of invading his privacy. Curiosity won.

As she scanned the rodeo flyer, her stomach twisted, her heart sank like lead. Several areas had been circled, including the list of scheduled events, prize money, championship points available. Travis had scrawled marginal notes, travel directions to a fair ground outside of Cheyenne, Wyoming, along with the phone number for someone named Clem, who was supposedly looking for a team-roping partner.

The rodeo would be held this weekend.

Peggy stared at the wrinkled sheet until her eyes stung and the words began to blur. Travis had wanted to go to Cheyenne, would have gone if not for her. Rodeo was his life, after all.

Or it had been, until Peggy had taken him away from it.

I'll always be here for you. Always.

Biting her lip, she refolded the sheet, laid it beneath his wallet and tiptoed out of the room. The babies were fussing louder now. Peggy went to tend to them.

She greeted her children with soft whispers, a mommy's kiss. She changed them, and fed them, and hummed soft lullabies, as she always did. But her mind was in chaos. Travis had promised to stay, a promise that had wrapped like a fist around her heart. When he'd spoken those cherished words, she'd wept with pure joy. But she hadn't asked for that commitment, hadn't coerced him into uttering those words. He'd said them freely, of his own volition.

Hadn't he?

Peggy carried the twins to their playpen, wound up their musical toy and went to put on coffee. Travis liked coffee first thing in the morning. He liked a big breakfast, too. Over the past few days she'd been amazed that he could consume so much food when the sun had barely crested the horizon.

Travis always brought Peggy a huge tray, with plates of steamy scrambled eggs, buttery toast, potatoes fried so crispy that her tongue wept with pleasure. She'd make a production of tasting each item, moaning with delight just to see his eyes glow. He took pride in everything he did.

He took pride in his profession.

Water sloshed from the carafe, splashed across the counter. She steadied her hand, finished filling the coffeemaker, then cleaned up the mess. She tried to concentrate on wiping the tiled counter dry, to focus on the steady drip of the coffeemaker, anything to keep her mind occupied.

Deep down, doubt gnawed at her.

Travis was a man of his word, but if she held him to a promise made in passion, she'd be stealing everything he held dear. He was a cowboy, a champion. Rodeo was in his blood. Born to the saddle, he was a man for whom the road held mystical appeal. Peggy could understand that intense yearning for travel, that desperate need to explore the next bend in the road seeking new places, new people, new adventures. A man like Travis could never grow roots, never be content living in one place.

He'd feel trapped, caged.

Peggy spun, sagged against the counter, heart pounding,

hands pressed over her ears, a futile effort to block out the noise in her head.

No, he wouldn't feel trapped. She wouldn't let him feel trapped.

Peggy snatched a box of pancake mix from the cupboard...*she could make Travis happy*...filled a mixing bowl to the brim...*she would make him happy*...grabbed a wooden spoon from the drawer and stirred the dry mix so frantically that it billowed like a sloppy white cloud.

Panicked, Peggy spun around, yanked milk from the fridge and poured half a quart into the bowl without bothering to measure.

Travis would be happy with her.

She plunged the spoon into the bowl, whipped wildly.

Travis would—

Milky lumps slopped onto the counter.

Be happy—

Onto her clothes.

With her.

Onto the floor.

The bowl spun and tipped over, pouring the contents over tile, down cupboards. A wet, lumpy mess pooled at her feet. It was ruined. Everything was ruined. Peggy wept.

"Yeah, sis, I know." Travis shifted on the sofa, switched the telephone to his left ear. He lowered his voice, forcing Peggy to move closer to the kitchen doorway to overhear. "She's doing good, real good. Even cooked breakfast this morning... I know, but it was all ready when I woke up and— Hmm? Oh." He coughed, cleared his throat. "Umm, well, never mind about that. I said, never mind, okay? Some things are none of your danged business. Now, about the job, do I have it or not?"

Peggy sagged against the doorjamb, twisting a dish towel

into a damp spear. Her stomach twisted, lurched. A sour taste stained her tongue.

"No more temporary, fill-in stuff, right? Full-time, with benefits, especially insurance."

She turned away, unable to bear it. Travis would rather have vultures peck his eyes out than drive a cab, yet he was on the telephone begging his sister for an opportunity to be miserable for the rest of his life.

Peggy had never forgotten the fury on Travis's face the day he'd been mugged, the disgust when he'd spoken about how much he loathed the job. Now he was ready to spend ten hours a day behind a steering wheel doing something he despised. He was willing to do it because he was a man of honor, a man of his word, and because he cared for Peggy enough to relinquish his freedom, to give up everything he held dear.

And she was willing to let him do it because she loved him.

No, not because she loved him. Because she feared losing him, because she needed him. *Needed him.*

She froze, horrified by the thought, more horrified by the truth. She *did* need Travis. She'd allowed herself to lean on him, depend on him, and was willing to let him destroy his own life for the enrichment of her own. That wasn't love. It was selfishness. It was weakness.

"You're supposed to be resting." Travis strode into the room, swept a reproachful gaze at the drainer stacked with clean dishes. "I told you I'd clean up the kitchen."

Peggy laid down the towel, wiped her palms on her robe. "You have enough to do without taking on my work, too."

"Your work, hmm?" He sauntered over, brushed a proprietary kiss on her forehead. "Now, that's real peculiar, seeing as how I never did see anybody's name etched in syrup across those dirty pancake plates. Besides, you've been up early, cooking and all. That's enough for one day."

"I'm fine, Travis."

"Did you take your medicine?"

"Yes."

"All of it? You always forget those little yellow pills."

She touched his wrist, stopping him as he reached toward the cabinet where her medication was kept. "I took them all, Travis."

The edge in her voice caught his attention. "Is something wrong, honey?"

"No." She snatched up the towel, pivoted around to wipe off the spotless table. Tears threatened. She blinked them away. "I don't like being treated like an invalid, that's all."

Travis said nothing for a moment, then Peggy heard the scuff of boot heels on linoleum. He came up behind her, so close that his body heat radiated into her spine. Warm palms caressed her upper arms. "I'm sorry, honey. I never meant to make you feel that way."

The towel stilled against the tabletop. She bit her lip, peeled her tongue from the roof of her mouth. "It's not your fault. You've been wonderful, really you have. I don't want you to think that I haven't appreciated everything you've done, because I have, but I'm all right now and—" she swallowed hard, forcing out the hateful words "—and it's time for both of us to get on with our lives."

His palms stiffened, flexed, dropped away from her shoulders. "I don't get it. Last night—"

"Last night was wonderful." Peggy closed her eyes, willed herself not to cry. "But it was a mistake."

A draft brushed her nape as he stepped away.

"Things happened too fast," she lied, staring at the painted wall directly beyond the table. "I'm not ready to make a commitment, not to you, not to anyone. I need... need space."

"Space." He said it dully, as if repeating a word he'd

never heard before and couldn't comprehend. "You need space."

"Yes." A sob caught in her throat.

Travis gave no indication that he'd heard it. "You want me to leave?"

Not trusting her voice, Peggy managed only a thin nod.

"Oh." From the echo of footsteps, she knew he was pacing the kitchen. The footsteps stopped. "Right away?"

She licked her lips, prayed she wouldn't faint. "I think it's best."

After a silent moment, she heard a shudder of air, as if he'd filled his lungs, then emptied them all at once. "Are you sure you'll be all right?"

She grasped the back of a chair. "Yes."

"And the babies...?"

"They'll be fine." Her knuckles went white. "We'll all be fine, Travis, just fine."

She heard him cross the room, pause at the doorway. "Is this really what you want?"

A tear slid down her cheek. "Yes, Travis, it's what I want."

An hour later, Travis slung his duffel into the back seat of his pickup and cast a doleful glance over his shoulder. A curtain in the front window vibrated. Peggy was watching him.

Tugging his hat down, he climbed into the truck and flipped the ignition. He let the truck warm up, not because the old diesel needed the extra revs, but because Travis needed the time to drink in the sight of Peggy's sweet face between the parted curtains. He wanted to memorize her freckled profile, the adorable tangle of red curls that bounced around her face like twisting flames. It would be his last image of her, and he wanted to drink it all in.

Pain stabbed through his chest. Travis cursed himself for

the weakness. He should have known better than to let himself care, to believe that Peggy saw anything in him that the rest of the world didn't. In the end, she'd recognized Travis for exactly what he was, a useless rodeo rat with nothing worth having and nothing to give.

Travis had always known Peggy deserved better. Now it seemed that she knew it, too. So he shoved the old truck into gear, and drove out of her life.

Fifteen

After keypunching the final figures, Peggy compared the tallied totals. They matched. She felt no relief, no pride, no sense of accomplishment. The chore was completed, period. There was no excuse to stay any longer, chalk up more hourly pay than she was entitled to. It was time to leave, to return to the shabby duplex still haunted by memories of Travis, a place where Peggy couldn't relax on the couch without remembering the popcorn fights they'd shared, the teasing laughter that always evolved into sweet, warm kisses. Nor could she climb into bed at night without the evoking memories of sweet lovemaking, stimulated by his musky scent clinging to the pillow.

It would help if she'd wash the pillowcase, of course. But she just couldn't bring herself to erase the final vestige of Travis's presence in her life. He'd only been gone a week. Peggy wasn't ready to let go. Not yet. Perhaps not ever. All she knew was that the old duplex had become a tomb, haunted by memories, stained by her secret tears.

God, she missed him, so much that her heart ached with longing. The only way she'd survived the loneliness was by playing Travis's rodeo video over and over and over again. He'd looked so happy in the film, so completely at home in his element.

The gift of freedom had been all Peggy had to give. As painful as her decision had been, she didn't regret it. How could she? Travis was where he belonged; he was happy. That's all that mattered.

Footsteps outside the dispatch center broke her reverie. She quickly exited the computer program and flipped off the machine just as Sue Anne wandered into the office sipping a can of soda.

Peggy swiveled away from the dark monitor, rubbing her palms on her thighs. "The month-end totals balance. I'll forward a draft of the statement to your accountant next week."

"You're a lifesaver." Clutching a can of soda, Sue Anne flopped onto the office sofa, kicking her feet up. "The twins are snoozing in their playpen. Seems a shame to wake 'em up, so how about staying for dinner? I've got a roast on the stove that's so big it took three of us to beat the danged thing into a pot. There's more than enough for an extra plate."

"I've already had dinner here twice this week. Jimmy is beginning to think I'm part of the family."

"You are, hon."

Peggy turned away, took a deep breath and wished that was true, but it wasn't. No matter how deep her feelings for the Conways, she could never be a real part of their family. But they would always be her dearest friends. She owed them so much.

Suddenly feeling weepy, Peggy made a production of clearing the computer table, drank the rest of her water and carried the glass into the kitchen.

Sue Anne followed, crossed her arms and propped a big hip against the counter. "Heard from Travis?"

Despite an involuntarily shudder caused by the sound of his name, Peggy managed to set the glass into the sink without breaking it. "No." She rubbed her palms together, glanced over her shoulder. "Have you?"

Sue Anne shook her head, narrowed her wise eyes and stared right into Peggy's soul. "You love him, don't you, hon?"

The question shouldn't have startled her, but it did. Flustered, she wrung her hands, rotated her shoulders and stammered something that sounded very much like the pathetic bleat of a bewildered lamb.

"I thought so." Heaving a maternal sigh, Sue Anne swaggered over to toss a chummy arm around Peggy's shoulders. "Didn't your mama ever warn you about cowboys?"

Peggy stared at the floor, saying nothing.

The big woman gave her an affectionate squeeze. "Don't you go worrying yourself. He'll be back."

"No, he won't." Peggy stiffened her spine and tried for a brave smile that might have worked if her chin hadn't been quivering. "Travis is where he belongs."

"He belongs with the woman who loves him."

"He has no idea how I feel."

"The hell you say!"

Peggy spun around, narrowed her gaze. "And don't you dare tell him, Sue Anne. I mean it. He'd feel duty-bound to do the 'honorable' thing by me, and I won't allow it. I simply won't allow Travis to give up everything he cares about just because I couldn't control my—" her face heated "—my urges."

Sue Anne's eyes stretched wide. A toothy grin followed. "Urges, hmm? Well, well, well. Fancy that."

"Sue Anne—"

"Oh, don't you fret. Your secret's safe with me."

Judging by the gleam in her dark eyes, Peggy doubted that. She sighed. "It doesn't matter, I suppose. The bottom line is that Travis will only be happy if he's traveling the country, seeing sights most people only 'dream of."

Sue Anne's grin faded. "Travis said that?"

"Not in so many words."

"Ah. But you could just tell what was on his mind, on account of you being in love with him and all."

Peggy tossed up her hands. "Travis was right. You *are* impossible."

Thirty minutes later, Peggy pulled up in front of the duplex and made several trips from the car to the house unloading babies and groceries. She'd just hauled the folded playpen out of the trunk when a mail truck tooled down the street and dipped toward the curb just behind her car.

The postal carrier hopped out, handed her a certified letter, then tipped his hat, climbed back in his little truck and drove away.

Peggy's heart sank when she saw the return address of the property management company to which she sent her rent payment, and she recalled the real estate agents who had been sniffing around the place over the past few weeks.

When she finally summoned the courage to open the envelope, she found exactly what she'd feared. The property had been sold. Peggy was being evicted.

"Hell of a ride, Stockwell! Too bad the horse took it without you." The raw-faced cowboy slapped Travis's bruised shoulder, then shuffled off, chuckling.

Travis whacked his hat on his thigh, reached back to rip the paper entry number off his back and limped past the livestock corral, spitting sawdust. At least he'd made the finals. Might have had a shot at the big money, too, if he hadn't glanced up from adjusting his grip and seen the glint of red hair in the grandstands.

He knew it wasn't Peggy, but couldn't keep himself from looking, anyway. Then the gate flew open, the bronc lurched out. One minute Travis was airborne; the next he was sucking dirt.

Now every bone in his body was jarred loose, and he was too parched to spit. Tugging his hat on, he wandered across the rodeo grounds toward a cluster of vendors hawk-

ing everything from cold beer and submarine sandwiches
to belt buckles and silver spurs.

Travis shuffled over, cast a longing glance at the beer
but settled for a soda. He still had one more event this
afternoon. This time, he'd keep his eyes off the stands.

He gulped the icy liquid, purchased another, wandered
back toward the arena and found himself waylaid by a sou-
venir booth displaying a tiny Stetson with baby-sized western boots and other miniature rodeo paraphernalia, including a white-fringed vest that would look terrific on Ginny.
It was a little big for her now, but she was growing so fast
and Travis figured it would probably fit in a couple of
months. And the little hat was just made for T.J.

"Can I help you, partner?"

"Hmm?" Travis glanced up at the hovering clerk. "No,
just looking. Thanks."

The clerk followed his eye. "That's real brushed suede,
just like the big guys wear. And this—" he fingered the
supple white fringe "—is hand-beaded. Pretty, ain't it?"

Travis nodded, but the items blurred under his stare, replaced by the image of two fat, drooly little faces. He could
practically hear the twins in his mind, their delighted little
squeaks as he wound up their musical toy. He could feel
their soft warmth in his arms, the wriggle of their tiny muscles growing stronger every day. God, he missed them.

And Peggy. Hardly a minute went by he couldn't see her
face in his mind, smell the flowery sweetness of her hair.
Thoughts of her crowded everything else to a small corner
somewhere in the back of his brain. The rodeo gave him
no joy anymore. He was empty inside. He was miserable.

He was in love.

But it didn't matter. Peggy didn't want him, and Travis
couldn't blame her. She needed a real father for those
babies, not some broken-down cowboy with nothing to his
name except an old truck and a pocket full of dreams.

So no matter how much it hurt, Travis was determined to respect her wishes, to stay out of her life, far away from her and from the babies he'd come to love as if they'd been his very own.

"So how 'bout it, mister? I can give you a great price."

Travis blinked, looked up. "Sorry, can't use 'em."

He stiffened his shoulders, trashed his soda and headed back to the arena, determined to put Peggy Saxon and her beautiful babies out of his mind forever.

But that night, as he drove toward another rodeo, another town filled with strangers, the little hat and vest were in the back seat.

"It's about time you called."

Travis shifted in the phone booth, plugging one ear to block out traffic noise from the interstate. "Been kind of busy, sis. So, how's everybody doing?"

"Well, let's see. Danny loves school, only calls when he wants money. Jimmy sprained his big toe and acts like he's gonna be crippled for life. And Ted's in love with a chesty blonde he met at the Pak 'n' Sav. That's about it."

He switched the receiver to his left ear and blew out a breath. "How's, umm, everybody else?"

"Asking about anyone in particular, are you?"

Pinching the bridge of his nose, Travis swallowed the urge to make a rude suggestion. "You know who I'm talking about."

"Sure I do. I'd just like to hear you say her name out loud."

"All right. Peggy, dammit. Are you happy now?"

She was silent a moment, then her voice softened. "The question is, are *you* happy?"

Travis had never been unhappier in his life. "Sure. Why not?"

"I just thought you might regret walking out, throwing Peggy and those babies to the wolves."

He straightened. "What the hell are you talking about?"

A pained sigh filtered over the line. "Do you care?"

"Don't mess with me, Sue Anne. I'm not so far away I can't come teach you some manners before I plant myself on Peggy's front porch and find out what the devil is going on."

"Well, that might be a little problem. Come next week, Peggy isn't gonna have a front porch. In fact, she isn't gonna have a house." Sue Anne paused for effect, then added dramatically, "They're bulldozing the duplex to build a new strip mall."

"Oh, Lordy." Travis clamped the receiver hard enough to crack plastic. "You mean she and those babies are going to be thrown out into the street?"

"Sad, isn't it?"

"There must be a mistake. No one on earth is cold enough to do that. I mean—" Travis spun in the booth, nearly choking himself on the cord. "What's going to happen, Sue Anne? What's she going to do?"

"Well, she's sure'n the devil not going to sit there with those babies and watch the walls come down around her ears," Sue Anne snapped. "She's leaving."

Travis's heart sank like a stone. "Where's she going?"

"The way I figure it, you lost the right to ask those questions when you walked out. Oops, the dispatch phone is ringing. Got to go."

"Damn it, Sue Anne, don't you hang—"

Grinning madly, Sue Anne cradled the receiver, unplugged the house phone so Travis couldn't call back and gave the silent dispatch unit an affectionate pat.

"That ought to do it," she muttered aloud, then cupped her hands behind her head, propped her feet on the desk and wondered if her brother would make it to Grand Springs by sundown.

After ripping a gluey line of sealing tape to bind the cardboard flaps, Peggy tossed the dispenser aside, flipped the carton over and loaded a lamp, shoe boxes of her cherished photographs and her beloved travel books. There was extra room in the carton, so she left it open, pushed it into the corner and glanced around, disheartened by the chaos.

Packing was second nature to her, but the immense volume of baby things added a whole new dimension to the moving process. She couldn't box up infant supplies in advance, because she used everything every day. Sometimes every hour.

She'd even discarded the notion of packing Homer and Bertha, fearing the twins wouldn't be able to sleep without the company of the stuffed Texan elephants that had shared their cribs from the beginning.

Moving day would be utter pandemonium. Still, there must be something she could do in advance to ease the final crunch.

Peggy wandered into the kitchen, which was muddled with smaller boxes bristling with cooking utensils. A soft trill caught her attention. She smiled at the furry orange face peering through the screen. "Hi, sweet boy. Are we ready for supper?"

The cat issued an agreeable meow, perked up as Peggy reached for the kibble box, then hung back as she went out to the porch. The wary animal still wouldn't permit her to touch him, so she refilled his plate, then watched from behind the screen door as the hungry stray slunk over to gobble up his meal.

She fretted about the poor little fellow, wondering what would happen to him when she was gone. If only she could get close enough to catch him, perhaps—

The front door suddenly vibrated as if being pummeled by a jackhammer. Peggy nearly jumped out of her skin. She spun around, clutched her throat and froze. There was another explosive burst, as if someone was trying to pound the door down.

She eyed a butcher's knife jutting from a half-packed carton, ignoring the rational voice in her mind that reminded her criminals rarely knocked.

The frantic pounding continued. "Peggy! Open the door."

Her mouth went dry. She tottered forward. That sounded like—

"Dang it, Peggy, I know you're in there. Open the dadgummed door."

"Travis," she murmured. It took a moment for the shock to subside. When it did, Peggy leapt forward, sprinted through the living room, hurdled a stack of linens and yanked open the door.

Words stuck in her throat, backed her breath into her lungs. He stood there in a sweat-stained T-shirt and floppy leather vest, wild-eyed, utterly disheveled and gloriously unkempt. She couldn't speak, couldn't breathe, couldn't do anything except stare mutely and wonder if this was some kind of cruel dream.

Travis swallowed hard, scanned her quickly, then his gaze settled on her face. His eyes softened, growing wary as he glanced over her shoulder into the cluttered room. His lips thinned. "It's true, then. You're leaving."

"Yes."

Apparently interpreting her nervous step back as an invitation, Travis opened the screen and strode inside. His tight gaze swept to a lopsided stack of cartons. "When?"

She clasped her hands to keep from hugging him. "This weekend."

Travis laid a hand on the sofa, eyeing the heavy furniture, the piled packing crates. "You can't manage all this on your own."

"Jimmy's bringing his pickup truck. He and Ted will help with the heavy stuff. It should only take three or four trips to get everything transferred."

"Transferred?" Travis frowned, cocking his head. Peggy didn't much care for the glint in his eye. "Transferred to where?"

"The management firm that rented me this place also manages an apartment complex on Mill Street," she replied, completely mystified by his stunned expression. "I'll be moving into one of the units."

"Mill Street is only a couple of miles from here."

"Yes, I know."

"But I thought you were leaving town. Hell, I thought you were leaving the danged state."

"Why would you think that...? Uh-oh." Peggy covered her mouth as Travis's eyes narrowed into mean little slits. She tried to swallow a smile, failed and finally extended a pleading hand. "Now, Travis, I'm sure it's all just an innocent misunderstanding."

Travis hooked his thumbs in his jeans, scowling darkly. "There's nothing innocent about my sister. She's devious as the devil himself."

"I'm sure Sue Anne meant well." Peggy's smile faded as the realization sank in. "So that's why you came back, to say goodbye?"

He shrugged, twitched, was suddenly fascinated by a twisted shard of tape stuck to the carpeting. "Not exactly," he muttered, poking the sticky lump with his booted toe. "I, uh, figured I might kind of, well, tag along."

"Tag along?"

"Just to, you know, make sure you got settled and such." Travis tugged his earlobe, avoided her gaze. "Then I figured I might hang around."

"Hang around," Peggy murmured, feeling like a confused parrot. She licked her lips and tried to form a cohesive thought by repeating herself yet again. "Tag along and hang around." It didn't make sense. Nothing made sense. "But why?"

"Oh, Lordy." Travis yanked off his hat and wiped a forearm across his brow looking miserable as a whipped puppy. "I'm not fixing to interfere in your life or anything, honest to God, I just want to...ah, well, you know."

"No, Travis, I don't know. I don't even have a clue."

He licked his lips and angled a glance toward the hall. "How're the twins? Bet they've sprouted plenty in the last three weeks."

"Travis—"

"Oh, all right." Tugging on his hat, Travis set a determined jaw and folded his arms like a shield. "Thing is, I just wanted to be close by in case you needed me. Now, don't go getting riled." He uncrossed his arms, holding his palms out like matching stop signs. "I know you can take care of yourself. God knows how many times you've told me. And I know you don't want me getting in your way."

"Oh, Travis, that's not—"

"Now, I don't blame you, honey, I surely don't. I haven't got beans to offer a woman like you, and someday you're going to find a man who'll make a fine husband and daddy." The words seemed to choke him, to force him to spit out every syllable like a bad taste.

Travis took a breath, avoided her stunned gaze and continued, running the words together as if he feared the slightest pause would be fatal. "But right now you're on your own, so I figured I'd kind of hang close just in case, you know, on account of if you ever needed a friend, I—" he coughed, folded his arms again "—I'd be there."

Peggy was touched to tears. "You'd do that...for me?" Her voice quivered with emotion. "But why?"

"I promised I'd never leave you," he said simply.

A lump of pure misery wedged in her throat.

She covered her eyes for a moment, gathered her courage, then faced him with as much fortitude as she could muster. "Under the circumstances, I wouldn't be fair of me to hold you to that promise, Travis, and I won't."

"I hold myself to it."

"But you'd have to give up the rodeo, that ranch in Texas you've been saving for—"

His head snapped up. "How'd you know about the ranch?"

"Sue Anne," she replied, waving that away as irrelevant. "The point is, that by keeping a promise I never asked you to make, you'll end up losing everything that's important to you."

Travis studied her eyes, then glanced away as if disappointed by what he'd seen. Or perhaps by what he hadn't seen. "I'll admit rodeo means a lot to me, and so does the ranch, but I reckon you and the babies mean a darn sight more." If he heard Peggy's shocked gasp, he made no indication. Instead, he continued to stare into space with sad eyes and a determined stance. "Now, I don't want you to be worried about me expecting something in return, because I respect how you feel about commitments and such—"

"It's a lie," Peggy blurted, then groaned at Travis's startled expression. She bit her lip, squared her shoulders and decided that no matter what the outcome, Travis deserved the truth. They both did. "When I said I wanted you to leave, that I wasn't ready for a commitment, it simply wasn't true. I lied."

Clearly, he was bewildered by the revelation. And hurt by it. "I suppose you had your reasons."

"Yes, I did." Reaching up, she tenderly touched his face, urging him to meet her gaze. "I lied because you are too noble, too selfless to be trusted with your own best interests. Don't you understand why I couldn't let you give up your life, your dreams?''

Travis shifted, scratched his forehead. "No, ma'am, can't say that I do."

Peggy clutched the open folds of his leather vest, hoisted up on tiptoes and whispered against his lips. "Because I love you, Travis Stockwell. If you can't see that, you're every bit as hardheaded and dense as your sister claims." She brushed a sweet kiss across his mouth, then withdrew nervously, waiting for his response.

His eyes were dark, veiled. "Do you really mean that?"

"The part about you being hardheaded and dense as a stone? Oh, absolutely."

"The other part, the love part."

"Yes," she whispered. "I really mean it."

Travis's Adam's apple twitched and his fingers flexed at her shoulders as if he wanted desperately to haul her into his arms. "I love you, too, honey, so much it hurts just to think about it. I'd be proud if you'd marry me, Peggy, but before you answer, I want you to know that I promise to get me a real job, one that pays enough so you and the twins will never have to worry about money again."

"You've got a real job, cowboy."

He shook his head, set a stubborn chin. "Following the rodeo circuit means being on the road half the year. I won't leave you and the babies to fend for yourselves."

"You won't have to." Peggy smiled and tickled a messy strand of sun-streaked hair peeking out from under his hat. "Trust me."

Sue Anne sniffed and wiped her moist eyes. "So, I guess that's everything?"

"I think so." Peggy rechecked the twins' car-seat straps, then exited the back seat of Travis's pickup and brushed her palms together. "Are you sure all that furniture isn't going to get in your way? I mean, we can always rent a storage shed—"

"Oh, pish. We got piles of room in that old garage, don't we, babe?" Sue Anne elbowed her husband, who blinked as if he'd just awakened on a new planet.

"Hmm? Oh, sure, sweet cakes. Lots of room." Jimmy beamed, slipping an arm around his wife's shoulders and glancing over at Travis, who was at the rear of the pickup. "Need any help?"

Travis stepped over the hookup tongue where the roomy fifth wheel was connected to the old diesel pickup truck. "Nope, all hooked up and ready to roll." He patted the trailer's shiny skin, and Peggy rejoiced at the glowing pride in her husband's eyes.

She met him at the curb and slipped an arm around his waist. "Our first home," she murmured, eyeing the gleaming fifth wheel that would provide all the comforts during their travels. They planned to follow the circuit for the next few years, until the twins were ready for school and they'd saved enough for the ranch Travis had dreamed about.

As for Peggy, she frequently pinched herself to make sure this wasn't all a wonderful dream. "I'm so excited. I swear, this is the most fun I've ever had standing up."

"Is that a fact?" Travis chuckled and kissed her cheek. "Maybe I can come up with something even better."

"Ooh, I can hardly wait." She batted her eyelashes. "My stars, Mr. Stockwell, I had no idea how truly inventive cowboys could be."

"The truth is, Mrs. Stockwell—" he lowered his lips to her ear and whispered "—you ain't seen nothing yet."

"Newlyweds," Sue Anne snorted. "Can't keep their horny hands off each other."

"Disgusting," Jimmy agreed, grabbing his wife's bottom.

Travis beamed, rubbing his hands together. "We'd better hit the road. We're due in Kalispell tomorrow."

Sue Anne's stoic expression crumpled beneath a flurry of hugs, manly backslaps and teary farewells. "Drive careful," she called as Peggy and Travis climbed into the truck cab. "Y'all call when you get there, hear?"

"We will, and don't forget that we'll be back for Thanksgiving." Peggy waved out the open window, then settled back in her seat, smiling.

Travis reached over and took her hand. "Any regrets?"

"Not a one," she replied, rubbing her cheek against his knuckles. "I'm looking forward to being a rodeo wife. Who knows, I might even take up barrel racing. Sue Anne makes it sound like great fun."

"I'll make you happy, honey. I swear."

Peggy's gaze bounced from her husband's solemn face, to the back seat where the twins were safely tucked in their carriers, and finally landed on the orange cat curled contently in the trailer window. "You already have, my love. You already have."

*   *   *   *   *

continues with

FOR HER EYES ONLY

by Sharon Sala
available in October

Here's an exciting preview...

June 6th

Thunder rolled outside the walls of Squaw Creek Lodge, ripping through the gray, overhanging clouds. Rain splattered against the shake-shingle roof before running onto the ground. It had been raining for so many days it seemed as if heaven was weeping. And while it was fashionable to cry at weddings, Jessica Hanson thought this was ridiculous.

She sat hunched over her computer, determined to concentrate on the payroll for the lodge employees, and not on the society wedding about to take place in the nearby ballroom. As she flipped through the time cards, her lower lip slid out of position just enough to pass for a pout. She'd known the couple who were about to get married but hadn't been invited. Although she *was* honest enough to admit that she hadn't been back in Grand Springs long enough to reestablish her place within her old circle of friends, and when she left town two years ago she'd broken all ties with them.

Luckily, Jessica had been back a little over two months, and had yet to see the man who'd been her reason for leaving. *Stone Richardson.* Just thinking his name made her heart hurt, and she blinked back a quick spurt of tears as she let the memory of him back into her mind. *Stone—as in...with a heart of.* Damn his ex-wife and damn his hard heart, anyway. It wasn't Jessica's fault his ex had done everything within her power to prove it was Stone's job as a cop that had ruined their marriage—and not her own lack

of understanding or willingness to accept him for who and
what he was.

Jessica's brief affair with Stone had ended without anyone ever knowing it had happened. Stone refused to trust
another woman enough to give their future a chance, and
Jessica hadn't been willing to settle for being a cop's sexual
outlet. Coming back to Grand Springs had been her way of
proving to herself that she was over him.

A sudden clap of thunder made the lights of the office
flicker. "No, no, no," Jessica begged, staring at the flickering screen. When the power held, she returned to her task.
Moments later, she hit the save key and a smile of satis-
faction crossed her face. Suddenly, the room went dark!

Outside her office, she heard the sound of a folding chair
tumbling to the floor, and then an unnatural silence. "Perfect. Just perfect," she muttered, and wearily laid her head
down on the desk while waiting for the power to resume.

A man's muffled voice sounded as he ran past the outer
door of her office, but Jessica thought he said something
about fuses and flashlights. Flashlights! There was one in
the file cabinet by the door. She pushed her chair back from
the desk and stood. Circling the desk with hands outstretched, she was forced to orient herself by touch alone.
When she bumped the edge of the desk with her knee, she
winced.

"Fish guts," she muttered, rubbing at the ache. She
moved again, still aiming for the file cabinets. The absence
of light threw her off balance and she staggered, stumbling
backward. Her sleeve caught on something sharp, and she
heard fabric rip. Fuming over the tear she'd put in her
blouse, she started forward once more.

Seconds later, something hard and round rolled beneath
her shoe. The sensation of moving through space without
seeing where she was going was frightening. All she knew
was that her feet were no longer on the floor and she was

on the way down. Then pain shattered her consciousness. She'd found the file cabinets...the hard way.

Lamplight flickered in a corner of the room.

Jessica groaned and clutched at her head as she rolled toward the glow, but the act of moving had not been wise. When the agony had subsided to a dull, pounding ache, she opened her eyes, focusing on the lamp and the soft, yellow glow across the room. A woman suddenly walked between Jessica and the light, but didn't look up.

"Help me," Jessica said, but the woman didn't move.

Jessica blinked slowly. The woman's image kept wavering in and out, and Jessica knew she was going to pass out again. Frantic for help, she lifted her arm, waving in the woman's direction as she tried once more to gain attention.

"Help me. Please, help me."

The woman turned and walked to the end of the desk, revealing her identity. Jessica went weak with relief. "Olivia! Thank God it's you."

It didn't seem odd to Jessica that Olivia Stuart, the mayor of Grand Springs, would be here at the lodge. After all, she was the mother of the groom who was about to be married. Where else might she have been?

"Olivia, you're going to have to help me."

To Jessica's disbelief, Olivia kept smiling. Suddenly, a second figure emerged from out of the shadows and grabbed Olivia from behind. One hand was clamped roughly over Olivia's mouth. Something glittered in the assailants's other, upraised hand. Moments later, when Olivia crumpled to the floor, Jessica began to scream. Led by the sounds of her distress, Jessica's co-workers soon found her—alone and unconscious, and bleeding profusely from a wound to the head.

Sometime later, Jessica woke up, disoriented by pain-killers and a headache of mammoth proportions. She knew little about what was going on around her until someone touched her arm.

"Take it easy, Jessie. You're in the hospital, and you're going to be all right."

Jessica blinked and then groaned. That voice and those wide, imposing shoulders were all too familiar. She looked up into stormy gray eyes and let her gaze wander to that stubborn square jaw before she looked away. *Stone Richardson...* Her heart raced and she knew...her two-year self-imposed exile hadn't worked.

Take 4 bestselling love stories FREE

Plus get a FREE surprise gift!

Special Limited-time Offer

Mail to Silhouette Reader Service™

3010 Walden Avenue
P.O. Box 1867
Buffalo, N.Y. 14240-1867

YES! Please send me 4 free Silhouette Special Edition® novels and my free surprise gift. Then send me 6 brand-new novels every month, which I will receive months before they appear in bookstores. Bill me at the low price of $3.34 each plus 25¢ delivery and applicable sales tax, if any.* That's the complete price and a savings of over 10% off the cover prices—quite a bargain! I understand that accepting the books and gift places me under no obligation ever to buy any books. I can always return a shipment and cancel at any time. Even if I never buy another book from Silhouette, the 4 free books and the surprise gift are mine to keep forever.

235 BPA A3UV

Name	(PLEASE PRINT)	
Address	Apt. No.	
City	State	Zip

This offer is limited to one order per household and not valid to present Silhouette Special Edition® subscribers. *Terms and prices are subject to change without notice. Sales tax applicable in N.Y.

USPED-696

©1990 Harlequin Enterprises Limited

Win a collector's edition framed poster from

36 HOURS

You could win a framed poster featuring the cover art for all twelve 36 Hours titles, or one of 50 second prizes of an unframed poster!

This unique collector's edition showcases the way all twelve covers were created from a single piece of art!

36 HOURS POSTER SWEEPSTAKES
OFFICIAL ENTRY FORM

To enter, complete an Official Entry Form or a 3" x 5" card by hand printing the words "36 Hours Poster Sweepstakes," your name and address thereon and mailing it to: In the U.S., 36 Hours Poster Sweepstakes, P.O. Box 9076, Buffalo, N.Y. 14269-9076; in Canada, 36 Hours Poster Sweepstakes, P.O. Box 637, Fort Erie, Ontario L2A 5X3. Limit: one entry per envelope, one prize to an individual, family or organization. Entries must be sent via first-class mail and be received no later than 9/30/97. No responsibility is assumed for lost, late, misdirected or nondelivered mail.

---

36 HOURS POSTER SWEEPSTAKES

Official Entry Form

Name: _____

Address: _____

City: _____ Phone: _____

State/Prov.: _____ Zip/Postal Code: _____

Silhouette® ™

KFP

36ENTRY

36 Hours Poster Sweepstakes
Official Rules—No Purchase Necessary

To enter, complete an Official Entry Form or 3" x 5" card by hand printing the words "36 Hours Poster Sweepstakes," your name and address thereon and mailing it to: In the U.S., 36 Hours Poster Sweepstakes, P.O. Box 9076, Buffalo, NY 14269-9076; in Canada, 36 Hours Poster Sweepstakes, P.O. Box 637, Fort Erie, Ontario L2A 5X3. Limit: one entry per envelope, one prize to an individual, family or organization. Entries must be sent via first-class mail and be received no later than 9/30/97. No responsibility is assumed for lost, late, misdirected or nondelivered mail.

Winners will be selected in random drawing (to be conducted no later than 10/31/97) from among all eligible entries received by D. L. Blair, Inc., an independent judging organization whose decisions are final. The prizes and their approximate values are: Grand Prize—a framed 9" x 48" poster featuring the 12 covers of the books in the Silhouette 36 Hours series ($400 U.S.); 50 Second Prizes—an unframed 9" x 48" poster featuring the 12 covers of the books in the Silhouette 36 Hours series ($50 U.S. each).

Sweepstakes offer is open only to the residents of the U.S. (except Puerto Rico) and Canada who are 18 years of age or older, except employees and their immediate family members of Harlequin Enterprises, Ltd., their affiliates, subsidiaries and all agencies, entities and persons connected with the use, marketing or conduct of this sweepstakes. All applicable laws and regulations apply. Offer void where prohibited by law. Taxes and/or duties on prizes are the sole responsibility of the winners. Any litigation within the province of Quebec respecting the conduct and awarding of prize may be submitted to the Régie des alcools, des courses et des jeux. All prizes will be awarded; winners will be notified by mail. No substitution for prizes is permitted. Odds of winning are dependent upon the number of eligible entries received.

Any prize or prize notification returned as undeliverable may result in the awarding of that prize to an alternative winner. By acceptance of their prize, winners consent to use of their names, photographs or likenesses for purposes of advertising, trade and promotion on behalf of Harlequin Enterprises, Ltd., without further compensation unless prohibited by law. In order to win a prize, residents of Canada will be required to correctly answer a time-limited arithmetical skill-testing question administered by mail.

For a list of winners (available after October 31, 1997), send a separate stamped, self-addressed envelope to: 36 Hours Poster Sweepstakes 5308 Winners, P.O. Box 4200, Blair, NE 68009-4200, U.S.A.

36RULE

When tomorrow is uncertain,
the only sure thing is love...

If you missed any 36 Hours titles, then order now and discover how, for the residents of Grand Springs, Colorado, the storm-induced blackout was just the *beginning!*